Sky Unfurled

Mc Randall

Copyright © 2025 by Mc Randall

Cover art and design by Mc Randall

Developmental and Copy Editing: Bonnie Embry

ISBN-13: 9798992442908

All rights reserved.

This book is a work of fiction. References to real people, events, establishments, organizations, or locations are intended only to provide a sense of authenticity, and are used fictitiously. All other characters, and all incidents and dialogue, are drawn from the author's imagination and are not to be construed as real.

Dedicated to my mom

For her unwavering support for my creative adventures

and never-ending love

Intro

The crisp autumn air swept across the Appalachian Mountains, rustling the leaves that had just begun to turn fiery shades of red and orange. Sky Treder stood on the back porch of her family's secluded house, her hands clutching the rail.

Ever since Sky was little, her house had never really felt like a home. Both her parents, Mr. Brad and Mrs. Denise Treder, were aspiring doctors—her father in medical practice and her mother in veterinary care. When she was born, they were both graduating from college with their medical degrees.

Her childhood started out carefree until she turned six years old. Her father would take her to the movies, play games, and have daddy-daughter dates all the time. They were thick as thieves. They would always be planning sneaky pranks on her mother.

Sky's mother was a good sport. She would laugh as confetti would pop out of the cabinets or silly string would rain down from the ceiling. She genuinely enjoyed watching her husband and daughter grow close. Mrs. Treder was a dutiful mom who made Sky's lunch every day for school—a brown paper bag filled with a peanut butter and jelly sandwich, a juice box, and a sweet note wishing her a great day.

But when first grade started, everything began to change.

Mr. Treder became swept up in researching new treatments for the sick and afflicted. His schedule quickly shifted until he was gone most of the day, only coming home late at night to collapse into bed. Mrs. Treder wasn't much better. She spent her days at Red-Field University, studying the development of animals big and small. She was even responsible for making life-changing discoveries in animal medicine.

By the time Sky finished first grade, her parents were off around the country, presenting their research and attending conferences. They had hired a nanny to come and care for her. When she turned ten, the nanny left, and her parents deemed her fit to stay home alone.

Sky had to grow up fast. She learned how to make her own food, do laundry, and get herself back and forth to school. This was also around the time her parents started traveling abroad. Their reputations became known across the globe, keeping them far from their home in Tennessee.

By age eleven, Sky knew how to handle things on her own. She thought she had everything under control until a fateful day that summer. She was playing games on her laptop, not a care in the world. She was in the middle of an intense online battle when a sharp, shooting pain traveled up her back. She tried to pass it off as growing pains, but the next few days only got worse. No amount of pain medication could ease the sensation of jagged hunting knives tearing through her shoulder blades.

She began spending hours in the shower, letting the rush of warm water wash away the streaks of blood that began to drip down her back. One night, the pain was so intense she couldn't sleep. She tossed and turned in her bed, clutching her pillow to muffle her screams. Her body felt like it was on fire, every breath fueling the flames.

When she finally woke up days later, groggy and sore, she didn't remember much of what had happened. But the pain in her back was gone, replaced by a dull ache. She stumbled to the bathroom to shower but struggled to take her shirt off. When she finally did, she caught sight of something in the mirror that made her heart stop.

Behind her were two large, feathery objects. They curved upward and downward with an almost angelic grace, their pristine white feathers shimmering faintly. The tips of the wings brushed just above her ankles.

In that moment, she knew what she was—a Humanimal.

Humanimals are people who develop animal-like characteristics, usually around ages six to eight. Sky had been a late bloomer, and she was completely caught off guard. She stared into the mirror, her mind racing.

From that moment on, she knew she had to keep this to herself. While the existence of Humanimals was well known, acceptance varied from place to place. In many communities, fear outweighed understanding. Normal children were often separated from Humanimal ones. Political figures claimed it was for "everyone's safety."

Not too far from Sky's house were two different schools. Norman Elementary was for the "normal" kids, while Foreman Falls was the local school for animal-like children. Sky couldn't stand the thought of leaving her one and only friend, Lydia, to attend a school for what some people called "freaks." Lydia had been Sky's best friend since third grade. Their friendship was more like a sisterhood.

But there was one glaring problem.

Lydia had never liked Humanimals. She spoke of them like monsters, often repeating what she had overheard her mother say at home. Lydia always felt a twinge of jealousy, wanting to be special or unique. She resented the fact that she wasn't different in some extraordinary way.

Sky knew that if Lydia found out, their friendship would be over.

Determined to hide her wings, Sky began binding them tightly to her back. She wore oversized jackets and long coats year-round to conceal them. She endured the discomfort and the heat, all to keep her secret safe. Having wings would only make life more difficult.

Despite everything, she clung to the hope that things would stay the same. Lydia was her anchor in a world that felt so lonely. If she lost Lydia, Sky wasn't sure who she'd be.

But every time she looked at her reflection, she was reminded of who she truly was—and the lengths she had to go to just to keep living a normal life.

Even though she had wings, she had never felt more trapped.

Her white wings, hidden beneath layers of gauze and a thick hoodie, ached to stretch out fully. She could almost imagine herself flying over the trees, her wings cutting through the wind, the freedom she craved just within reach. But that wasn't her reality. Not yet. Maybe not ever.

But even out here, where the closest neighbor was miles away, she couldn't take the risk.

It was the first day of her junior year at Norman High, and Sky's stomach churned with nerves. Another year of keeping secrets, another year of dodging the mandatory health checks. She couldn't afford a single slip-up, not when Lydia—the only person she trusted—might turn against her if the truth came out.

Her phone buzzed on the railing, lighting up with a text from Lydia: "Don't be late! We've got Calc first period. You know Mrs. Jensen won't tolerate tardy geniuses."

Sky smirked. Lydia always knew how to pull her out of her thoughts, even if unintentionally. She grabbed her bag and took one last glance at the mountain view.

One

The hallways of Norman High buzzed with the chaos of students finding their lockers, chatting with friends, and scrambling to avoid being late for their first classes. Sky weaved through the crowd, her head down, her dirty blonde hair acting as a curtain to shield her from unwanted attention. Lydia caught up to her, practically bouncing with energy.

"Sky! There you are. Did you finish the Summer Calc homework? I mean, of course you did, but did you double-check number seven? That one nearly killed me."

Sky laughed softly. "Yeah, I did. I can show you at lunch."

"You're a lifesaver," Lydia said, adjusting her glasses. Her green eyes sparkled with the excitement of a new school year. "C'mon, we're going to be late."

The morning passed uneventfully as the two girls navigated through their classes. Sky's heart raced when she heard the lunch bell ring, though. The dreaded health check was next, and she had to be ready.

When they reached the nurse's office, students were already lined up in a neat row. A small sign hung on the door: "Annual

Health Check Sponsored by NisenX." Inside, nurses guided each student to prick their finger and wipe a sample of blood onto a card labeled with their name.

Sky had planned for this moment. Earlier that morning, she'd stopped by a local cafe where a man had suffered a nosebleed. While no one was watching, she'd snagged a tissue soaked with his blood and stashed it in a small plastic baggie in her pocket.

As the line moved forward, Sky's hands trembled slightly. She slipped the tissue out and pressed it onto her index finger, smearing the blood just enough to make it look authentic. When her turn came, she wiped the sample onto the card, handed it to the nurse, and walked away without a second glance. Her heart thundered in her chest as she stepped outside, finally able to breathe again.

"All done?" Lydia asked, waiting for her by the lockers.

"Yeah," Sky said, forcing a smile. "Piece of cake."

The rest of the day went on without incident. By the time the final bell rang, Sky was ready to head home and decompress, but an announcement crackled over the PA system.

"Attention students! This Friday, Norman High will join several other schools for a Back-to-School Bash at Troy Stadium. Come support your football teams,

marching bands, and dance lines in an evening of fun and entertainment!"

Sky groaned. She hated events like this—loud, crowded, and full of jocks and band nerds. She was about to suggest skipping it when Lydia turned to her, practically vibrating with excitement.

"You're coming, right?"

"Do I have to?" Sky muttered.

"Yes! I'm in the marching band. Flute player extraordinaire! You have to come support me."

Sky sighed, Lydia had been in band since 7th grade, she couldn't let her down. "Fine. But only for you."

"You're the best," Lydia said, grinning. "I'll pick you up at six. Wear something cute!"

Sky doubted she'd ever be able to pull off "cute," but she nodded anyway. As she walked home, her mind wandered back to the health check. Another year, another successful dodge. But she couldn't shake the feeling that her luck might run out someday—and when it did, everything would change.

Two

Friday evening came faster than Sky had anticipated. She stood in front of her mirror, pulling on her signature navy blue trench coat over a plain t-shirt and jeans. Large holes she'd cut into the back of the coat allowed her wings to breathe, but keeping them hidden inside was a challenge—especially tonight. She'd run out of gauze and hadn't had time to pick up more.

Lydia arrived promptly at six, honking her car horn until Sky came outside. The drive to Troy Stadium was filled with Lydia's chatter about the marching band's lineup. Sky nodded along, trying to mask her growing unease about the crowd.

The stadium was massive, packed with teens and teachers from several schools. Lydia ran off to get ready for the performance, leaving Sky to find a seat. She climbed to the very top set of bleachers, the ones that hung over the lower level, and looked out over the field. The band's music filled the air, and Sky couldn't help but cheer when Lydia's section took center stage.

Over to her far left, a group of Norman High football jocks were laughing and joking loudly. Sky ignored them, focusing on the music. As the performance ended, she made her way toward the stairs to leave, but Lydia appeared, still in her band uniform, carrying her hat and flute.

"What did you think?" Lydia asked, her face flushed with excitement.

Sky beamed. "The music of Journey always sounds great to hear!"

They stood about fifteen rows from the ledge closest to the field when a snickering laugh interrupted them. Sky and Lydia turned to see the group of jocks gesturing toward them, their laughter mocking.

Lydia, never one to back down, narrowed her eyes. "What's so funny?"

Tristen, the main jock, smirked. "That wasn't real music, just a bunch of nerds walking around a field like idiots."

Lydia bristled and stormed up to him, her finger jabbing the air in front of his face. "You don't know what real talent is. You just throw around a dumb ball and get praised for it."

The two exchanged heated words while Sky watched from a distance, torn between staying out of it and stepping in. When Lydia started shoving Tristen, Sky's heart sank. The jock grabbed Lydia's flute and dangled it over the edge of the bleachers.

"No!" Lydia cried, reaching for it as the jocks laughed. Tristen teased her, pretending to let go, before finally tossing the flute. Lydia lunged for it, her momentum carrying her over the edge.

Sky acted on instinct. She sprinted down the steps, tossing off her coat mid-run. Her white wings unfurled, catching the glare of the stadium's floodlights as she leapt into the air. She reached Lydia just in time, grabbing her hand. Sky, never having flown before, struggled to stabilize the flight. They teetered side to side, making for an awkward landing.

Sky could feel her wings straining under the unfamiliar weight. Awkwardly, she descended to the stadium entrance, setting Lydia down roughly to the ground. The sound of the battered flute hitting the concrete echoed in the stunned silence.

Breathing heavily, Sky looked up to see the entire stadium staring at her. Lydia's wide eyes filled with tears as she whispered, "Sky?"

Sky avoided her gaze, glancing back at the crowd. "I'll see you at school Monday," she said softly, then tucked her wings in and ran off into the night, heading for the only place she felt safe—home.

Three

Sky spent the entire weekend dodging Lydia's calls and texts. She had no idea what to say or how to explain what happened at the stadium. Every time her phone buzzed, she glanced at the screen and turned it over, letting the messages go unanswered. Deep down, she knew things would never be the same, but she wasn't ready to face the consequences just yet.

Finally, Monday came. Sky's stomach twisted in knots as she walked into school, keeping her head down and her long blonde hair draped over her face like a shield. She could feel the stares of her classmates, hear their whispers as she passed. Words like "freak" and "monster" floated through the air, cutting into her already fragile nerves.

She headed straight to her locker, determined to keep her routine as normal as possible. As she fumbled with the lock, trying to ignore the weight of the stares, a shadow fell over her. Sky glanced up to see Vice Principal Reynolds standing there, his expression unreadable.

"Miss Treder," he said, his tone calm but firm. "Come with me to the principal's office."

Sky's heart sank. She nodded mutely, hiding her face behind her hair as she followed him through the now-silent hallway. The whispers grew louder behind her, but she didn't look back.

When they reached the office, Vice Principal Reynolds gestured for her to go inside. Principal Greta sat behind the desk; her hands folded neatly in front. Beside her stood the school nurse, holding a blood testing kit.

"Sky," Principal Greta began, her tone kind but serious. "Is there something you'd like to tell us?"

Sky's mouth went dry. She stuttered, struggling to find the words, but nothing coherent came out. Principal Greta sighed and gestured to the nurse.

"We need to confirm what we all saw on Friday night," she said. "Please extend your hand."

Sky hesitated, her heart pounding in her chest. The nurse stepped forward and gently took her left hand, pricking her index finger with a small lancet. Sky flinched at the sting, watching as the drop of blood soaked into the test strip.

The second her blood touched the strip it turned bright yellow. Sky blinked in surprise. She'd never seen yellow on the tests before. Principal Greta's expression softened, but there was a hint of resignation in her eyes.

"That's what I expected," she said quietly. "Sky, you're in the wrong school. We'll need to transfer you to Foreman Falls High immediately. It's a school designed specifically for students like you. We have already sent your records there."

Sky's stomach dropped. "But... I don't..." she stammered, but Principal Greta held up a hand to stop her.

"This isn't a punishment," she said. "It's for your own safety and well-being. Please clean out your locker and meet Vice Principal Reynolds when you're done. He'll drive you to Foreman Falls."

Sky nodded numbly and left the office. The hallways felt even quieter now, the weight of a hundred pairs of eyes pressing down on her. She reached her locker and began emptying it, stuffing her books and belongings into her bag. Out of the corner of her eye, she saw Lydia standing at the end of the hallway, her expression a mix of sadness and confusion.

Sky hesitated, clutching a book to her chest. Neither of them knew what to say. Finally, Sky turned away, slamming her locker shut and walking toward the front office.

On the ride to Foreman Falls, Sky was silent. Vice Principal Reynolds tried to make small talk, but Sky barely responded, her thoughts consumed by what lay ahead. She hated the attention she'd gotten at the stadium and at school. What would it be like in a place full of kids just like her?

As they pulled into the parking lot of Foreman Falls High, Sky's anxiety only grew. The red brick building loomed before her, a stark reminder that her life was about to change forever.

Four

Sky stepped out of the car and was immediately greeted by a cheerful older man standing at the school's entrance. He extended his hand toward her, his smile wide and welcoming.

"Welcome to Foreman Falls, Ms. Treder!" he said warmly.

Sky hesitated before shaking his hand, still reeling from everything that had happened. The man's joy felt misplaced, almost jarring.

"I'm Principal Henderson," he added. "We're so happy to have a new student join us."

Sky gave him a small nod, unsure how to respond. Principal Henderson led her inside, his enthusiasm undeterred by her silence. The main office was lined with awards and achievements, plaques commemorating the school's academic and athletic successes.

"Please, have a seat," Principal Henderson said, gesturing to a chair across from his desk. Sky sat down, clutching her bag tightly as he took his seat. "Foreman Falls has a long history," he began. "We were one of the first schools in the country established exclusively for Humanimal students. We're incredibly proud of our championship football team, our award-winning cheer squad, and our excellent academic programs."

Sky nodded absently, her mind wandering as he spoke. She couldn't shake the feeling of being an outsider, even in a place meant for people like her.

"I hope you'll find your place here," Principal Henderson said, his tone gentle. "If you need anything at all, my door is always open."

A knock at the door interrupted them. Principal Henderson smiled and stood, opening the door to reveal a girl in a red and white cheerleader uniform. She was short, no more than five feet tall, with flawless milk chocolate skin and sleek black hair pulled into a high bun. Her brown eyes sparkled.

"Sky, this is Nia," Principal Henderson said. "She's one of our best cheerleaders and will be showing you around today."

Sky stood reluctantly, eyeing the girl warily. Nia's smile was so bright it was almost blinding.

"Hi, Sky!" Nia chirped. "It's so nice to meet you. You're going to love it here!"

Sky doubted that but followed Nia out of the office anyway. As they walked, Nia chatted non-stop, introducing herself as a junior and one of three cheer captains. She spoke glowingly about her experiences at Foreman Falls, her energy infectious even if Sky wasn't in the mood to catch it.

Nia showed her the lunchroom, the nurse's office, her classrooms, and finally, her locker. It was located near the gym, almost directly across from the locker room doors.

"Sorry about the placement," Nia said with a grimace. "Nobody likes being next to the football lockers. It's basically their party corner."

Sky sighed, not thrilled with her new setup. "It's fine," she muttered.

Nia checked the time and gasped. "I've got to run! AP Physics waits for no one. Good luck with the rest of your day!" She waved and hurried off, her cheerleader uniform bouncing as she jogged away. Sky noticed two small tan ears poking out of Nia's head but didn't bother to ask what kind of Humanimal she was.

Left alone, Sky stared at her locker, fiddling with the jammed lock. She struggled for a minute before a voice behind her asked, "Need some help?"

She turned to see a tall guy, easily six feet, with light skin, dark brown, windblown hair and a bright, disarming smile. His hazel eyes, a mesmerizing mix of greens and browns, gleamed warmly.

"The lockers over here get beat up all the time," he said, stepping closer. "They just need a good shove."

Before Sky could respond, he gave the locker a firm push, and it popped open. She turned to thank him but froze, words catching in her throat. His presence was magnetic, and she couldn't seem to look away.

"There you go," he said, his smile never wavering. "I'm Ryan, by the way."

"Thanks," Sky managed to mumble, her voice barely audible.

"No problem," Ryan said, nodding before heading back to his group of friends, all of whom were wearing varsity jackets. One of them called out, "Ryan, let's go!" and he jogged off, his dark feathers visible under his jacket as he moved.

Sky stared after him, stunned. He had wings—just like her. But his seemed so natural, so effortless, unlike the burden she carried. She shook her head and turned back to her locker, trying to focus on unpacking. She couldn't afford to get distracted, especially not by some jock, no matter how nice he seemed.

Five

Sky went to her morning classes, keeping her head down and avoiding interaction. When lunch finally rolled around, she walked along the farthest walls of the cafeteria, trying to blend into the background. After grabbing a tray of chicken and fries, she scanned the room for an empty seat.

Her thoughts were interrupted by a cheerful voice. "Over here, Sky!"

She looked up to see Nia waving her arms enthusiastically from across the room. Sky sighed, reluctant to join a table full of cheerleaders, but she didn't know anyone else. Ducking her head, she made her way over and sat down on Nia's left.

Sky had barely taken a bite when one of the other girls at the table asked, "So, where did you transfer from?"

Sky glanced up at the three girls staring at her, then shrugged. "Nowhere important."

The girls exchanged looks and started whispering to each other. Sky ignored them, focusing on her food as Nia leaned over and whispered, "Don't mind them. They're always gossiping about something."

"Then why hang out with them?" Sky asked.

Nia laughed. "I usually talk to my boyfriend anyway."

Sky raised an eyebrow. "Your boyfriend?"

Nia's smile widened. "Yeah, Bryant. He's one of the offensive linemen."

Sky rolled her eyes. "A cheerleader dating a football player? How original."

Nia giggled. "Hey, you can't knock it till you try it. Not all football jocks are dumb. Well," she gestured toward a nearby group of loud, laughing players, "most of them are."

Just then, a massive guy approached the table. He was tall and wide, his dark skin contrasting with his bright smile. Two small brown ears poked out from his shaven head, and his fingernails were short and sharp. Sky tensed until Nia greeted him with a kiss on the cheek.

"Sky, this is Bryant," Nia said, grinning. "My big snuggle bear."

Bryant blushed but hugged her back. Sky raised an eyebrow. "So, he's a bear and his name is Bryant?"

"Yeah, so?" Nia said, laughing.

Sky shrugged, deciding it must be an inside joke. As the couple chatted, Sky couldn't help but feel a pang of loneliness. She'd never been on a date, never had anyone look at her the way Bryant looked at Nia. She sighed and focused on her food, trying to ignore the hollow feeling in her chest.

Her thoughts were interrupted again by another voice. "Bryant!" a guy called, jogging over to their table. Sky looked up to see Ryan, his ever-present smile lighting up the room. He gave Bryant a quick bro hug before turning to Sky.

"Hey," Ryan said, his hazel eyes locking onto hers. "I never got your name earlier."

Sky froze, her cheeks flushing red. She struggled to find her voice, but Nia jumped in to fill the silence.

"Her name's Sky," Nia said. "She's new here, transferred from Norman High. She's kind of shy."

Ryan nodded, his gaze still on Sky. "Why'd you transfer?"

Sky nervously mumbled, "I...I was different from them. Not normal."

Sky couldn't handle the attention. Without another word, she bolted from the table, leaving her lunch behind. She ran to her next class, Avian Anatomy, and slipped into the farthest seat in the back corner. Her heart was still racing as she tried to calm herself down.

The classroom filled quickly, the only open seat remaining was the one next to Sky. She exhaled slowly, hoping to go unnoticed. Just as the tardy bell rang, the door swung open.

"Late again, Mr. Daniels," the teacher, Mrs. Fields, said with a sigh.

"Sorry, ma'am," Ryan said, grinning sheepishly. "Won't happen again."

Sky's heart sank as he walked to the back of the room and sat down beside her. He glanced at her and flashed that same disarming smile.

"Looks like we're both bird brains," he joked lightly, gesturing to the class.

Sky couldn't believe it. Of all the people to end up next to, it had to be him.

Six

Class couldn't end quickly enough. As soon as the bell rang, Sky rushed out the door, avoiding any chance of another awkward interaction with Ryan. The rest of the school day passed in a blur, but she couldn't shake the feeling that Ryan was everywhere—lunch, class, and even his locker, which turned out to be near hers.

When the final bell rang, Sky trudged to her locker to drop off her textbooks. She was just starting to pack up when Nia appeared beside her, practically bouncing with excitement.

"What are you doing after school?" Nia asked, her bright brown eyes sparkling.

Sky hesitated. "Nothing, really. Probably walking home."

Nia's face fell in mock horror. "Walking? No way! I can give you a ride. But you'll have to wait until after cheer practice."

Sky didn't relish the thought of waiting around, but the long trek home didn't sound appealing either. "Okay," she said softly.

Nia clapped her hands together. "It's a plan! Come on, you can hang out in the gym."

Sky followed Nia to the gym and sat on the bleachers closest to the doors, pulling out a book to read. From her seat, she could see

Nia stretching with the other cheerleaders. Each girl was unique, their animal characteristics on full display. On the way to the gym, Nia had mentioned she was part hamster. The others included a few chickens, a squirrel, a chipmunk, some coyotes, and even a chameleon. Tails swished, scales shimmered, and the occasional howling wail echoed through the gym—a symphony of diversity.

Sky hadn't realized her seat gave her a clear view into the school's workout room until she glanced up. Inside, the football team was hard at work, doing treadmill sprints, jumping jacks, and weightlifting. She quickly focused back on her book, not wanting to risk spotting Ryan or Bryant.

After about an hour, the cheerleaders finished their practice. Nia, wiping sweat from her face, approached Sky with a grin.

"Thanks for waiting," she said. "Let me just change, and we can go."

Sky nodded, watching as Nia headed to the locker room. The football team also began wrapping up their workout, and soon a group of sweaty, boisterous guys emerged from the training room. Sky kept her eyes on her book, but a voice broke her concentration.

"What's your problem?" someone asked.

Sky looked up to see a guy staring at her. He had tanned coffee-colored skin, jet-black hair, and a mane of fur around his collarbones. His sharp teeth glinted when he spoke, and his dark, pointed ears twitched slightly.

"Excuse me?" Sky said, startled.

Before the guy could respond, Ryan stepped in. "Cool it, Trevor."

Trevor smirked. "She doesn't seem like a Humanimal. Must be some normal kid who snuck in."

He gestured toward Sky with a sharp clawed hand, "What are you, anyway? You've got no ears, no tail, no scales. Kinda plain, don't you think?"

Sky felt her cheeks flush with embarrassment, but before she could think of a reply, Trevor leaned closer. "Or are you hiding something?" he added, his voice low and mocking.

"Back off," Ryan said, stepping between them. His tone was calm but firm. "She's new. Leave her alone."

Trevor chuckled and raised his hands in mock surrender. "Relax, man. Just having a little fun."

Ryan didn't move until Trevor turned and walked away, joining a group of other football players who laughed as they disappeared down the hall. Once they were gone, Ryan glanced back at Sky.

"You okay?" he asked, his hazel eyes filled with genuine concern.

Sky nodded quickly, though her heart was still racing. "I... I'm fine."

Ryan gave her a small smile. "Don't let him get to you. Trevor likes to act tough, but he's harmless."

Sky wasn't so sure, but she nodded anyway. "Thanks," she mumbled, looking down at her book.

Ryan hesitated for a moment before stepping away. "See you around, Sky," he said, his voice light as he headed off to join Bryant and the rest of the team.

Sky exhaled deeply, her hands gripping her book tightly. She wanted to disappear, to vanish from this awkward and overwhelming new world. But before she could dwell on it, Nia's cheerful voice broke through her thoughts.

"Ready to go?" Nia asked, her gym bag slung over one shoulder and her hamster-like ears twitching slightly.

Sky nodded and stood, grateful for the distraction. As they walked out to Nia's car, the conversation shifted to lighter topics. Nia talked about cheerleading, the upcoming football game, and how much she loved being part of the team.

Seven

The next few days at Foreman Falls High were relatively uneventful for Sky. She went to her classes, completed her homework, and spent her free time with Nia. Each morning and afternoon, Nia picked her up and dropped her off, making the commute far less daunting. Sky would wait for cheer practice to end before heading home, grateful for Nia's lively company.

By Friday, however, the atmosphere at school had shifted. It was game day, and the halls buzzed with energy for the upcoming pep rally and football game. Sky never understood the need for pep rallies every Friday. To her, it seemed like the jocks were glorified enough without needing more fuel for their egos.

During her free period, Sky walked with Nia toward her locker, their conversation circling back to the rally later that day. Across the hall from Sky's locker, Trevor, Bryant, and their group of football friends stood joking and laughing loudly. Sky ducked her head, trying to ignore them as she headed for her destination.

But Trevor's voice cut through the noise. "Hey, what's the hurry? Aren't you excited for the game?"

Sky didn't respond, keeping focus on her locker as she sorted her books.

Trevor turned back to his friends, his grin widening. "Aw, newbie's being shy. What a shame. She's kinda pretty, though."

Her face flushed red. She could feel the heat rising in her cheeks as Trevor noticed her reaction.

"Oh, look," he teased. "She's embarrassed. Don't worry, newbie. You'd feel a lot more comfortable acting like one of us instead of trying to be some normal kid."

Nia's glare shot toward Bryant, expecting him to say something in Sky's defense. But Bryant looked away, clearly unwilling to get involved. Disappointed, Nia muttered under her breath before turning to Sky.

"Do you want me to beat him up?" Nia asked, half-joking but with a sharp edge in her voice.

Sky shook her head, whispering, "It's fine. Don't worry about it."

Nia gave the group of boys a death stare as she walked away. Trevor, oblivious to her warning, grabbed a red Gatorade bottle from one of his friends and turned back to Sky.

"You need to relax, newbie," he said with a fake smile. "We're all friends here. You just need to cool off."

With that, he tipped the bottle, dumping its contents over Sky's head. The cold, sticky liquid soaked her from head to toe, turning her coat and hair a vibrant red.

At the end of the hall, Nia froze before storming back toward them. She grabbed the empty bottle from Trevor's hand and smacked him across the face with it. "You're a jerk," she snapped before wrapping an arm around Sky and leading her towards the girls' locker room.

Ryan, having just turned down the hallway, saw Trevor smiling ear to ear. Just past him, rushing towards the gym, were Sky and Nia. He could see a trail of red following them, and a Gatorade bottle in Trevor's hands. It didn't take long to put two and two together.

He sprinted down the hall asking Trevor, "What did you do?" His voice was strong and unwavering. Trevor laughed, "I was just helping the new girl chill out." He turned back to his friends and gave them high fives.

Ryan felt anger, "If you ever do that again I swear..." "You don't have to be so mad," Trevor said, "It was just a joke. Maybe you should cool off too."

Ryan knew it wasn't a joke, not to Sky. She had to be feeling humiliated, and that didn't sit right with him. He stood there in the hallway, trying everything he could to not smack Trevor in the face, noticing a slight red mark on his cheek. Ryan chuckled, realizing that Nia must have given him a piece of her mind.

Sky's eyes welled with tears as she followed Nia. "These guys are worse than the ones at my last school," she murmured, her voice trembling.

Nia quickly grabbed handfuls of paper towels, trying to dry Sky's hair and trench coat. "We'll fix this," she said firmly. "You'll be fine."

Sky shook her head, "It's no use. I'm soaked and I don't have anything else to wear."

"I've got extra cheer sweats in my locker," Nia said, already running to fetch them. While Nia was gone, Sky rinsed her hair in the sink, trying to wash out the sticky drink. By the time Nia returned, her hair was damp but clean.

"This is all I've got," Nia said, holding out a pair of gray sweatpants with "Foreman" printed down one leg and a bright red athletic shirt that read "CHEER" in bold white letters.

Sky's stomach twisted, "I... I can't wear this," she said, her voice barely above a whisper.

Nia tilted her head, "Why not?"

Sky hesitated, "I won't be able to hide my…" she trailed off, looking back towards her wings.

Realization dawned on Nia's face, but she didn't press. "It's okay. The shirt's super stretchy. It'll work for any species."

Sky managed a small smile as she slowly removed her coat. A few white feathers drifted to the floor, and she unfurled her wings cautiously, checking them for any stains. Behind her, Nia gasped.

Sky turned to see Nia covering her mouth, her eyes wide. "Do you… see anything on them?" Sky asked nervously.

Nia shook her head, her expression softening. "No. They're… beautiful."

Sky's cheeks flushed as she maneuvered her wings into the shirt, threading them carefully through the fabric. The material stretched to accommodate her, and Nia handed her the sweatpants to complete the outfit. Once dressed, Sky glanced at herself in the mirror. The red shirt and gray pants were far from her usual style, but they fit well. Her wings, though visible, blended into the shirt's design.

Nia grinned and grabbed a hair tie from her bag. "You can't leave your hair all wet like that. Sit."

Sky sat as Nia worked quickly, pulling her damp hair into a high ponytail. When she finished, Sky looked in the mirror again, surprised by her reflection.

"I've never seen this much of my face before," she admitted.

"You're beautiful," Nia said firmly. "You should pull your hair back more often."

Sky smiled shyly, but her stomach tightened as she walked to the door. She dreaded the stares that would come her way. She had never worn fitted clothes or let anyone see her wings before.

"Just walk straight to class," Nia said, patting her shoulder. "I'll handle those idiots."

Taking a deep breath, Sky stepped out of the locker room. She kept her eyes forward, heading straight for her next class. The hall grew quieter as she passed the group of boys who had laughed at her earlier. She felt their stares and glanced up briefly, catching their shocked expressions. Their jaws were practically on the floor. Beside her locker was a familiar face.

Sky's eyes met Ryan's for a moment. His hazel gaze softened, and she felt a strange twist in her chest. Tears pricked her eyes, and she bolted down the hall, unable to handle the attention.

Behind her, Nia approached the group. Without hesitation, she slapped Trevor hard across the face. "You should be ashamed of yourselves," she snapped, her voice venomous. Her glare shifted to Bryant, who avoided her gaze, his expression filled with guilt.

The group quickly scattered, heading to their classes. Ryan stayed behind, lingering near Sky's locker. His heart felt heavy, his mind racing. He didn't understand the emotions swirling inside him—concern, guilt for not being there in time to help, and a fierce need to protect her. But one thing was clear: he couldn't ignore what had just happened, and he couldn't ignore Sky.

Sky struggled through the rest of her classes. Everywhere she went people stared, girls whispered, while the guys seemed surprised or caught off guard. By the time the pep rally began Sky decided she couldn't handle the crowd or the noise. She slipped away to the library, her safe haven.

The distant sounds of the band playing, kids cheering, and a speaker rallying the crowd filtered faintly into the quiet sanctuary of books. Sky made her way to a small, padded window seat tucked in a secluded corner. She curled up there, trying to focus on her homework, but her mind was a storm of emotions. Tears welled up and began to stream down her face. It was all too much – the attention, the humiliation, the overwhelming shift in her life.

She cried quietly, lost in her own world, until a faint buzz of her phone broke through her thoughts. It was a text from Nia:

Nia: Where r u?

Sky wiped her tears and typed back: Library

A few minutes later Nia appeared, her cheerful demeanor replaced with concern. She walked over, handing Sky a tissue. "Hey," she said softly, "How are you holding up?"

Sky took the tissue and dabbed at her face, "Honestly, freaked out."

Nia sat down beside her, her expression serious, "What's freaking you out the most?"

Sky hesitated, "The attention. Everyone staring, talking about me... it's overwhelming. But..." she paused, a small smile breaking through her tears, "it does feel good to have my wings free."

Nia grinned, "See, I told you wings like yours are too pretty to hide!"

Sky chuckled softly, appreciating Nia's unwavering support. Together, they left the library and headed toward the parking lot. The pep rally was still going strong in the distance, but Sky was relieved to be leaving it all behind.

"I have to be at the game tonight around 6:30," Nia said as they walked. "Do you want to come? It might distract you from everything that happened today."

Sky shook her head gently, "Thanks, but I think I need a break from everyone at school. I just want a relaxing weekend."

Nia nodded. "Fair enough. But I'm coming by tomorrow to check on you, okay?"

Sky smiled. "Okay. Thanks, Nia."

When they reached Sky's house, Nia dropped her off with a quick wave before heading back to school. Sky let herself in, the familiar silence of the house greeting her. She slipped off her shoes, set her bag down, and made her way to the living room.

Needing comfort, she turned on a cheesy kids' movie about a horse and his family—a nostalgic favorite. She made herself a mug of hot chocolate, grabbed a blanket, and curled up on the couch. As the warm, sweet drink soothed her, Sky let the events of the day wash over her. It had been one of the hardest days she could remember, but for now, she was relieved to finally be alone.

Eight

Saturday started off quiet for Sky. She spent most of the day lounging around the house, trying to enjoy the calm after such a chaotic week. But by mid-afternoon, Nia showed up, her usual energetic self, and announced that they needed to revamp Sky's wardrobe.

"You can't just hide those gorgeous wings," Nia said as she dragged Sky out to her car. Sky sighed, knowing she was right. Now that everyone at school had seen her wings, there wasn't much point in trying to keep them hidden.

Nia drove them to the mall and led Sky into a store called Gear Bound. The shop catered specifically to Humanimals with unique clothing needs, and Nia wasted no time diving into the racks of shirts designed for winged species. She helped Sky pick out several new tops—some made of athletic material that hugged the base of her feathers, while others featured keyhole backs for easier movement.

By the time Nia was satisfied with their haul, Sky had an entirely new collection of shirts that actually fit her wings. To celebrate, Nia took her to her favorite Chinese restaurant in town.

Sky scarfed down a plate of honey chicken while Nia chattered about her plans to confront Bryant.

"I'm going to beat him to a pulp for not standing up for you," Nia said, stabbing her fork into a piece of orange chicken.

Sky smiled, grateful for Nia's loyalty. "You don't have to do that," she said, though she secretly appreciated the thought.

Nia changed the subject, talking excitedly about the football team's victory on Friday and their upcoming homecoming game. "Next Friday is going to be insane!" she exclaimed. "There's a special pep rally, the game itself, and of course, the dance."

Sky raised an eyebrow. "The dance?"

"Yeah! I've been helping plan it for weeks. You have to come."

Sky hesitated, staring at her plate. "I already don't feel comfortable at school. Why would I go to a dance?"

Nia pouted. "Please, Sky! I've worked so hard on this. You have to come."

Feeling the pressure, Sky finally relented. "Fine. I'll go."

Nia squealed with joy. "Yes! And that means we're going dress shopping after school on Thursday."

Sky groaned at the thought of getting dressed up but nodded. They finished their meal and headed home, ending the day on a lighthearted note.

Sunday was calm and lazy. Sky spent the day putting away her new clothes and wondering how she would look in them. She tried on a few shirts, marveling at how natural her wings felt in the keyhole designs. By the evening, she had settled back into her usual routine, grateful for the quiet before the start of another week.

Monday morning arrived too quickly, and Sky's nerves were on edge. She sifted through her newly organized drawers, finally settling on an outfit that Nia had helped her pick: fitted dark blue skinny jeans, burgundy ankle boots with a knitted fold, and a pastel blue shirt with a large keyhole back. She tied her hair back with a scrunchie adorned with white ribbons.

When Nia pulled up to Sky's house, her reaction was immediate. "You look amazing!" she shouted, practically bouncing out of the car.

Sky smiled shyly. "Thanks."

"Wait," Nia said, rushing inside. "You just need one more thing."

Before Sky could protest, Nia had her sitting in front of her mom's vanity. In minutes, Nia applied eyeshadow, eyeliner, mascara, and blush, her hands moving with practiced ease.

"Do you want to see?" Nia asked, stepping back to admire her work.

Sky shook her head, feeling self-conscious. "No."

Nia shrugged. "Your loss. You look incredible."

They climbed into the car and headed to school, Sky trying to brace herself for the day ahead.

As soon as they arrived, Nia had to practically drag Sky out of the passenger seat. Sky clutched her sling bag tightly, nerves buzzing as she stared at the school entrance. "I can't do this," she muttered.

"Yes, you can," Nia insisted. "Come on, you look amazing."

Reluctantly, Sky followed Nia inside, her eyes fixed on the ground in front of her. "Look up," Nia said firmly. "Show off a little."

Sky hesitated before lifting her gaze and managing a small smile. Most students were too busy with their own conversations to notice her at first, but as she passed by, heads began to turn. By the time she reached her locker, Sky felt the weight of all those glances and whispers.

Waiting by her locker were Bryant and Ryan. Nia immediately bristled. "I've got this," she said, motioning for Sky to handle her books while she turned her full attention to Bryant.

Sky glanced at Ryan and noticed him blushing slightly. She supposed the new outfit had caught his attention. As she grabbed her books for the day, she could hear Nia letting Bryant have it.

"You just stood there," Nia fumed. "Friday was unacceptable. Until you figure out how to make things right, we're taking a break."

Bryant looked crushed. "Come on, Nia. Don't do this."

Nia was already storming off, throwing a parting glare at Ryan. "I expected a lot from you, too," she snapped.

Sky watched as Bryant chased after Nia, though she was already halfway down the hall. Sky couldn't help but smile slightly at how fast Nia could move.

Closing her locker, Sky jumped slightly as Ryan stepped closer. "Can we talk?" he asked quietly.

Sky's chest tightened. The last thing she wanted was another awkward conversation. She shook her head and muttered, "I can't," before rushing off to her first class.

The rest of the morning passed in a blur. Sky did her best to smile as more students greeted her in the hallways. It felt strange—the sudden friendliness—but she tried to "fake it till she made it." By lunchtime, however, she was exhausted.

She and Nia sat far away from the football players in the cafeteria. Sky noticed Bryant glancing longingly at Nia, while Ryan's gaze occasionally drifted toward her. Sky couldn't help but wonder if he felt sorry for her.

After lunch came Anatomy class—Sky's least favorite. Most of the other students were smaller bird species like ducks, chickens, finches, and bluebirds. The only other predator in the class was Ryan. The difference between them and the smaller birds was stark. Sky's white wings might have seemed swan-like, but she knew from her paperwork that she was a peregrine falcon with a rare condition that gave her white feathers and fair skin. She was unique, and that set her apart even more.

Today's lesson focused on high-speed flight techniques. The teacher paired her with Ryan to read chapter 25 on predatory speed and flying strategies. Sky focused on her textbook, jotting down notes, determined to avoid conversation.

Ryan, however, scooted his desk closer. "I'm glad I'm not the only real flyer in this class," he said lightly.

Sky ignored him, keeping her eyes on her notes.

Ryan gently pushed her book down. "Can we talk?"

Sky hesitated, anxiety bubbling up again. "I... I don't know," she said quietly.

"Please," Ryan said. "I'm sorry for what Trevor did. I should've done something."

Sky looked at him, her emotions a mix of hurt and uncertainty. "Why apologize? Did Nia put you up to this?"

Ryan shook his head. "No. I should've gotten there sooner on Friday."

Sky sighed, her gaze drifting to her wings. "Jerks are everywhere," she muttered. "My old school wasn't that different."

Ryan's brow furrowed. "Did you have friends there?"

Sky hesitated before answering. "I had one good friend, but we're not talking anymore."

"Why not?"

Sky gestured to her wings. "We're... not the same."

A wave of sadness washed over her as she thought about Lydia. They hadn't spoken since that night at the stadium. Ryan seemed to sense her hurt.

"At least you have a few friends here," he said gently. "Nia's great."

Sky nodded. "Yeah. She's... something."

"She talks about you all the time," Ryan added. "To Bryant, mostly. Or at least she did before she started giving him the cold shoulder."

Sky chuckled softly. "He deserves it."

Ryan smiled, his hazel eyes meeting hers. "We all do. I'm sorry, Sky. I promise I won't let Trevor or anyone else treat you like that again, not if I can help it."

There was a sincerity in his voice that made Sky believe him. "Thank you," she said quietly.

The conversation shifted back to the textbook, and they finished their assignment in relative silence. When class ended, Sky packed up her things and headed out, determined to find Nia and regroup.

Nine

Sky and Nia were outside after school, sitting on the bleachers overlooking the upper field where the cheerleaders practiced. Below them, on the lower field, the football team was running drills. Cheer practice had just ended, but the football team was still busy. Nia leaned forward, her elbows on her knees, glaring down at the players.

"Bryant apologized to me," Nia said, her tone a mix of satisfaction and annoyance. "He got down on his hands and knees. I've never seen him so sorry. Honestly, it kind of felt good."

Sky smiled faintly. "Did you forgive him?"

Nia shrugged. "Yeah, eventually. We're back to normal now. But he knows he's on thin ice. And," she added with a wicked grin, "he's supposed to beat that jerk Trevor at some point."

They continued watching the field. The snap was made, and Bryant moved out of the way, allowing another player to plow straight into Trevor. Trevor went flying, landing hard on the turf.

Nia burst out laughing. "Oh, that was a hit!"

Sky couldn't help but join in. "He definitely had that coming."

As their laughter died down, Sky glanced at Nia. "Ryan apologized to me, too, for what Trevor did."

Nia raised an eyebrow, "Really?"

Sky nodded and explained the awkward conversation they'd had during Anatomy class. "He seemed genuine," she added.

Nia giggled, covering her mouth.

"What?" Sky asked, frowning slightly.

"Ryan Daniels? Apologetic? That's a first," Nia said. "He usually just blends in with the other meatheads."

Sky blinked, surprised, "Really?"

"Oh, yeah. Ryan is one of the schools' heartthrobs," Nia explained. "Girls are always fawning over him, and he just brushes them off. He doesn't really talk to anyone, let alone apologize. So the fact he's being nice to you? It's...interesting."

Sky looked down at the field, her eyes finding Ryan easily. He wore number 19, standing out among the other players with his confident stance. She felt her cheeks flush and quickly looked away.

Nia noticed, her eyes narrowed, a teasing grin spreading across her face. "Oh my gosh. Do you have a crush on THE Ryan Daniels?"

Sky's face turned even redder. "Football guys aren't my type," she said quickly, trying to brush it off.

"Oh, sure," Nia said, her voice dripping with sarcasm.

Sky rolled her eyes but couldn't stop the smile tugging at her lips, "Let's just go home."

They stood, gathering their bags. As they walked toward the parking lot, Sky glanced back at the field one last time. Her thoughts drifted to Ryan—the way he'd looked at her during their conversation, the sincerity in his voice when he apologized. Could he really like her? No, she thought. That didn't seem possible. He was probably just being nice.

But what if it meant more?

Ten

It was Thursday, and the school day had just ended. As soon as they reached the parking lot, Nia practically sprinted to the car, her excitement bubbling over.

"I am so, so happy we're going dress shopping!" Nia exclaimed, clapping her hands together.

Sky trailed behind, shaking her head. "I'm not exactly looking forward to it."

Nia ignored her, unlocking the car and hopping into the driver's seat. Sky reluctantly climbed in, bracing herself for what she knew would be an overwhelming experience. On the way to the mall, Nia rambled about colors, styles, and fits.

"I think red would look amazing on me," Nia said, steering the car into the mall's parking lot. "But for you? Maybe blue? Or something with sparkles... Oh, maybe a soft pastel!"

Sky barely managed a polite nod as they walked into the mall. Nia led the way to a store called Formal Fashions, a boutique specializing in dressy clothing for Humanimals. The moment they stepped inside, Nia went into overdrive, pulling dress after dress from the racks and piling them into Sky's arms.

"This one's perfect," Nia said, holding up a glittering red gown. "And this one!" She grabbed a sleek emerald dress without waiting for Sky's response.

By the time they reached the fitting rooms, Sky was juggling a mountain of gowns. Nia pushed open a door and motioned for her to go in. "Okay, let's see what looks good!"

Sky hesitated, glancing at the pile of dresses. "I don't really feel comfortable doing this," she admitted.

Nia's face softened. "Alright, fine. But you're not off the hook yet."

While Sky sat on a bench outside the fitting rooms, Nia spent nearly an hour trying on dresses. Each time, she emerged to twirl dramatically, asking for Sky's opinion. Finally, she found "the one"—an ombre sunset gown that shimmered in the light.

As Nia paid for her dress, Sky wandered through the store, letting her fingers trail over the racks of fabric. Her eyes landed on a baby blue gown made of tulle that sparkled faintly under the lights. It was sleeveless, with a sweetheart neckline and a design that would perfectly accommodate wings.

"That dress would look stunning on you," Nia said, suddenly appearing at her side.

Sky blinked, surprised. "Really?"

Before she could protest, Nia grabbed the gown and all but shoved her into a fitting room.

"Just try it," Nia urged. "If you hate it, I won't say another word."

Sky sighed but slipped into the gown. When she stepped out, Nia's reaction was immediate. Her eyes welled with tears.

"You look gorgeous," Nia said, her voice thick with emotion.

Sky blushed, smoothing the fabric over her hips. The dress fit perfectly, the soft blue contrasting beautifully with her white wings.

"You're getting it," Nia declared.

"But-"

"No buts!"

Nia dragged her to the register, and before Sky could argue, the dress was purchased. As they left the mall, Sky carried the garment bag, feeling a mix of embarrassment and excitement.

On the drive home, Nia chattered about homecoming plans. "Bryant's going to have a matching tux," she said. "And he's picking us up."

Sky sighed. "Great. I'll be the awkward third wheel."

Nia rolled her eyes. "You're not a third wheel! Besides, you never know. Maybe Ryan will show up without a date."

Sky's stomach twisted at the thought. "Yeah, right," she muttered. "He'll probably have some random girl on his arm."

Nia didn't reply, but Sky's mind was already racing. She stared out the window, wondering what the night would bring and trying not to dwell too much on the possibility of seeing Ryan. She still couldn't shake the memory of his apology—or the way he'd looked at her.

"Maybe he was just being nice," she thought, but a small part of her couldn't help but wonder.

Eleven

It was Friday, Homecoming Day, and the school was abuzz with excitement. For Sky, the day passed fairly normally, though the energy in the air was hard to ignore. When the pep rally began, she hesitated but decided to attend for once. She stood to the side of the bleachers, watching as the football team ran out through a line of cheerleaders, their energy visible. The crowd erupted into cheers, and the band played upbeat tunes to pump everyone up.

The rally was filled with typical antics—jocks in tutus and pompoms performing silly routines, impromptu dance battles, and spirited class games between the freshmen, sophomores, juniors, and seniors. Sky smiled at some of the ridiculousness but quickly grew bored. Slipping away unnoticed, she made her way to the library and her favorite nook.

The library was quiet, the distant sounds of the rally barely audible. Sky settled into her small window seat, pulling out her notebook and pencil. This was her safe place, where she could think and create without interruption. She stared out the window, searching for inspiration, and began scribbling a poem, the words flowing effortlessly as her thoughts wandered.

Her concentration broke when a familiar voice spoke. "What are you doing back here?"

Sky looked up, startled, to see Ryan standing in front of her. He wore his usual jeans and sneakers, paired with his bright red football jersey bearing the number 19 in white. The way he looked in his uniform made her heart skip a beat.

"I.. uh..." she stammered, trying to form a coherent response. Finally, she said, "I'm not a fan of big crowds."

Ryan grinned and grabbed a chair, flipping it around to sit on it backward. "Neither am I."

Sky blinked in surprise. "That can't be possible. You're a hotshot football guy."

He laughed, the sound light and genuine. "Yeah, but the attention gets old. Just a bunch of girls screaming at me while the guys joke around."

Sky muttered under her breath, "Your problems seem so real."

Ryan caught her comment and chuckled. "It's harder than it looks, you know. That's why I almost never hang out after games. I go home, read comics, play guitar, or have lengthy discussions with my dad about being successful."

Sky tilted her head, curious. "What does your dad do?"

Ryan's expression shifted slightly, his confidence dimming. "William Daniels."

Sky's eyes widening. "William Daniels? As in one of the top executives at NisenX? I think he's the vice president."

"Yep," Ryan said, his tone resigned. "That guy."

Sky hesitated before saying, "It must be hard being his son."

Ryan gave a small smile. "Yeah. Everyone expects the best from me. More than I can really do."

Sensing that he didn't want to delve deeper into the topic, Sky changed the subject. "Why did you come to the library? The pep rally seemed exciting."

Ryan shrugged. "I noticed you slip out the back and wanted to see where you went."

Sky's face flushed red. He laughed lightly. "You do that a lot, you know. Having fair skin makes it hard to hide your emotions."

She ducked her head. "I just feel more comfortable back here."

"I get it," Ryan said. "I'd rather hang out here than in a locker room full of dumb jocks."

Sky chuckled. "I didn't realize a jock would recognize the stupidity of the others."

Ryan feigned offense, a wide grin spreading across his face. "What do you mean by that?"

"Just that you're... different," Sky said, a teasing edge to her voice. "And you seem to know it."

Ryan leaned back. "I only play football to get away from my parents. It's a nice break, even if the guys aren't the brightest."

He glanced at her notebook. "What are you writing?"

Sky quickly pulled the notebook to her chest. "Nothing. I just like to write in my free time."

Ryan smirked, reaching for it. "Let me see."

"No!" Sky said, pulling it away. "These are for my eyes only."

Ryan held up his hands in surrender. "Okay, okay."

After a moment, he asked, "Are you coming to the game tonight?"

Sky sighed. "Nia is forcing me to go."

"Good," Ryan said, standing up as the distant sound of the school's anthem reached their ears. "It'll be nice to see you in the crowd."

Sky watched him leave; her cheeks still warm. "See you tonight," he called back with a smile.

She could only smile in return, her mind racing. "Wow," she thought. "He's... something."

Twelve

The night of the football game had arrived, and the high school stadium was packed. Sky hesitated for a moment before stepping inside, overwhelmed by the noise of the crowd and the bright lights illuminating the field. Cheers erupted as she walked around the track surrounding the field, taking in the energy of the night.

Her eyes scanned the scene until they landed on Nia, who was cheerleading along the 50-yard line. Sky noticed the scoreboard: Foreman - 0, Gramble - 7. Her school was losing, but the crowd didn't seem to mind—there was still plenty of time to turn things around.

Sky made her way to the fence where Nia stood. The moment Nia spotted her, she ran over and enveloped Sky in a big hug. "You made it!"

"Barely," Sky said, smiling faintly. "Your fifty or so texts convinced me."

Nia grinned. "I knew that would work! Come on, sit with us."

Sky hesitated but eventually agreed, letting Nia led her to the cheerleaders' bench along the fence. It was a chilly night, and Sky tucked her wings into the thin hoodie she wore, wishing she'd dressed more warmly. But being on the field felt cozier than sitting in the windy bleachers.

Sky settled in and watched the game unfold. Trevor, the quarterback, threw an interception, and the crowd groaned as the opposing team scored another touchdown. The scoreboard changed to Foreman - 0, Gramble - 14. The crowd booed, and Sky saw Trevor throw his helmet to the ground in frustration, yelling at his teammates to "get it together."

The coach called a timeout and gathered the players. Sky watched as he turned to Trevor, his expression stern. "Cool it, or I'll have you benched," the coach warned. Then he looked at Ryan, number 19, and asked, "You want to give it another go?"

Sky tilted her head, curious. "What does he mean by 'another go?'" she thought, realizing Ryan must not have done well earlier in the game.

Ryan stood there, helmet in hand, scanning the crowd as if searching for something... or someone. His eyes landed on Sky, and a big smile spread across his face. He turned to the coach and nodded. "I've got this."

The team took their positions on offense, and Sky found herself watching Ryan intently. He lined up on the far side of the field, and Trevor prepared to receive the hiked ball. The moment the play started, Ryan took off, leaping a few feet into the air. Trevor spotted him and launched the ball in his direction. Ryan caught it perfectly, spun on his heel, and sprinted toward the end zone. His speed was unreal—it was as if he blinked across the field. The crowd erupted as Ryan scored their first touchdown of the night.

Sky couldn't help but be impressed. "That was something," she thought, a small smile tugging at her lips.

From that point on, the game shifted dramatically. Foreman High dominated, racking up points until the scoreboard read Foreman - 37, Gramble - 14. The final seconds of the game were electric, with the crowd cheering wildly, the football team chanting "Foreman High!" in unison, and the band playing the school's anthem. Sky found herself caught up in the excitement, clapping and even cheering by the end.

As the celebration died down, the crowd began to disperse. The homecoming dance was next on the agenda. Nia ran up to Sky, practically glowing with excitement, having just jumped into Bryant's arms. "We have to go now if we're going to get ready!" she exclaimed, grabbing Sky's hand and pulling her toward the exit.

Sky glanced back at the field, her eyes catching on number 19. Ryan was waving at her, his smile as bright as the stadium lights.

She felt her cheeks flush as she turned away, letting Nia drag her off.

"I wonder if I'll see him at the dance," she thought, her heart fluttering at the possibility.

Thirteen

Homecoming dance was finally here, and Nia had been talking about it nonstop all week. After the game, Sky and Nia headed to Nia's house to get ready. The atmosphere was electric as they hurried to clean up and change into their dresses. Sky felt exposed in her strapless baby blue gown, her wings resting delicately above the tulle. Nia reassured her there was nothing to worry about.

As Nia began braiding Sky's hair, Sky marveled at how intricate and regal it looked. By the time Nia finished, her hair resembled Cinderella's from the live-action movie, adorned with subtle sparkles that caught the light. Nia added the final touch: makeup. Sky sighed, never liking the idea of wearing makeup, but before she could protest, Nia tossed down the brushes and exclaimed, "Finished!"

Sky hesitated but decided to look in the mirror. She stared at her reflection, completely blown away. Her eyes shimmered with a pale, sparkly eyeshadow, and the dark brown eyeliner and mascara made her blue eyes sparkle like an ocean under the moonlight. Her cheeks flushed as she teared up, overwhelmed by how beautiful she looked.

"Perfection," Nia declared, beaming.

Sky's thoughts were interrupted by the doorbell. Nia squealed, "Bryant is here!" and dashed downstairs. Sky followed to see Bryant's reaction. He was starstruck, taking in Nia's sunset-pink-to-orange ombré mermaid gown and wispy bun adorned with pearls. Bryant, in a classic black tux with a hot pink flower on his lapel, held a corsage that completed Nia's look perfectly.

Sky stood back, watching the couple with a smile. Bryant asked if they were ready, and Nia's mom insisted on taking pictures in the front yard. After a round of photos, they climbed into Bryant's black jeep—Nia in the passenger seat and Sky in the back. Sky appreciated the extra space, letting her wings rest comfortably.

When they arrived at the venue, Sky was awestruck. The building looked like a grand mansion; its exterior illuminated by string lights. Inside, the theme "Starry Night" came to life. Stars twinkled across the ceiling, and streamers of blue and white cascaded from the rafters. Balloons scattered the floor, and at least 150 students filled the room. A large DJ station had a banner reading, "Foreman Falls High Homecoming! Sponsored by NisenX."

Sky rolled her eyes. "Of course, NisenX sponsored this," she muttered.

Bryant was taking selfies with Nia when his phone rang. After a brief conversation, he turned to them. "Ryan's truck died. I'm going to pick him up. Be back soon."

Nia and Sky chatted along the wall while Bryant left. Nia explained the effort it took to make the decorations, especially the stars. Sky complimented her hard work, saying she could never have done something so beautiful. Nia's face lit up with gratitude but froze when she heard the "Cupid Shuffle" start playing.

"I have to dance!" Nia exclaimed, running to join her cheer squad on the floor. She begged Sky to come but got only a polite decline. "Think about it!" Nia shouted as she disappeared into the crowd.

Sky stayed back, happy to see her friend having a blast but still feeling out of place. She slipped out the farthest door, finding a small deck overlooking a breathtaking valley. The navy-blue lake shimmered under the full moon, and string lights dotted the landscape. She leaned against the railing, taking it all in, grateful for a moment alone.

The solitude didn't last long. Footsteps approached from behind, startling her. She turned quickly, tripping slightly, but strong arms caught her. Looking up, she saw Ryan, dressed in a fitted black tux with white lapels. His deep brown wings stretched behind him, the shades of brown matching his hair perfectly.

Sky's mind went blank. "Wow," she blurted.

Ryan smiled. "Same."

He stepped back, taking in her appearance. The moonlight danced on her wings, and her pink lips curled into a shy smile. "You look... wow," he said, struggling for words.

Sky thanked him quietly, turning back to the valley. Ryan moved to her side, asking why she was out in the cold. She blushed, realizing she hadn't even noticed the frigid air. "Less people," she said.

"Agreed," Ryan replied, standing close. The tension between them was noticeable.

Sky congratulated him on the game. He chuckled. "Didn't start that way."

"I missed the first quarter, so it doesn't matter," she said.

Ryan smiled warmly. "I'm glad you showed up."

"Nia would've killed me if I didn't," she admitted.

Ryan's gaze softened. "Still, thanks."

Sky tilted her head. "For what?"

"For helping me focus," he said. "I was lost in my head until I saw you."

Sky scoffed. "There's no way I'm the reason you did better."

"You are," Ryan said firmly.

They stood in silence until Ryan asked, "Want to see something cool?"

Sky nodded, and he led her inside, down a hallway, to a closet with a wooden ladder. "Follow me," he said, climbing up.

Sky hesitated. "Is this safe?"

"Trust me," Ryan said. She followed, wings tucked tightly. At the top, Ryan offered his hand, helping her onto the roof. The view took her breath away: lakes, a distant city, and endless fields under the starlit sky.

"Woah," she whispered.

"Thought you'd like it," Ryan said, sitting on the edge. Sky joined him, letting the breeze catch her wings. He explained the mansion's history and how he learned to fly from this very roof.

"From all the way up here?" Sky asked, amazed.

"I crashed a lot," Ryan admitted with a laugh. "Mostly into that lake."

She pictured herself from the school bash, barely avoiding a terrible landing.

Sky admired his skill. Ryan noticed and asked, "Want to take off from here?"

Sky hesitated. "I... I can't fly," she admitted.

Ryan was stunned. "Why not?"

"I've always had to hide my wings," she said quietly.

Ryan took her hand gently. "I'll show you."

They stood, and Ryan guided her to face the valley. He encouraged her to stretch her wings, running his hands lightly along their edges. She shivered at the sensation but closed her eyes, focusing on the wind. For the first time, she felt free.

"Feel every feather," Ryan said. "That's where it starts."

Sky smiled, laughing softly as the breeze lifted her wings. When she turned to thank him, the glow of the sky illuminated his outstretched wings, and she was in awe.

"That felt amazing," she said.

Ryan grinned. "You have no idea."

The cold eventually got to Sky, and she tucked her wings in. Ryan noticed and draped his jacket over her shoulders. She blushed, thanking him.

"Let's head back," he said. They climbed down, and Sky slipped on the last rung. Ryan caught her again, laughing. "You've got to stop falling for me."

Sky laughed, following him back to the dance. They found Nia and Bryant swaying to the last slow song of the night. Bryant drove them home, with Ryan sitting beside Sky in the back seat. She felt a warmth she didn't want to end.

At Nia's house, Bryant kissed Nia goodnight while Ryan grasped Sky's hands. "I had an amazing time," he said softly.

Sky smiled. "It was definitely something."

He kissed her forehead gently before leaving with Bryant. Sky, still wearing Ryan's jacket, made her way inside. Nia drove her home afterwards.

She plopped onto her bed, thinking it was the most amazing night of her life. Her phone buzzed. A text from Ryan: "Hope you don't mind; I got your number from Nia. Just wanted to make sure you made it home safe."

Sky smiled, texting back: "Not a problem. I did. Thanks."

Ryan responded with a wing emoji, and Sky couldn't help but grin.

Fourteen

That whole weekend, Sky and Ryan texted back and forth. Their conversations covered everything from school classes to family life. Sky opened up about her parents and their busy careers, which often left her feeling forgotten. Ryan listened sympathetically, sharing little glimpses into his own life.

When Monday morning arrived, Sky and Nia walked into school, both still glowing from their wonderful homecoming night. As they entered the building, Sky immediately spotted Ryan waiting by her locker. Nia noticed too and smirked. "I'll leave you two to it," she teased before heading off, likely to find Bryant.

Sky approached her locker, a smile already forming. "Good morning," she said shyly.

"Morning," Ryan replied, his grin widening. Their conversation was light and easy, filled with laughter and teasing. The moments felt effortless as they talked, and before they knew it, it was time to head to class.

At lunch, Ryan walked straight over to sit beside Sky, ignoring the curious glances from other students. He leaned closer and asked, "Can you meet me at the practice fields during study hall?"

Sky tilted her head, curious. "Why?"

"You'll see," he said with a mysterious smile. Unable to resist, she nodded. "Okay."

When study hall came, Sky made her way to the upper practice field, where Ryan was waiting. The crisp afternoon air carried the faint scent of grass, and the field was quiet and empty. She approached cautiously. "So, what are we doing out here?"

Ryan grinned. "Study hall is the perfect time to practice flying."

Sky's nerves kicked in immediately. She looked around, scanning for any potential onlookers. Once she was sure no one else was there, she relaxed slightly and nodded. "Alright."

Picking up right where they had left off at homecoming, Ryan began teaching Sky the basics of flying. At first, her movements were awkward and unsure, but with each passing day, her confidence grew. Time seemed to fly by—weeks passed, and Sky improved with every lesson. To her amazement, she found herself mastering techniques faster than she thought possible.

During those lessons, Sky and Ryan grew closer. The tension between them was undeniable, filled with unspoken words and fleeting touches. Their connection deepened with every shared moment, though neither dared to acknowledge it outright.

Outside of study hall, their bond continued to flourish. They talked whenever they could, whether in hallways or through stolen glances between classes. While Nia practiced cheer routines, Sky found herself watching the football field, her eyes always drawn to number 19. Ryan's skill as the team's star receiver was undeniable, and Foreman High's football team racked up win after win, earning their spot in the playoffs.

The week of the semi-finals brought an electric energy to the school. Sky couldn't help but feel proud of Ryan, though she remained cautious about the growing attention he received from other girls. Erica and Patricia, two of the cheer team captains, seemed especially jealous. They couldn't understand why Ryan, the school's heartthrob, spent so much time with someone like Sky. Their glares and whispered comments were impossible to miss.

Sky made a point to avoid Erica and Patricia whenever possible, keeping her head down in the hallways and steering clear of the cheerleaders' table at lunch. She knew this week would be intense, but she wasn't about to let their jealousy ruin her happiness.

Fifteen

It was Monday afternoon, and Sky sat on the hill above the football field, watching the players below. Nia was practicing with the cheer team nearby, working with the others on assembling new t-shirt cannons for Friday's game.

Nia plopped down beside Sky, brushing her hair out of her face. "So," she started with a knowing grin, "how's flying practice going?"

Sky smiled, her cheeks pink. "It's amazing. I was gliding down the hill the other day—about six feet off the ground. It felt... freeing. Exhilarating. Like nothing I've ever done before."

Nia grinned even wider. "See? Told you those wings were too gorgeous to hide."

Sky chuckled softly but didn't reply. Nia nudged her shoulder. "Speaking of wings... are you and Ryan officially boyfriend and girlfriend yet?"

Sky's face turned bright red. "I... I would know if we were, right? I've never had a boyfriend before."

Nia's jaw dropped. "Wait, what? How? You're so pretty and smart!"

Sky looked away, embarrassed. "No guy's ever been interested in me before. I was always too quiet, too shy."

Nia crossed her arms, shaking her head in disbelief. "I can't believe that. Especially now. You've totally come out of your shell."

Sky blinked. "What do you mean?"

"I mean," Nia said, gesturing at her, "you're walking through the halls more confidently. You're smiling all the time. You're even talking so much more. You're like a whole new person, and I am so proud of you."

Sky's heart warmed at the compliment. Before she could reply, Nia grabbed her hand. "Okay, show me how good a flyer you are now."

Sky hesitated, looking nervously at the field below. "I don't really want to... not in front of everyone."

"Oh, come on," Nia said, rolling her eyes. "Most of the girls are heading inside, and those guys are too busy running drills to notice."

Sky glanced down at the field, her eyes finding Ryan effortlessly. He was soaring through the air, catching throw after throw with ease. She sighed. "I guess."

Nia jumped up in excitement as Sky stood. Facing the hill, Sky unfurled her wings slowly, feeling the breeze brush against her feathers. She stepped back several feet, taking deep breaths to calm her nerves. Then, bolting forward, she launched herself off the edge of the hill. The wind lifted her, and she soared higher than she ever had before.

She couldn't help but shout with glee. Below, Nia raced along the ground, cheering her on. Sky paused mid-air, marveling at the view, as she started to descend an updraft swept in, bringing trouble.

"I... uh, don't know how to get out of this draft!" she called to Nia.

"I have no idea either!" Nia shouted back, laughing.

Sky glanced over at Ryan, watching to see if he would land and how he did it. She was about to try a slow descent when a sharp object slammed into the side of her head. The world went black as she began free-falling.

Ryan, already hovering nearby, heard the thwack and saw her plummet. In a blur, he bolted forward, catching her mid-air. He flew them to the side of the hill, gently laying her down as Nia rushed over.

"What happened?" Nia demanded, panic in her voice.

Off to the side, Erica and Patricia burst out laughing. Erica held a t-shirt cannon, with a smug look on her face.

"Back off, or I swear—" Nia started, but the girls shrugged and walked away, still giggling.

Ryan crouched beside Sky, patting her cheeks. "Sky. Sky, wake up."

Nia grabbed a nearby t-shirt, using it to press against the long scratch on Sky's forehead. Blood trickled down, but Nia knew head wounds always looked worse than they were.

Sky groaned, her eyes fluttering open. She winced. "What happened?"

"Take it easy," Ryan said gently. "You're okay."

Nia scowled. "Erica thought it'd be funny to hit you with a rock."

Sky rolled her eyes. "Not surprised."

Nia stood, fuming. "I'm getting the nurse," she announced, sprinting off.

Ryan stayed, keeping the cloth pressed to Sky's head. She gave a weak laugh.

"What's so funny?" Ryan asked.

"I was expecting to crash land anyway," she said.

Ryan chuckled. "You're something else, you know that?"

Soon, Nia returned with the nurse, a short, stout woman. Ryan and Nia helped Sky to her feet, but she immediately wobbled, a wave of dizziness hitting her. Ryan steadied her as they made their way to the nurse's office.

The nurse patched up the scratch, assuring them it was minor and would heal quickly. "But," she added, "you need to take it easy for a couple of days."

Sky groaned. "Great."

Ryan placed a hand on her shoulder, flashing her a reassuring smile. "I'll make sure she does."

The nurse recommended rest, and Nia muttered something about "taking care of business" before leaving. Ryan offered to take Sky home, insisting he could miss the last few minutes of practice.

Sky smiled. "Thanks, Ryan."

Sixteen

Sky and Ryan were driving in his dusty red Ford truck, heading to her house. The trucks interior smelled faintly of leather and pine air freshener, and the radio played softly in the background. Sky rested her head on the passenger-side window, watching the trees blur past.

As they pulled up to her house, Sky reached for the door handle, but Ryan was already outside, running to her side. "You're not following doctor's orders," he said with a teasing smile, pulling the door open for her.

Ryan wrapped his arms around her, lifting her gently from the truck. She couldn't help but notice how strong and muscular he was. Her cheeks flushed pink, and Ryan tilted his head. "Why are you so red?" he asked.

"Oh, nothing," she replied quickly, looking away.

Ryan smirked but didn't push further. He carried her inside and set her down on the ivory woven couch, then stood up, "Where's your medicine cabinet?"

She gestured toward the kitchen. "Far left upper cabinet."

Ryan nodded and disappeared briefly. Moments later, he returned with two Tylenol and a glass of water. Handing them to her, he said, "Take these."

Sky took the pills, swallowing them with a sip of water. "Thanks. I hope they kick in soon because my head feels like someone's stabbing it."

Ryan frowned. "Those girls are the worst. I still can't believe they thought that was funny."

"Let's not talk about them," Sky said, placing a small frozen pea ice pack on her head. "Tell me something good instead."

Ryan smiled. "Okay. You were amazing out there today. Flying that high? That was incredible."

Sky's face brightened. "Thanks. It did feel amazing... until the rock."

They both chuckled softly. Ryan sat down beside her on the couch. "So, what now? What do you usually do to relax?"

Sky admitted, "I watch cheesy movies and drink hot cocoa."

Ryan declared, "Perfect!" He got up and headed to the kitchen, where he made a cup of hot chocolate. When he returned, he handed it to Sky. "Hope this is okay. I might have added too much of... everything."

Sky laughed, taking a sip. It was overly sweet but comforting. She reached for her faux fur blanket, patterned like rabbit's fur, and draped it over herself. Ryan raised an eyebrow. "Mind sharing? Your house is freezing."

Sky nervously grinned and lifted a corner of the blanket. "Sure."

Ryan scooted closer, their legs touching. Sky felt a warmth spread through her, more intense than the first time she had been near him. Her heart raced as she tried to focus on her drink and not the way his proximity made her feel.

Ryan turned on a rom-com featuring Will Ferrell and Adam Sandler. "I love these guys," he said, settling in.

Sky smiled, trying to focus on the movie. As the pain medication began to work, her migraine eased, and she felt her eyelids grow heavy. She leaned against Ryan's shoulder, her head resting there as she drifted off.

By the time the credits rolled, Ryan had also fallen asleep. He stirred, blinking at the screen, then looked down. Sky was curled up, her head resting on his lap, looking peaceful. He froze for a moment, his heart pounding as he took her in.

Her golden hair framed her face perfectly, and her features were soft and serene. He couldn't help but think about how incredible she was—her bravery, her wit, her smile. The way her blue eyes sparkled when she talked about something she loved. She was unlike anyone he had ever met.

Ryan's thoughts spiraled. "She's amazing," he realized. "The most amazing person I've ever met. And somehow, in such a short time, I'm falling for her."

He didn't know how to tell her or if she even felt the same way. But for now, he was content just to be here with her.

Smiling to himself, he reached for the remote, turned off the TV, and leaned back. The room was quiet, the warmth of her presence enough to lull him back to sleep. He rested his head against the couch and drifted off, cherishing the moment.

Many hours had passed. Sky began to wake up, her mind groggy as the faint light of the rising sun crept through the windows. The world felt warm and still, and as her senses returned, she realized something was different. Her "pillow" wasn't soft—it was warm. Slowly, she opened her eyes and tilted her head upward. There, asleep against the couch, was Ryan.

Her heart stopped. She was lying on Ryan's lap.

Panic swelled inside her. What should she do? How had this happened? Before she could formulate a plan, she shifted slightly, and Ryan stirred. His eyes fluttered open, and he looked down at her with a groggy smile.

"Good morning, sleepyhead," he said, his voice still thick with sleep.

Sky's face turned beet red as she quickly sat up, brushing her hair back. "I—I'm so sorry! I didn't mean to fall asleep like that... let alone until morning."

Ryan chuckled softly, leaning forward to gently push a stray strand of hair out of her eyes. "It's no problem. I'm just glad you're feeling better."

Sky managed a small smile but felt her cheeks burn even more.

Ryan glanced at his leather band watch and frowned. "It's 4 a.m. I need to run home before my mom wakes up and realizes I'm not there."

Before he left, Ryan knelt down beside her. "Let me check your cut first," he said, carefully unwrapping the bandages. Sky sat still, trying not to fidget, though her insides were a jumble of nerves. When the bandages came off, she was surprised to see the cut had already shrunk to a thin, small line.

"Looks much better," Ryan said. He applied fresh bandages with practiced care, his touch gentle. Sky tried her best not to move, though the proximity made her heart race. She felt jittery and flustered, but Ryan seemed completely at ease.

"All set," he said with a smile as he stood. "I'll head home, get ready for school, and come right back to pick you up. Tell Nia she doesn't need to bother."

"Sounds good. Thanks."

Ryan flashed her one last grin before heading out the door. Sky stood by the window, watching him drive off in his dusty red truck. As the taillights disappeared, she leaned against the wall, her heart still pounding. How was she going to explain this to Nia?

Her thoughts drifted back to Ryan—the warmth of his smile, the way he cared for her, and the feeling of waking up beside him. She couldn't help but smile, realizing how happy he made her. His morning smile, in particular, had a way of melting her completely. She sighed, shaking her head as she tried to steady her emotions. This boy was something else.

Seventeen

Sky and Ryan made it to school just in time. True to his word, Ryan had gone home, eaten breakfast with his mom, and came right back to pick her up. The car ride had been filled with laughter as Sky sang along to the radio. Ryan mostly laughed, enjoying her enthusiasm and playful nature.

By lunchtime, Sky and Ryan were sitting together in the cafeteria when Nia came bounding over. Without waiting for an invitation, Nia grabbed Sky by the arm. "I need to borrow her for a minute," she announced to Ryan, who just chuckled and nodded.

Nia dragged Sky into the empty hallway, her face alight with curiosity. "Alright, spill it. What happened after yesterday's incident?"

Sky hesitated, her cheeks warming. "Nothing much. Ryan gave me a ride home. We watched a movie, drank hot chocolate. Nothing crazy."

Nia narrowed her eyes. "Uh-huh. And?"

Sky looked away. "And... by the end of the movie, I fell asleep on the couch."

Nia folded her arms, waiting. "Next to Ryan?"

Sky nodded slowly.

Nia squealed, clapping her hands in excitement. "That is adorable!"

Sky covered her mouth. "Shhh!"

Nia lowered her voice to an enthusiastic whisper. "Still. Adorable."

Sky couldn't help but smile. "It was... pretty amazing."

When they returned to the cafeteria, Nia gave Sky a knowing look as they rejoined Ryan and Bryant. The next few days passed in a blur. Sky and Ryan grew even closer, their connection deepening with each shared moment. Ryan seemed to find excuses to hug her more often, touch her shoulder or hand gently. Every time he did, Sky felt goosebumps ripple across her skin.

By Friday night's game, Sky had made her own sign to cheer for number 19. Foreman Falls won decisively, securing their place in the finals. To celebrate, Ryan invited Sky, Nia, and Bryant over to his house. Sky, in particular, was excited; she'd never seen Ryan's home before. Ryan was usually hesitant to bring friends over, especially with his father around, but this weekend his dad was out of town.

Eighteen

On Saturday morning, Sky practiced wing stretches and graceful landings in her yard. After a few clumsy attempts, she heard Ryan's familiar voice. "Not too bad," he teased, trying to contain his laughter as she face-planted.

"Oh, like you were perfect when you started," she shot back, grinning.

"Fair enough," Ryan said, holding out a hand to help her up.

After some playful banter, Sky changed clothes, and they headed to Ryan's house. She thought her own house was large, but Ryan's was enormous. The driveway alone was a massive circle, wide enough for three lanes of traffic. The house stretched far and wide, at least the length of a football field. Floor-to-ceiling windows gleamed in the sunlight, and a stone awning covered the double crystal doors. Beside the entrance was a sleek tablet screen embedded in the wall.

Sky's jaw dropped. "Your dad must be stinkin' rich working for NisenX."

Ryan shrugged. "He's always thought bigger is better."

As they parked, Sky stepped out of the car, still mesmerized. Ryan took her hand, grounding her. He placed his palm on the tablet, and it lit up with the words, "Welcome home, Ryan."

Sky stared. "That's amazing."

"Meet RAD," Ryan said. "Our smart home system. It runs the house."

Inside, the grand entrance was breathtaking. The floors were polished white stone, and a sweeping staircase curved upward. To the left was a sprawling kitchen with two gray quartz islands, and to the right was a room with a grand piano. Straight ahead, a long hallway hinted at more wonders. Sky was speechless.

From the kitchen, a woman's voice called out, "Ryan, is that you?"

"Hey, Mom!" he replied, leading Sky toward the voice. They found a woman with long brown hair tied back, wearing a sophisticated blouse and dress pants, topped with a red checkered apron that read "NisenX." She was cooking something fragrant with noodles and vegetables.

Karen Daniels turned, and Sky immediately saw the resemblance to Ryan. "Oh, honey, you've never brought a girl home before!"

Sky blushed furiously as Ryan groaned. "Mom, you're embarrassing her."

Karen extended her hand. "I'm Karen Daniels, but please call me Karen."

Sky shook her hand. "I'm Sky. Ryan and I go to school together."

Karen smiled warmly. "I thought I recognized you from the football games. You're the one with the number 19 sign!"

Ryan quickly interjected. "Nia and Bryant are coming over soon to celebrate last night's win."

Karen beamed. "Wonderful! Would you like some chow mein?"

Ryan nudged Sky. "You have to try it. Mom's cooking is top-notch."

Sky nodded eagerly, and soon they were eating heaping bowls of noodles. Karen joked about how Humanimals ate so much, saying Ryan could easily eat enough for three grown men. Sky laughed as Ryan turned red. It was the first time she'd seen him embarrassed.

After thanking Karen, Ryan led Sky upstairs. The winding staircase opened to another expansive hallway with doors lining both sides. "When are Nia and Bryant supposed to get here?" Sky asked.

"Not for another hour," Ryan said casually.

Sky raised an eyebrow. "Why did you pick me up so early, then?"

"I wanted to show you something," he said with a mischievous smile.

He led her to a door second from the end on the right. Inside, he told RAD to turn on the lights, revealing a room filled with workout equipment, some specially designed for Humanimals with wings. Mirrors covered the walls, dumbbells were stacked up along the base boards, and benches with large wing holes sat ready for lifting weights.

Sky gasped. "This is amazing!"

"It gets better," Ryan said, pulling back the curtains at the far wall to reveal a wooden deck with a zipline extending to a distant treehouse.

Sky stepped onto the deck, mesmerized by the view. Fields stretched to the forest beyond, and the setting sun bathed everything in warm light. Ryan explained how he had learned to fly using the zipline, demonstrating the harness designed to allow wings full range of motion.

"You can try it," he offered, holding out the harness.

Sky's eyes lit up. "Really?"

Ryan adjusted the straps for her smaller frame and hooked her to the line. "Ready?"

Taking a deep breath, Sky nodded. "Definitely."

She leapt off the deck, the wind rushing past her as she gained speed. Closing her eyes for a moment, she imagined flying freely. When she pulled the release cord, she soared ahead, exhilarated. Ryan's cheers echoed behind her, but she barely heard them. She was flying.

Too soon, the maple boarded treehouse loomed ahead. Sky braced herself and crash-landed onto the platform, rolling to a stop. Breathing hard, she got to her hands and knees, laughing in pure joy.

Ryan landed beside her. "Are you okay?"

Sky jumped to her feet, her face glowing. "That was amazing! It felt... like nothing I've ever experienced. The wind, the speed, everything."

Ryan laughed, watching her excitement as she jumped up and down, her feet leaving the ground each time. "You can come over anytime to practice," he said.

Sky threw her arms around him in a tight hug. "Thank you for this."

The hug lingered, their faces inches apart. The golden light of the sunset illuminated Sky's features, and before he could stop himself, Ryan leaned in and kissed her. The moment was brief but electric.

Ryan felt a rush of emotions surge through him. His heart was pounding, his mind spinning with thoughts of Sky. She wasn't just someone he cared about—he was certain now there was something stronger between them. The way her blue eyes lit up, the warmth she radiated, and her uncontainable joy captivated him completely. As he pulled back, he smiled at her, his chest tightening with a mixture of exhilaration and nervousness. He wasn't sure how she felt, but in this moment, he realized how deeply he was falling for her.

They pulled apart at the sound of familiar voices. "Lovebirds, come down already!" Nia called, climbing the treehouse ladder with Bryant.

After a lingering glance at Sky, who looked just as dazed and radiant as he felt, Ryan turned and headed over to greet Bryant. His steps were light, but his mind was elsewhere. She was amazing—more than amazing. She was everything.

Sky's mind raced. The kiss had felt perfect, more than she could have imagined. Every feather on her body seemed to stand on end, and a wave of warmth and goosebumps rippled from her arms to her spine. She barely noticed Nia's teasing or Bryant's greeting as she replayed the moment in her head.

"Did something happen?" Nia asked, her eyes narrowing playfully.

Still blushing, Sky shook her head and joined the others, her thoughts still spinning.

Nineteen

The group spent the evening immersed in fun—watching movies, playing card games, and tossing around a football. Sky tried her best, even though throwing or catching wasn't her forte, much to everyone's amusement. By midnight, they all went their separate ways. Bryant offered Nia a ride home, while Ryan drove Sky.

The car ride was filled with unspoken feelings. Sky couldn't stop thinking about the kiss they had shared, wondering if Ryan felt the same. Little did she know, he was battling the same desire, wanting to kiss her again but holding back.

When they arrived at her house, Ryan walked her to the door. They lingered in the doorway, exchanging quiet goodnights. Sparks flew between them, but the moment passed as they reluctantly parted ways.

Time seemed to blur in the days that followed. Sky and Ryan spent every waking moment together whenever they could, often hiding in the library's secret nook. Their relationship strengthened, building an unshakable bond.

Friday finally arrived—the day of the big championship game. Nia helped Sky get ready, painting her face with the red and white school colors and number 19. Excitement buzzed in the air as the stands filled with cheering fans.

The game was a nail-biter, with Foreman Falls and Drewry High neck and neck at 28-28. In the final ten seconds, Foreman's quarterback, Trevor, huddled his team. They shouted, "Foreman High!" before lining up for the game-winning play.

The ball was snapped, and Trevor launched it skyward. Ryan surged into action, catching the ball midair. He weaved through defenders, dodging tackles with precision. With a final leap, he crossed the goal line, clutching the ball just over the line as the buzzer sounded.

The stadium erupted in cheers as the announcer declared Foreman Falls the 5A Football Champions! Fans poured onto the field, and Sky searched the crowd for Ryan. Before she could find him, arms wrapped around her, pulling her down onto the grass.

Sky spun around to see Ryan, covered in dirt and grass, grinning ear to ear. "You did it!" she screamed, throwing her arms around him.

"We did it!" he said, lifting her off the ground and spinning her in circles.

Their moment was cut short as Ryan's teammates called him over to celebrate. Sky joined Nia, both buzzing with excitement.

They overheard Trevor announcing a party at his house the next night. The crowd cheered, but Sky and Nia exchanged unimpressed glances, rolling their eyes at Trevor's need for attention.

Later, as Sky and Ryan headed back to his truck, a stern voice stopped them. "Congratulations, son," the voice said.

They turned to see a tall man in an impeccably tailored charcoal suit, his metal-rimmed glasses glinting under the stadium lights. His expression was cold, his posture commanding. Ryan's face drained of color. "Dad, you came?" he asked hesitantly.

"Of course," William Daniels replied. "I had to support my son, the champion."

Ryan's hand gripped Sky's tightly, his unease palpable. Introducing Sky as his friend, Ryan looked more anxious than proud. Mr. Daniels scrutinized her, his handshake firm and unyielding.

"So, you're Sky Treder," he said, a faint, knowing smile appearing. "The transfer student—a Peregrine Falcon, I hear, with leucism. Unique."

Sky froze. How did he know that?

"I keep track of everything at Foreman Falls," Mr. Daniels explained, his tone clinical. "As head of health checks nationwide, I make it my business to know."

Ryan quickly ushered Sky away, but his father's parting words lingered. "Focus on what matters, Ryan. Not distractions."

In the truck, Sky held Ryan's hands, asking if he was okay. He brushed it off, apologizing for the encounter, though the tension between them lingered.

The next day, news of Trevor's party flooded social media, boasting it would be "the party of the year." Sky, uninterested in the chaos, texted Nia to ask if she was going.

Nia replied: "Not a chance. Bryant and I have much better plans than partying with drunk teens."

Sky: "Your plans sound perfect. Have fun!"

Sky texted Ryan, knowing he was stuck at home.

Sky: "How's the homework?"

Ryan: "Boring as hell. Dad's making me read NisenX reports. I don't care about that company!"

Sky: "NisenX owns everything. It's so annoying."

Ryan: "😡"

Sky: "🐉👤"

Their emojis, code for sneaking off to fly, were met with regret from Ryan.

Ryan: "Wish I could, but Dad's watching me like a hawk."

Sky: "Trevor's party will be amazing, though. 😊"

Ryan: "Stay far away from that mess."

Twenty

Later that evening, Sky lounged on the couch when a news bulletin flashed across the screen.

"A GROUP OF ARSONISTS HAS TARGETED NISENX CENTERS IN WESTERN TENNESSEE. THREE LOCATIONS HAVE BEEN DESTROYED. AUTHORITIES SUSPECT THE ANTI-HUMANIMAL GROUP, THE REFRAMERS."

Sky stiffened. The ReFramers were notorious for their hatred of Humanimals, believing them to be unnatural and dangerous. They protested Humanimal rights, aiming to eradicate them from society.

Sky's phone buzzed. Lydia's name appeared—a surprise after months of silence.

Lydia: "Stay away from the party. Not safe."

Sky's heart raced. What did Lydia know? Why warn her now? Without hesitation, Sky grabbed her jacket. She had to find out what was going on, even if it meant stepping into Trevor's chaotic party.

Sky, being a fairly great flyer, headed over to the party. It wasn't hard to find since the address was plastered all over social media. As she approached the house, she took in its tall, two-story modern design with a slanted roof and mostly glass walls. Lights spilled out from the interior, casting a glowing aura around the place. The music was deafening, pounding through the air and almost hurting her sensitive ears.

She landed lightly near the front steps and peered inside through the massive windows. She recognized many faces: Erica, Trevor, Patricia, and the rest of the football team and cheer squad, along with dozens of other teens she had never spoken to. The kitchen counter was stacked with bottle after bottle of liquor and wine. Everyone had a red Solo cup in hand, laughing and downing drinks. Sky gagged at the thought of the bitter alcohol and decided to avoid the chaos.

Circling around to the back of the house, she came upon a large cement patio. A pool, still covered by a tarp, sat unused. Couples were sprawled across the backyard lawn, locked in various stages of drunken makeouts. Sky wrinkled her nose and quietly avoided them. Not that it mattered—most of the teens were too drunk to notice anything beyond their immediate vicinity.

As she continued around the house, she spotted a side door slightly ajar, leading down to what appeared to be a basement. She hesitated, the faint sound of voices drifting up through the opening.

Cautiously, she approached the door, pressing her ear against it. Two voices were talking, their tones hushed but urgent.

Voice 1: "The electrical system runs through here. If we overload it and time it right, the whole house will lose power."

Voice 2: "And the cameras?"

Voice 1: "Taken care of. Once the grid is down, nothing's going to record anything. Clean escape."

Voice 2: "What about the pool? We still setting the cord?"

Voice 1: "Yeah. One of you needs to sneak up and drop it in. Make sure the switch is set first. And don't get caught."

Sky's stomach churned as she realized they were planning something dangerous.

Voice 1: "You—get the car ready. Park it just out of sight in the next driveway. You—set the timer. Make sure the whole system fizzles out right after we're gone. I'll oversee everything."

Sky's pulse quickened as she heard footsteps approaching the door. She shot up into the sky, wings slicing through the chilly air. Perched high above, she watched as three figures dressed in black hoodies and jeans slipped out of the basement. They moved with purpose, each heading in different directions around the property.

The basement door clicked shut, but not before Sky caught a glimpse of something that made her heart sink: a beaded bracelet on the last figure's wrist. She knew that bracelet.

Lowering herself cautiously, she landed near the door and carefully pushed it open, avoiding any creaks. A short set of concrete steps led down into the dimly lit basement. At the far end of the room, a lone figure stood hunched over the electrical panel, hands moving deftly as they worked.

Sky's breath caught in her throat. Gathering her courage, she stepped closer and said, "Lydia?"

Twenty-One

Sky froze as the figure turned around. Standing right in front of her was Lydia—her messy hair disheveled, glasses slightly askew, and her face etched with shock.

"Sky? What are you doing here?" Lydia whispered, her voice a mix of surprise and frustration. "I told you not to come!"

Sky's voice quivered, anger and hurt rising to the surface. "You think you can text me something so vague after months of silence and expect me not to worry?"

Before Lydia could respond, Sky threw her arms around her in a tight hug. For a moment, Lydia hugged her back, but she quickly pushed Sky away, her expression conflicted.

"You need to leave," Lydia said, glancing around nervously.

"Why?" Sky demanded. "Why are you even here at some stupid high school party?"

Lydia turned away, staring at the nearby stained cement wall. "I don't see why you care."

Sky grabbed Lydia's shoulder, forcing her to face her. "What's that supposed to mean? You're the one who ghosted me!"

The two stood face to face as Lydia's voice cracked with emotion. "You lied to me, Sky. You kept this huge secret for who knows how long. You were my best friend—my *only* friend—and you didn't trust me."

Sky recoiled at the accusation. "I didn't mean to hurt you! I was scared you'd leave me if you found out. Just like my parents did." Her voice softened. "I couldn't lose you too."

Tears streamed down Lydia's cheeks as she raised her voice. "I wouldn't have left..." Her words faltered, her anger dissolving into uncertainty. "...At least, I don't think I would have."

Sky's heart broke at the sight of her oldest friend, the one who had been her anchor since the third grade, struggling to even look at her.

"Oh, Lydia..." Sky whispered, her voice filled with regret.

Before either of them could say more, a drunken voice echoed from the stairs. "Well, what do we have here?"

Both girls turned to see Trevor swaggering down, his steps uneven but his gaze sharp. In an instant, two large jocks grabbed them, pinning their arms behind their backs. They were dragged to the kitchen, where Trevor began pacing in front of them, a smirk plastered across his face.

"I'm surprised anyone would dare crash *my* championship party," he slurred, his words dripping with mockery. He gestured lazily toward the girls. "So, you two know each other?"

Sky glared at him. "What does it matter?"

Trevor laughed, his razor-sharp teeth glinting under the rainbow lights. "Found a few more like Lydia snooping around outside," he said. Lydia's face paled.

"Oh, but don't worry," Trevor continued. "I've got some friends showing them around."

Sky's stomach twisted in fear. "Lydia didn't do anything," she pleaded. "Let her go!"

Trevor's smirk widened. "Wrong again," he said, pulling a small device from his pocket—a crude contraption with wires and a timer. "This little gadget was rigged to the electrical panel downstairs. A power outage followed by an uncontrollable fire. Sound familiar?"

He turned to Lydia, his face inches from hers. "Tell me, how do I know your friend here wasn't in on it?" He turned to Sky, his eyes gleaming with malice.

"She wasn't!" Sky protested. "I stopped her before anything happened."

Trevor chuckled darkly. "Sure you did." He straightened, addressing the crowd with a theatrical flourish. "Normals—so desperate to be special like us that they'd rather destroy us than join us." He clicked his tongue. "I think it's time we teach this 'Normo' a lesson."

A lackey handed Trevor a small white pill. He held it up for Sky to see, his grin wicked. "Sky, since she's your friend, you get to decide. Take this little pill, or…" He turned to Lydia, dragging a claw along her cheek, drawing a thin line of blood. "Or I show her what these claws can really do."

Lydia winced; her face filled with fear.

Sky's heart pounded as she looked between Lydia and Trevor. "What is it?" she asked.

Trevor's smile turned feral. "It's called Ragger. Made by NisenX to give Predators like us an… edge." His voice lowered; his tone almost gleeful. "Small doses are fun, but a whole pill? Let's just say it's a *wild ride*."

Sky's gaze locked with Lydia's, whose fear was now unmistakable.

"Give it," Sky said firmly.

Trevor's laughter boomed as he grabbed her face, forcing her mouth open. He dropped the pill in, and Sky swallowed with difficulty.

"Fantastic," he sneered, demanding she open her mouth to prove she'd taken it. Satisfied, he gestured to his lackeys. "Bring them."

Sky and Lydia were hauled upstairs and shoved into a large office. Trevor turned back, smirking as he blocked the door. "Good luck," he said mockingly. "Maybe Lydia will learn to stay in her lane." With that, he slammed the door shut.

Sky tried the handle, but it wouldn't budge. She turned to Lydia, panic creeping into her voice. "We're locked in."

From the other side of the door, muffled voices promised trouble.

Lydia paced behind a brown sofa, her voice trembling. "What's going on? What's Ragger?"

Sky leaned against the wall, pressing her palms to her temples. "I don't know. Some drug NisenX made. I think people use it to get high."

Lydia's voice rose. "Why did you even come here? You've made everything worse!"

Sky snapped back. "Why did you do something as stupid as crashing a party for a bunch of drunk zoo animals?"

Lydia buried her face in her hands. Sky's retort died in her throat as she noticed something—a black mark peeking through a tear in Lydia's hoodie.

"What's that on your arm?" Sky asked softly.

Lydia quickly covered it. "None of your business."

Before Sky could press further, a pounding sensation exploded in her head.

"Sky, what's wrong?" Lydia asked, her voice tinged with fear.

Sky gasped, clutching her head. "My heart's racing. I feel... angry."

Her breathing quickened as she slid to the floor, trembling. Lydia knelt beside her, panicking. "You have to fight it! Stay with me!"

Sky snapped to her feet, her eyes wild. "Why do you even care?" she shouted, slamming her fist into a mirror. It shattered, leaving shards of glass sprinkled with blood.

Lydia screamed, backing away. "Sky, please! Remember who you are! We're best friends!"

Sky blinked, regaining a sliver of control. She threw her phone toward Lydia and doubled over, her body trembling.

"Call Ryan," Sky rasped, her voice strained.

Lydia scrambled for the phone, her hands shaking as she unlocked it. Finding Ryan's number, she dialed.

When he picked up, his voice was curt. "Sky, I can't talk right now."

"This is Lydia," she stammered. "Sky's in trouble. Some lion guy forced her to take something—Ragger—and now she's…" A crash interrupted her, and she ducked behind the sofa. "Please, hurry!"

"I'm on my way," Ryan said, his voice resolute.

The line went dead as the sound of shattering glass echoed through the room.

Twenty-Two

Sky was fighting desperately to release the overwhelming anger without hurting Lydia. She began punching the wall, her fists pounding relentlessly until the drywall cracked under the force. She grabbed anything within reach—a chair, a lamp, even a small side table—and hurled them across the room. The sound of breaking objects filled the air, drowning out Lydia's pleas. Sky could barely cling to the fear she felt for hurting her oldest friend; it was buried under a surge of primal rage.

"I have to get out of here," Sky muttered through gritted teeth, her feathers ruffling and quivering as her instincts screamed for release. She could feel it building inside her, a terrifying drive to attack, to unleash. Her eyes locked on Lydia, and she tensed, ready to leap. Her muscles coiled like springs, and every feather on her wings bristled in anticipation.

Lydia, still crouched behind the couch, tried to reach her. "Ryan is on his way! Just hold on, Sky! You'll be okay, I promise!"

But Sky didn't hear a word. It was as though the roar of a car engine filled her mind, drowning out everything else. Her breath came in ragged gasps as her gaze bore down on Lydia.

"Duck," Sky growled, her voice low and menacing.

Lydia froze, confused. "What?" she stammered, trying to assure Sky that everything would be fine. "Sky, I—"

"NOW," Sky snarled, her voice so deep and stern that it left no room for argument. Lydia caught a glimpse of Sky's eyes, and what she saw sent chills down her spine. Sky's pupils were stretched unnaturally, giving her eyes a dark, predatory look. They weren't the eyes of her best friend anymore. They were the eyes of a predator, wild and violent.

Lydia dropped to the floor just in time. With a powerful thrust of her wings, Sky launched herself through the air and plowed straight into the wall of windows. The glass shattered in a deafening cascade, the shards catching the light as they rained down around her. Sky didn't stop; she didn't even look back. She knew she had to run, to escape, before she did something she couldn't take back.

The frosty night air hit her like a slap as she soared out into the open. She flew low over the backyard and into the woods, her wings cutting through the air with furious speed. The dark forest swallowed her up, the trees closing in around her like a sanctuary from the chaos she had left behind.

Back inside, Lydia remained on the floor, her hands trembling as she clutched Sky's phone. Shards of glass were scattered around her, glinting in the dim light. She didn't dare move, paralyzed by fear and the memory of those eyes. The predator that had stared back at her wasn't the Sky she knew. It was something else, something terrifying.

Lydia's whispered words broke the silence. "Ryan... please hurry."

She looked down at the phone in her hands, noticing the screen was still active. "Hello? Ryan? Are you there?" she asked desperately. The line was silent for a moment before the call cut out abruptly.

Ryan didn't bother with his car, knowing he could fly to the party much faster. The urgency in Lydia's voice and the mention of Ragger burned in his mind. He soared through the night, his wings slicing the air, and within minutes, he landed heavily on the front porch of Trevor's house. The thudding music and loud chatter spilled out into the yard, but Ryan barely registered it. He shoved the door open, ignoring the startled stares of partygoers, and scanned the crowd.

Trevor was sitting on the stair steps, laughing his head off with a drunken slur. Ryan's rage ignited. He stormed over, grabbed Trevor by his mane, and slammed him against the wall.

"Where is she?" Ryan growled, his voice low and dangerous.

Trevor, blinking slowly and clearly inebriated, chuckled. "She's having a blast with her little friend upstairs," he said mockingly.

Ryan's grip tightened, and Trevor winced in pain. "I'm not asking again. Where is she?"

Trevor snickered, then gestured lazily toward a door jammed with a chair. "Over there," he slurred.

Ryan released him and moved to the door, but Trevor's drunken voice called out behind him. "Man, you've gone soft. That winged freak's got you whipped, huh?"

Something inside Ryan snapped. He turned sharply and drove his fist into Trevor's jaw, sending the lion sprawling to the floor. "If you ever hurt Sky again, you'll regret it," Ryan snarled, his hazel eyes blazing with fury.

Trevor groaned, too stunned to respond, as Ryan ripped the chair away from the door and swung it open. The sight inside shook him to the core. The room was in shambles—furniture overturned, the walls scarred with dents and cracks, and shards of glass scattered everywhere. Blood droplets trailed across the floor toward the shattered windows.

"Sky?" Ryan called out, his voice trembling with a mix of fear and desperation. "Lydia?"

A weak voice came from behind the couch. "Are you Ryan?"

Ryan rushed over to find Lydia huddled behind the couch, pale and shaking. "Where's Sky?" he asked urgently.

Lydia pointed toward the shattered windows. "She... she went that way. She just... flew out." Her voice cracked with fear as she glanced at the wreckage.

"Go home," Ryan ordered, his tone leaving no room for argument.

He didn't wait for her response. He bolted through the shattered wall, his wings propelling him into the dark woods. The cold air stung his face, and the trees blurred past as he darted between them, searching for any sign of Sky.

His mind raced. He knew the effects of Ragger all too well. He'd seen it in his father's-controlled experiments—how it turned people into primal, uncontrollable beasts. The effects were short-lived, but intense enough to leave lasting damage.

A scream pierced through the trees. Ryan's heart dropped as he pinpointed the source and veered sharply toward it. He found Sky in a small clearing, her fists relentlessly pounding a tree trunk. Her feathers were ruffled and splattered with blood, and her eyes were wild—blackened with stretched pupils, like a predator's.

"Sky!" he called, landing a few feet away. "Are you okay?"

She snapped her head toward him, and he saw the rage etched into her face. "Ryan, get away!" she growled, her voice deeper and more feral than he'd ever heard.

"Sky, you're going to be fine. You just need to…" His words were cut off as she launched into the air, landing on a nearby tree branch.

"Stay back!" she shouted, but her tone was a mix of anger and fear.

"Sky, focus on me," Ryan pleaded. "You're almost through this, I promise. Just hold on."

She leapt from the branch, throwing a punch his way. Ryan dodged, noting the flicker of blue returning to her eyes. "It's almost over, Sky. Just fight it!" he urged.

She lunged at him again, but her movements were slowing. He caught her bloodied fists and held them tightly, even as she screamed in frustration.

"Lydia… my parents… they all left me!" Sky shouted, tears streaming down her face. "I've always been alone!"

Ryan's heart broke as he held her trembling hands. "Sky, you're not alone," he said softly. "You have Nia, Bryant, and… and me."

Sky's eyes flared with a brief burst of energy. "You? You're the hardest part of it all!" she yelled, her punches weakening with each word. "You make me… feel things…"

She stumbled, and Ryan caught her as she collapsed. "Why?" he asked gently, holding her in his arms.

Through her tears, she choked out, "Because I...think I love you. And I... I'm so scared you'll leave me, just like everyone else."

Ryan's breath caught as her words sank in. She sobbed against his chest, her body shaking as she finally let go of the pain she'd been carrying. He wrapped his arms tightly around her, feeling a wave of emotions crash over him. Fear for her safety, pain for her struggles, and an overwhelming realization of his own feelings.

"Sky," he whispered, his voice breaking. "I love you too."

He held her close, his wings folding protectively around her as they lay on the forest floor. The night was still, save for the rustle of leaves and the sound of Sky's soft sobs. Ryan knew he'd do anything to protect her, to keep her from feeling alone ever again.

Twenty-Three

Sky started to wake up, her eyes cracking open slowly. Her entire body felt like it had been run over by a semi-truck, and her head throbbed in a dull rhythm. She glanced around the room, her vision groggy as she tried to piece together where she was. On the wall, she spotted a small shelf adorned with golden trophies. Her eyes wandered to family pictures, though she couldn't quite make out the faces in her current state. Then her gaze landed on a framed red jersey with the number 19 boldly printed in white. Panic set in as realization struck her—she was in Ryan's room, in Ryan's bed.

Her heart raced, and she attempted to sit up, only to fall back down with a sharp wince. Looking at her hands, she noticed they were both wrapped in gauze, with additional bandages scattered along her arms. What happened to me? she thought.

Suddenly, the door across from the bed swung open, and a puff of steam escaped from the bathroom beyond. A tall figure stepped into the room, and Sky's breath caught in her throat. It was Ryan. Steam still clung to his skin, and he was rubbing a towel through his damp hair. He was dressed in red joggers that hung loosely on his hips, and his bare chest glistened slightly from the shower. His abs were defined like they had been sculpted by an artist; each muscle etched perfectly. His strong shoulders framed a broad chest, and his wings extended slightly behind him, feathers catching the light as they moved. Sky felt her cheeks flush. She couldn't tear her eyes away from him and felt a mix of admiration and embarrassment. Was it even legal to look that good?

Ryan's eyes immediately caught the slight flinch Sky made as she tried to sit up again. He quickly crossed the room, concern strewn across his face. "Take it easy," he said gently, placing a hand on her left arm to help her lay back down and propping her up with a pillow.

Sky stared at him, still dazed. "What happened?" she croaked, her voice hoarse.

Ryan began to unravel the gauze around her left hand. "You went to Trevor's party last night," he said softly.

Sky shook her head slightly, trying to comprehend. "Are you sure? I don't remember…"

"Yeah, you were there," Ryan confirmed. "And so was your friend Lydia."

Sky's brows furrowed in confusion. "I don't remember much of anything. What happened?"

Ryan paused, studying her face. "What's the last thing you do remember?"

Sky thought for a moment, her eyes darting as she tried to piece together fragmented memories. "I remember texting you... you told me not to go. I remember lights, lots of lights... and people. I think they were drunk. And I felt... really upset. No, mad." Her voice trailed off.

Ryan nodded grimly. "Yeah, there were plenty of drunk idiots there." He continued unwrapping her left hand, revealing red, scratched knuckles. "Do you remember beating the crap out of a tree trunk?"

Sky looked at him, baffled. "Why would I do that?"

Ryan sighed. "Because Trevor forced you to take something."

Sky's breath hitched. "What did he make me take?"

Ryan finished with her left hand and began unwrapping her right. "It's called Ragger. It's a drug developed by NisenX. Originally, it was meant for soldiers, to give them bursts of energy and... well, primal rage. But it's illegal now. Some idiots still use it in small doses to get high, but Trevor thought it'd be funny to give you a full dose."

Sky stared at him, horrified. "Rage? That doesn't explain the tree."

Ryan leaned forward slightly; his expression serious. "Trevor locked you and Lydia in a room together, thinking it'd be entertaining to watch you go primal. You didn't hurt her, though. You busted through a wall of windows and flew off instead."

Sky's jaw dropped. "I flew through a wall of glass?"

Ryan nodded. "Yeah. Found you shortly after, punching a tree trunk in the woods."

Sky looked away, ashamed. "Did I... say anything?"

Ryan hesitated, not wanting to burden her with the emotional confession she'd made in her rage. "Nothing that made much sense. You were just... yelling."

Sky frowned. "I'm sorry."

"You don't need to apologize," Ryan said. "Lydia called me from your phone. That's how I knew to find you."

Before Sky could respond, a voice called from the hallway. "Is she awake yet?"

Ryan smiled as Karen, his mom, peeked around the corner. "Yeah, come in," he said.

Karen entered the room and knelt beside the bed, her kind eyes scanning Sky. "How are you feeling, sweetheart?" she asked gently.

Sky managed a weak smile. "Like I got hit by a car."

Karen chuckled. "Well, that sounds about right. I used to be a nurse before I started working with my husband's company as chief of the medical wing. So, I wanted to make sure you're okay."

Sky looked at Ryan, who nodded. "She's good at this," he assured her.

Karen examined Sky's hands and the bandages on her arms. "You're healing nicely. Just try not to fight any more inanimate objects."

Sky and Ryan both laughed, and Karen smiled warmly. "The drug's effects should subside within 24 hours. You'll feel like yourself again soon."

"Thank you," Sky said sincerely.

Karen patted her hand. "Take it easy, okay?" She stood and left the room, shouting over her shoulder, "And put a shirt on, Ryan!"

Ryan laughed, running to his closet. He pulled on a gray NFL t-shirt before turning back to Sky. "So, what do you want to do now?"

Sky hesitated. "Is your dad still home?"

Ryan shook his head. "Nah, he got called to an emergency at work."

Relief washed over Sky's face. "In that case, I'd love to do the zipline again."

Ryan quickly shot down the idea. "Not until you've rested. That stuff takes a toll."

Sky groaned. "Fine. What else do you have?"

"How about the movie room downstairs?" Ryan offered. "I know how much you love movies."

Sky smiled. "Better than being stuck in a stranger's bedroom."

Ryan smirked. "Pretty sure we're past strangers." He scooped her up in his arms, ignoring her protests, and carried her down the stairs.

The movie room was incredible. Rows of theater-style seats faced a massive projector screen. In the back were a popcorn machine, every kind of candy imaginable, and a soda machine. Sky's jaw dropped. "Why didn't we watch movies here before?"

Ryan grinned. "Didn't want to show off."

Sky rolled her eyes as he carefully set her down. "Your house is insane," she said.

"Your house feels more like home," Ryan replied as he started the popcorn machine. "Want anything?"

Sky shook her head. "Still feeling bleh."

Ryan returned with a bucket of popcorn, settling beside her. "What should we watch?"

Sky smirked. "Not action. My head can't take it."

Ryan laughed, settling on a Will Ferrell movie. As the film began, Ryan glanced at Sky. His thoughts drifted to the woods, to her confession. He wanted to say something but decided against it. She needed time, and he'd wait. Smiling to himself, he shifted his attention back to the movie. For now, just being beside her was enough.

Twenty-Four

Sunday eventually came to an end, with Sky and Ryan spending the day indulging in a full movie marathon. By the halfway mark, Sky realized how cold she felt due to her torn and tattered shirt. Ryan, ever attentive, ran out and quickly returned with his varsity football jacket in hand.

"Here," he said, draping it over her shoulders. "It's even got holes for your wings."

Sky shyly grinned as he wrapped it around her. The warmth and faint scent of Ryan reminded her of homecoming night when he'd done the same. She couldn't help but feel a quiet flutter in her chest.

By the time the sun set, Ryan drove Sky home, making sure she was safely inside before heading back to his place. The next morning, Ryan picked her up as usual, and they headed to school. The only remnants of the party incident were a few scratches on Sky's knuckles and a faint, barely visible scar on her forehead from the rock collision. Walking into school, Ryan stayed protectively close to Sky, his arm brushing against hers.

As they reached the lockers, Nia came running down the hallway, her face a mix of worry and frustration. She skidded to a halt in front of Sky and immediately started questioning her.

"What happened to you? You didn't respond to any of my texts yesterday!" Nia exclaimed.

Sky exchanged a glance with Ryan before explaining. "It's... a long story."

Nia crossed her arms, narrowing her eyes. "Well, start talking."

Sky took a deep breath and explained the events of the party—Lydia's warning text, confronting her in the basement, Trevor forcing her to take Ragger, and how everything spiraled out of control. She described how Ryan found her in the woods and stayed with her through the aftermath.

Nia's face turned beet red with anger. "That's it! I'm going to murder Trevor. Where is he? I'll rip that stupid mane off his smug face!"

Bryant, who had just walked up, chuckled nervously. "Relax, babe. Last I heard, Trevor's parents were furious about the party. He got suspended after the cops' found drugs on him."

Ryan scowled. "Suspended? Why wasn't he expelled?"

Sky rolled her eyes. "Trevor's parents must have pulled strings. Ugh."

Nia muttered under her breath about "how money fixes everything" as the group dispersed to their respective classes. At lunch, they gathered around their usual table. The atmosphere was lighthearted as Nia shared plans for the cheer squad's next performance. But Ryan's attention was suddenly drawn to the hallway.

"Don't look now," he whispered to Sky, "but that jerk is here."

Sky followed his gaze and spotted Trevor at his locker, presumably gathering his books to do schoolwork from home. Her stomach tightened, and a wave of anger surged through her. The memory of the party and Trevor's smug face was enough to reignite her fury.

Nia stood; fists clenched. "That's it. I'm going over there."

But Sky was faster. She bolted from the table, Ryan following close behind. She stormed up to Trevor and, without hesitation, shoved the books from his hands. They scattered across the floor as he turned to face her, his expression smug.

"What do you want?" he sneered.

Before he could say more, Sky sent a forceful punch into his gut, knocking the wind out of him. Trevor doubled over in pain, gasping for air. Nia arrived just in time to knee him hard between the legs. Trevor crumpled to the floor, groaning in agony.

Bryant and Ryan caught up, standing back and watching in stunned silence as the girls unleashed their fury. A teacher's voice suddenly rang out from the hallway. "What's going on here?"

Ryan quickly grabbed Sky by the arm, pulling her away. "Nothing, sir," Bryant said smoothly, stepping forward. "Just a misunderstanding."

The teacher eyed the scene—Trevor on the floor, Sky and Nia glaring down at him—before shaking his head and walking away. The group hurried back to the lunchroom, where they burst into laughter at the absurdity of the situation.

Ryan sat beside Sky, staring at her with a mix of awe and admiration. Her fierce determination and fiery spirit only made him like her more. The way she stood up for herself, unafraid to confront someone as intimidating as Trevor, was captivating. His thoughts swirled with feelings of admiration and love, wondering how he had gotten so lucky.

Sky, still catching her breath, muttered, "I was ready to beat him to a pulp."

Nia grinned. "I was about to rip the fur off his smug face."

Bryant laughed, planting a kiss on Nia's cheek. "Remind me never to get on your bad side."

Nia smirked. "You'd better not."

The bell rang, signaling the end of lunch. Ryan and Sky walked together to Avian Anatomy, his arm resting protectively around her shoulders. Sky felt self-conscious wearing Ryan's jacket, knowing everyone could see it. She stared at the floor, a blush creeping across her cheeks. But deep down, she couldn't help but feel incredibly lucky. For the first time in her life, she felt truly cared for, and it was a feeling she never wanted to lose.

Twenty-Five

Sky and Ryan walked into Avian Anatomy class together, their usual seats at the back of the room waiting for them. The teacher, Mrs. Fields, stood at the front, a large diagram of migratory patterns projected on the screen behind her. The topic for the day was seasonal behavior in bird species.

Mrs. Fields began, her voice calm and methodical. "As we've been discussing, many avian species engage in seasonal migration, often traveling thousands of miles to find more suitable climates or resources. But what's remarkable is the social cohesion many of these species display during these migrations." She clicked a remote, and an image of geese flying in a V-formation appeared.

"Take geese, for example," she continued. "Not only do they travel in highly organized formations to reduce wind resistance, but they also exhibit an extraordinary bond. If one bird becomes injured or unable to continue, another will stay behind with them until they are able to rejoin the group or until the end of their journey. This loyalty is seen in their nesting habits as well—many geese remain with a single mate for life. This kind of connection provides stability and support for survival in harsh conditions."

Sky listened intently; her gaze fixed on the screen. She'd always found it fascinating how birds formed such strong bonds, and as she glanced at Ryan beside her, she couldn't help but wonder if humans—or rather humanimals—were capable of the same.

A girl sitting near the front raised her hand, and Mrs. Fields gestured for her to speak. "Mrs. Fields, what about imprinting? Is that real?" she asked.

Mrs. Fields rolled her eyes slightly. "Imprinting is often exaggerated in popular culture. While it's true that certain bird species form immediate bonds at birth, what you're referring to—romantic or lifelong emotional imprinting—is largely a myth. Humanimals often attribute unexplained emotions to it, but there's no scientific evidence."

Another student, a girl with reddish feathers framing her face, chimed in. "But my uncle says he imprinted last year. He bumped into a girl on the street, and now they're married. They're different species of birds, but he swears it's real."

Mrs. Fields sighed but nodded. "Fine. Since there seems to be so much curiosity, let's discuss it. Imprinting, as it's described in folklore, occurs when two humanimals—or a humanimal and a human—form an immediate, inexplicable bond. The phenomenon supposedly transcends physical attraction and is described as a sense of purpose and completion when with the other person."

The class leaned in, intrigued. Mrs. Fields began pacing the front of the room. "Some avian species, like penguins or albatrosses, mate for life, forming a bond so strong that they can recognize their mate's call even after years of separation. The myth suggests that humanimals, particularly avians, can experience a similar connection."

The girl who had asked the initial question raised her hand again. "So... it's like love at first sight?"

Mrs. Fields shook her head. "Not exactly. For some, the connection might seem instant, while for others, it's something that builds over time. The common thread is the intensity of the bond—a feeling that every thought and action revolves around the other person. It's said to bring a mix of nervousness, excitement, and comfort all at once."

The class murmured with interest, but Sky's mind was elsewhere. She stared at her desk, her thoughts racing. When she'd first met Ryan, she'd been nervous, stumbling over her words and avoiding eye contact. But there had been something else—a pull she couldn't explain, as though her world had shifted to revolve around him without her consent. Was this what Mrs. Fields was describing? Or was she just overthinking?

She thought about Ryan's smile, the way it lit up his whole face and made her feel safe. She thought about how her heart raced when he touched her hand or how her stomach fluttered when he looked at her as if she were the only person in the room. She couldn't help but wonder if he felt the same.

Mrs. Fields' voice interrupted her thoughts. "Of course, this is just a myth. There's no scientific evidence to support the existence of imprinting. It's a romanticized idea that many cling to, but it's not real."

Sky's chest tightened. Was it really just a myth? If it wasn't real, then what was she feeling? Her mind swirled with questions as she glanced at Ryan out of the corner of her eye. He was listening intently, his brow furrowed in thought. Did he feel the same pull she did, or was she imagining it all?

Ryan suddenly turned his head and caught her staring. He smiled, and her heart skipped a beat. She quickly looked away, her cheeks burning. Maybe it was just a myth, but the way she felt about Ryan was undeniable. Whether it was imprinting or something else entirely, she couldn't deny that he made her feel complete in a way she'd never experienced before.

Twenty-Six

Class ended, and Ryan and Sky went their separate ways. As Sky jetted off to her next class with determination, Ryan leaned against the wall of lockers, watching her disappear down the hallway. He couldn't help but smile, his thoughts consumed by her.

Ryan remembered the first day he saw Sky. She'd been wearing a long navy-blue trench coat, her hair cascading down to hide her face. She seemed scared, almost like she wanted to vanish into the crowd. He'd noticed her struggling with her locker, and it had been the perfect excuse to approach her. The moment she'd looked up at him, her wide blue eyes meeting his, the hairs on the back of his neck had stood on end. His heart had quickened, and for a moment, he couldn't think straight. He didn't know what was happening, but he'd known one thing for certain—he wanted to talk to her more. To be around her.

As Ryan walked to his next class, his mind wandered to everything he'd learned about her since then. Sky was shy and reserved, yet incredibly strong and resilient. She had this quiet determination that he admired. When she smiled, it was as if the whole world paused just to catch a glimpse of her light. He couldn't help but grin at the memory of her blushing and turning away whenever he teased her. And her laugh? It was like music—soft, genuine, and addictive.

In Avian Anatomy earlier, they'd been listening to the teacher discuss imprinting. Ryan had felt an unexpected pang of recognition as the teacher described the symptoms of this supposed bond. Nervousness, excitement, a sense of purpose—those were exactly the feelings he'd had for Sky from the moment they'd met. He'd spent months trying to make sense of it. He'd never been interested in anyone before, not even the countless girls who fawned over him at school. But Sky was different. She didn't fawn. She didn't try to impress him. She was just... real. Kind, patient, and unguarded in a way that made him want to protect her.

By the time the final bell rang, Ryan had decided he'd spend every free moment with her now that football season was over. He leaned against the lockers, waiting for her to round the corner. On cue, Sky appeared. Her ponytail swayed with each step, her wings catching the light and moving gracefully behind her. And then there was that smile—the one that made his chest tighten and his thoughts blur. Man, she's incredible, he thought.

Sky walked up to her locker, fumbling with the lock. "Football season's over," Ryan said casually, leaning against the locker next to hers. "I've got a lot more free time now."

Sky glanced at him, her blue eyes meeting his for a fleeting moment before she turned back to her books. Those eyes, he thought, were like a stormy sky after a fresh rain, deep and endless. "Oh yeah?" she said coyly. "Bet you have a lot of stuff planned."

Ryan leaned closer, his voice dropping to a playful whisper. "Not really. Just hanging out with you, I guess."

Sky shrugged, her lips twitching into a small smile. "What makes you think I want to hang out with some hot-shot football guy?"

Ryan grinned. "Why wouldn't I want to hang out with someone as amazing as you?"

Sky felt a shiver race down her spine at the nearness of his voice. She turned away, pretending to organize her locker, trying to mask the flush spreading across her cheeks and ears.

Suddenly, Nia appeared, her cheerful voice breaking the moment. "What are you two planning for this week?" she asked, her eyes darting between Sky and Ryan.

Sky opened her mouth to respond, but Ryan beat her to it. "Actually, we've got plans," he said, his voice confident.

Sky blinked, looking at him with surprise. "We do?"

Ryan nodded. "Yep. We're going on our first official date."

Sky's face lit up with joy. Nia clapped her hands together, grinning. "Take it easy, you two. Don't ruffle too many feathers!"

Bryant strolled up, wrapping an arm around Nia. "I guess that means we've got the weekend to ourselves, huh, babe?"

Nia smirked. "Your 'babe' could use some me-time."

Bryant feigned a pout, snuggling closer to her shoulder. "Not without me."

Nia rolled her eyes but smiled, tugging him toward the exit. "We'll talk later," she said, leaving Sky and Ryan alone in the now-empty hallway.

Ryan turned to Sky; his tone softer. "How about we head to my place? Mom's making sesame chicken tonight, and I know it's your favorite."

Sky grinned. "Only if I get to use that zipline of yours."

Ryan leaned in close, his voice a low whisper. "Of course."

Sky's breath caught in her throat, her heart racing as his words sent an electric warmth through her. She nodded, unable to form a coherent response. Hand in hand, they walked towards Ryan's truck, their nerves buzzing with quiet emotions after such an eventful day.

Twenty-Seven

Sky and Ryan sat on the wooden deck of his house, their legs dangling off the edge as they watched the sun begin its slow descent. The warm glow bathed the world in golden light, reflecting off the trees and the rolling hills beyond. Both were tired but happy after spending the afternoon racing through the sky and playing on the zipline. Ryan leaned back on his hands, glancing at Sky with a wide smile.

"You've really improved since Homecoming night," he said, his tone filled with admiration.

Sky beamed at the compliment. "Flying is the most amazing thing I've ever experienced. It's hard not to just stay up there, you know? Everything feels so simple in the sky. No problems. No drama. Just… freedom."

Ryan nodded, his gaze drifting upward. "Yeah. Life up there is definitely easier than down here."

Sky stood up, stretching her wings. "I could bolt into the sky right now and never look back," she said with a teasing grin.

Ryan smirked. "So why not?"

Sky didn't hesitate. With a mischievous smile, she leapt into the air, her wings spreading wide. They caught the wind perfectly, and she soared upward, higher and higher. She climbed until Ryan's house became a tiny speck below her. From this height, the world unfolded like a breathtaking painting. The clouds were close enough to touch, the city lights in the distance shimmered like stars, and the sun cast long, vibrant shadows across the earth. It was thrilling.

Within moments, Ryan joined her, his powerful wings slicing through the air as he ascended to her level. "You're definitely a professional flyer now," he said, his voice carrying easily over the wind.

Sky laughed; the sound carried away by the breeze. "I want to try something," she said, her eyes sparkling with excitement.

Ryan raised an eyebrow. "What's that?"

Sky didn't answer. Instead, she angled her wings downward and dove. The wind roared in her ears as she picked up speed. Faster and faster, she fell, the ground rushing toward her in a blur. Her heart raced with adrenaline, but there was no fear, only pure exhilaration. Her wings cut through the sky with ease, each feather perfectly aligned to minimize resistance. She felt alive, as though she and the wind were one.

As the ground neared, Sky adjusted her wings, shifting her body to catch the upward draft. She felt a powerful gust of air push against her, lifting her back into the sky with an effortless grace. The maneuver was flawless, and she slowed to a gentle glide, her chest heaving with elation.

Ryan flew over to her, his face a mix of awe and curiosity. "How did you do that?" he asked.

Sky grinned. "I've been reading up on peregrine falcons. They have insane speed, and I wanted to see if I could pull it off."

Ryan shook his head, clearly in awe, "Color me impressed. You killed it, Sky."

Sky was breathing heavily, the adrenaline leaving her both excited and drained. Ryan noticed her fatigue and took her hands gently. "Let's head back down. You've earned a break."

She hesitated, her eyes scanning the horizon. "Do we have to? Life's so much better in the clouds."

Ryan smiled, flying closer until they were almost nose to nose. "I guess we can stay a little longer."

The tension between them crackled like bolts of lightning. Sky's breathing quickened, but not from exertion. Ryan felt his own heartbeat pick up as he gazed into her eyes, the world around them fading into insignificance.

"What do you want to do now?" Sky asked softly, her voice barely above a whisper.

Ryan's smile widened. Without thinking, he wrapped his arms around her, pulling her close. Their lips met in a kiss that was charged, more intense than anything they'd shared before. Up here, high above the world, it felt like nothing else mattered. The wind danced around them, ruffling their hair and wings. Ryan held her tightly, feeling her heart race against his chest. Every moment felt timeless.

When they finally separated, their foreheads touched, both of them breathing heavily. Sky's voice was barely audible as she whispered, "Wow."

Ryan smiled, his eyes locking onto hers. He took her hand, and together they descended, landing on the treehouse's wooden deck. They sat close on the dusty couch inside, the silence between them comfortable yet thrilling. The sun had dipped below the horizon, painting the sky in shades of deep purple and orange.

Finally, Ryan broke the silence. "Do you remember our lesson from school today?"

Sky, leaning against his shoulder with his wing draped protectively around her, asked, "Which one?"

Ryan hesitated, looking straight ahead. "From Avian Anatomy."

Sky's heart skipped a beat, and she sat up slightly. "Yeah, I think so. Why?"

Ryan's cheeks flushed, and he avoided her gaze. "Do you believe in that sort of stuff?"

Sky turned away, the awkwardness between them noticeable. "I'd like to think so. I mean, stuff like that's in every fairytale for a reason, right?"

Ryan nodded slowly. "I think I've felt something like it before."

Sky's curiosity was piqued. "When?"

Ryan glanced at her; his voice soft. "A few months ago. This new girl showed up at school. She was quiet and reserved, struggling with her locker. I went over to help her out."

Sky's cheeks burned red. "And?"

Ryan smiled, his hand reaching up to gently cup her cheek. "When her eyes met mine, I was at a loss for words. I knew in that moment there was something special about her."

Sky's blue eyes glistened with tears, their vibrant hue capturing Ryan's full attention. They reminded him of the ocean under a clear sky, deep and endlessly captivating.

"I haven't been able to get my mind off her since," he admitted.

Sky's voice was shaky as she whispered, "I met someone pretty incredible too. But I was too nervous to be around him."

Ryan frowned. "Why?"

Sky's gaze dropped. "Because I knew I was falling for him. And I was scared... scared he'd be like everyone else in my life. That he'd just... go."

Tears streamed down her face, and Ryan used his thumbs to gently wipe them away. His hands cupped her face as he whispered, "That will never happen."

Sky felt the weight of his words, the sincerity in his voice melting away her doubts. She smiled as Ryan leaned in, pulling her into another kiss. This one was softer but no less meaningful. Sky let herself fall into him, her worries fading away. In his arms, she felt something she hadn't felt in a long time: joy. Pure, unadulterated joy.

For the first time, Sky felt free—free to fly, free to be herself, free to love and be loved. And in that moment, with Ryan holding her close, she knew she'd found something extraordinary.

Twenty-Eight

A few days later, school let out for Thanksgiving break. The day before Thanksgiving, Ryan picked Sky up to take her to his house. Karen, Ryan's mom, was already busy prepping for tomorrow's feast in the kitchen, a symphony of delicious smells filling the air.

Karen greeted Sky with a big smile and an even bigger hug. "Hi, Sky! Nice to see you again!"

Sky hugged her back. "It's nice to see you too! Is there anything I can help with?"

Karen gestured toward the kitchen island, which was covered in ingredients. "Oh, there's plenty to be done. How about you wash, peel, and get the potatoes ready to cook?"

Sky nodded eagerly. "Sure, I can do that." She walked over to the far end of the kitchen island and got to work.

Ryan, standing by the door, asked his mom, "What can I do to help?"

Karen gave him a knowing smile. She leaned in and whispered, "Go help Sky. I'm sure you'd rather be over there anyway." She winked at him as a faint blush spread across his face.

Ryan joined Sky at the counter, grabbing a potato and a peeler. "Looks like I'm on potato duty too," he said, flashing her a smile.

They spent the next few hours prepping potatoes, green beans, and rolls. They laughed as Ryan tried to balance a potato on his nose, only for it to tumble to the floor. Sky teased him about his lack of culinary skills, and Ryan countered by saying he'd just stick to eating. The atmosphere was warm and lighthearted.

When it was time for Sky to head home, she hugged Karen goodbye.

Karen smiled warmly at her. "Hey, Sky, do you have any plans for Thanksgiving?"

Sky hesitated, glancing at Ryan. He looked embarrassed, realizing he hadn't asked her about it earlier.

"I'm usually home alone for the holidays," Sky admitted.

Karen shook a rolling pin in Sky's direction. "Well, you have plans now. You'll be joining us for dinner at five o'clock sharp!"

Sky's heart swelled with gratitude. "Thank you. I'd love to."

She looked at Ryan, who grinned and said, "I was going to drag you over here anyway."

As they drove home, Sky couldn't help but smile. For the first time in a long time, she felt truly wanted. Not just by Ryan, but by his family too.

It was Thanksgiving Day, and Sky was nervously getting ready for Ryan to pick her up. She stood in front of her mirror, debating what to wear, knowing full well that Ryan's mom and dad would most likely be there. After rifling through her closet, she finally settled on a burnt orange blouse with ruffled edges. The back had a heart-shaped cutout, perfect for her wings to stretch through comfortably. She paired it with her darkest gray jeans and navy-blue high-top sneakers. Her hair was braided to the left side, and she applied a light layer of makeup. Weeks of Nia's makeup lessons had finally paid off—she could handle the basics now.

"You've got this," Sky told herself in the mirror, taking a deep breath. "It's just a family celebrating Thanksgiving. Nothing to stress about."

She was about to head downstairs when she heard a knocking at her window. Being on the second floor, there was only one person it could be. She drew back the curtains to see Ryan hovering outside, a charming grin plastered across his face. He was dressed in a burgundy button-down shirt and dark blue jeans, his wings stretched wide against the morning sun.

Sky opened the window, leaning out onto the roof. "Why didn't you just come to the door?" she asked, laughing.

Ryan shrugged with a mischievous smile. "I thought we could take a different route to my place today."

Sky raised an eyebrow. "You can't be serious."

Ryan stepped back, spreading his wings further. "Dead serious. You can fly just as fast as me, if not faster. So, why not?" He held out his hand to her.

Sky rolled her eyes but couldn't help smiling. "You're ridiculous," she said before stepping out and leaping into the air. The wind caught her wings immediately, lifting her higher. Together, they soared above the trees, neighborhoods, and houses, the crisp autumn air filling their lungs. In the distance, Ryan's house came into view.

Before they landed, Ryan stopped Sky mid-air. "Hey, just a heads-up. This might be a little... awkward."

Sky frowned. "Why?"

Ryan hesitated. "My dad's home."

Sky's heart sank a little. She could see the concern on Ryan's face. "It'll be okay," she reassured him. "We'll just take it moment by moment." She reached out to touch his arm, her blue eyes meeting his. "We've got this."

Ryan smiled, though the worry didn't completely leave his face. "You're amazing, you know that?"

They landed in front of the crystal doors of the Daniel's home, greeted by Karen, who opened the door with a beaming smile. "Sky! So glad you could join us for Thanksgiving! Ryan didn't stop talking about you coming over."

Sky blushed as Karen pulled her into a warm hug. "Thanks for having me," Sky said, her voice shy but genuine.

Karen stepped back and added, "And Ryan's dad was able to get off work to join us, which is a rare treat."

Ryan and Sky exchanged a glance, both feeling the weight of that statement, and followed Karen inside. She led them to the grand dining room, and Sky's jaw nearly dropped. The agarwood table was enormous, capable of seating at least twenty people. It was covered with a feast fit for royalty: mashed potatoes, stuffing, green beans, casseroles, and a perfectly roasted turkey sitting proudly in the center. Crystal glasses sparkled under the chandelier, and silverware gleamed against pristine white napkins.

Sky had never seen so much food in one place before. She felt a mix of awe and intimidation as she took it all in. Karen gestured for them to sit while she went to fetch her husband. Ryan pulled out a chair near the end of the table and gestured for Sky to sit beside him.

"My dad's not exactly the happiest person," Ryan muttered under his breath. "Dinner's probably going to be quiet and boring."

Sky chuckled quietly. "I wouldn't be surprised."

Footsteps echoed from down the hall, one set light and quick, the other heavy and deliberate. Karen entered first; her smile unwavering as she took a seat across from Ryan. Behind her was Mr. Daniels, his presence commanding the room. He wore a perfectly pressed white button-down shirt with a brown-striped vest and khaki trousers. His shoes were polished to a shine, adorned with small gold pins bearing the letters NX. His metal-framed glasses glinted under the chandelier as his piercing gaze landed on Ryan and Sky.

"Glad to see my son brought a friend from school," Mr. Daniels said in a tone that was more formal than friendly.

Karen's smile widened. "Sky's not just a friend. She's Ryan's girlfriend."

Mr. Daniels raised an eyebrow. "I wasn't aware Ryan was even dating. But with your glowing school record, Ms. Treder, I suppose it's a good influence. Maybe you'll rub off on my son."

Ryan's jaw tightened, and he looked away. Sky felt the tension rise and tried to focus on the plate in front of her. Karen quickly motioned for everyone to sit, and Mr. Daniels took his seat at the head of the table, his movements precise and calculated.

As they began to eat, the air was thick with unspoken words. Plates were piled high with food, especially Sky's and Ryan's, while Karen and Mr. Daniels ate more modest portions. The silence was broken when Mr. Daniels asked, "So, Sky, how are your parents?"

Sky nearly choked on her drink, caught off guard. "Uh, they're doing fine. As far as I know."

Mr. Daniels nodded; his expression unreadable. "Remarkable careers they have. A world-renowned veterinarian and a leading doctor. I had the privilege of meeting them at a seminar a few months back. Brilliant minds, much like yourself."

Sky forced a smile. "Thank you." She looked down at her plate, trying to hide her discomfort.

Mr. Daniels turned his attention to Ryan. "Maybe she could tutor you. Your academic performance could certainly use some improvement."

Sky quickly interjected, "Actually, Ryan's been helping me a lot. He's a great tutor."

Mr. Daniels' eyes flickered with mild surprise before he nodded. "Is that so?"

The conversation shifted as Mr. Daniels began talking about NisenX, his pride in the company, and its groundbreaking research. Sky felt unease creeping in as he mentioned "monitoring unique individuals" like herself and Ryan. His tone was clinical, almost cynical, as he talked about genetic studies and the potential to revolutionize medicine.

"Being the unique creature that you are, Ms. Treder," he said, his gaze fixed on her, "I'd be delighted to have you visit my office sometime. My colleagues would be thrilled to study your wings up close."

Sky pulled her wings tighter against her back, feeling exposed. "I'll think about it," she said quietly.

Ryan's hand found hers under the table, giving it a reassuring squeeze. "She's not really into that kind of thing, Dad," he said firmly.

Mr. Daniels' eyes narrowed slightly. "I was merely offering."

The tension was substantial, and Karen quickly tried to change the subject, but the unease lingered. When Mr. Daniels' phone rang, he excused himself to take the call, leaving the table.

Karen turned to Ryan and Sky with a soft smile. "Why don't you two take a walk while I clean up? You could use some fresh air."

Ryan started to protest, but Karen waved him off. "Go on. I've got this."

Grateful for the escape, Ryan and Sky stepped outside, the cool evening air a welcome relief. They walked hand in hand toward the treehouse, their favorite retreat. Ryan's grip on her hand tightened.

"I'm sorry about him," he said, his voice heavy. "He's always been like this."

Sky shook her head. "It's okay. He didn't mean to—"

"No," Ryan interrupted, his voice rising. "He meant every word. My dad's never been kind. When I was little, he..." Ryan's voice cracked. He took a deep breath and continued. "He took me to work with him all the time. They studied me. Took blood samples. Scanned me. I was just a kid, and he let them treat me like a lab rat."

Sky's heart ached as she listened. She wrapped her wings around him, offering silent comfort.

"Thanks," Ryan said, his voice barely above a whisper. "You're the only person who's ever really understood."

Sky tightened her embrace. "I'm not going anywhere," she whispered.

For a moment, the world felt quiet and safe. But in the back of their minds, both of them heard Mr. Daniels' voice, his words lingering like a storm on the horizon.

Twenty-Nine

The middle of December brought a biting chill to the air, with skies so gray they seemed to weigh heavily on the earth below. The icy wind whispered through the school corridors, carrying the faint promise of a storm. The mood matched the weather—tense and uncertain. As much as Sky and Ryan were inseparable, there was an unease brewing in the background of their lives. Ryan's father had been relentless, asking him almost daily to visit NisenX, but Ryan's refusals were steadfast. Sky knew the topic troubled him, so she refrained from pressing with questions.

On a particularly cold Wednesday morning, the hallways of Foreman Falls High buzzed with the usual clatter of students rushing to class. Sky sprinted down the corridor, her sneakers skidding slightly on the polished floor. Spotting Ryan by his locker, she collided into him with such force that he barely managed to steady them both, his strong hands gripping her shoulders.

"Whoa, Sky! You okay?" he asked, his voice full of concern.

She looked up at him, her blue eyes wide and frantic. "We need to go somewhere," she said breathlessly. "Like, right now."

Ryan didn't ask any questions. He could tell by her tone and the anxious way she gripped her phone that this was serious. Without a word, he followed her as she weaved through the crowds, leading him to the library. Once inside, they headed to her secret nook—a quiet, hidden spot near the large arched windows. The two sat down across from each other on the wide windowsill, the frosty glass behind them amplifying the bitter air outside.

Ryan leaned forward, his voice gentle. "Alright, Sky. What's going on?"

Sky held her phone tightly, her knuckles white. She bit her lip, hesitating before she finally whispered, "My parents emailed me."

Ryan's eyebrows rose in surprise. "Isn't that a good thing?" he asked cautiously.

Sky shook her head, her expression heavy with a mix of frustration and sadness. Without a word, she handed her phone to Ryan, the screen glowing with the email. Ryan took it, his eyes scanning the message as Sky folded her hands in her lap, nervously twisting her fingers.

Subject: Exciting News

Dear Sky,

We hope this email finds you well. We've just wrapped up the seminar here in London and are preparing for our next steps. Excitingly, we've been offered positions with NisenX at their headquarters in Atlanta, Georgia. This is a fantastic opportunity for us to continue advancing our work in veterinary medicine and human health.

We understand this might come as a surprise, but there's no need to worry. We'll still make time to visit you in Tennessee when our schedules allow. In fact, we're hopeful we'll be able to stop by for Christmas this year.

Please continue to focus on your studies and take care of yourself. We're very proud of you.

Love,

Mom and Dad

Ryan finished reading and let out a slow breath, handing the phone back to Sky. "Wow," he said softly, understanding the weight of her feelings. "No wonder you're upset."

Sky clutched the phone, her shoulders slumping. "They've always been gone, Ryan," she said, her voice cracking. "And now they're going to work with your dad? This is a disaster."

Ryan reached out, placing a comforting hand on her shoulder. "I get it," he said. "But hey, they might actually stop by for Christmas. That's something, right?"

Sky's face twisted with unease. "I really hope they don't."

Ryan tilted his head. "Why not?"

She hesitated before gesturing toward her wings, which were tucked tightly behind her. "They don't know about... this. They've never seen them."

Ryan frowned. "What? You've never told them?"

"No," Sky admitted. "They've been gone so much... and when it happened, I didn't know how to bring it up. What if they freak out?"

Ryan squeezed her shoulder reassuringly. "Don't stress too much. If they're jerks about it, you can always come stay at my place."

Sky let out a small laugh, tears glistening in her eyes. "With your dad around? No, thank you!"

Ryan chuckled, the tension breaking momentarily. "Fair point."

Outside the window, the sky had darkened considerably. Thick, swirling clouds churned ominously, casting shadows over the landscape. The air seemed heavy, as if the atmosphere itself was holding its breath. In the distance, faint rumbles of thunder echoed, rolling across the horizon like a warning.

"Looks like a storm's coming," Ryan murmured, gazing out at the foreboding sky. The clouds twisted and coiled like restless serpents; their edges tinged with an eerie, greenish hue. Trees swayed violently in the rising wind, their bare branches clawing at the darkening heavens. The distant flash of lightning illuminated the scene for a brief second, stark and unsettling.

Sky stared out the window, her thoughts swirling as much as the storm outside. "I have a bad feeling about all of this," she said quietly.

Ryan turned back to her; his expression serious. "We'll figure it out. I promise."

For a moment, the storm outside was forgotten as they sat together, drawing strength from each other's presence.

Thirty

It was that following Friday, and the air was crisp with December's bite. The day started like any other at Foreman Falls High, with students shuffling through the halls and the hum of idle chatter filling the air. Then, the PA system crackled to life, silencing the buzz.

"Good morning, Foreman Falls! As school is winding down for the year, we want to remind you to ace those final semester exams! Also, there is a career fair at NisenX HQ this weekend—a great opportunity to explore the job and career options they have to offer! For more information, please check the school's website. Thank you, and have a great day!"

Sky was sitting in calculus when the announcement rang through the halls. She frowned, her pencil frozen mid-equation. She didn't recall Ryan mentioning anything about this career fair, but something about it made her uneasy. As soon as the bell rang, she slung her bag over her shoulder and headed straight for Ryan.

She found him leaning casually against the row of lockers, his jacket slung over his shoulder, his dark hair slightly tousled. Sky didn't waste time with pleasantries. "What is this career fair garbage?" she asked, her tone sharp.

Ryan rolled his eyes. "It's my dad's latest stunt. He thinks if he sponsors something for the school, I'll feel obligated to go."

Sky shook her head, her irritation mirroring his. "No way. We're not going."

Ryan let out a sigh and leaned back against the lockers. "I wish it were that simple. My mom's making me go. She thinks it'll look bad if I don't show up, and she's…" He hesitated, rubbing the back of his neck. "She's not giving me a choice."

Sky's face softened as she picked up on his disappointment. "If you have to go," she said firmly, "then so am I."

Ryan's eyes widened in alarm. "Sky, no. Absolutely not. There's no way I'm letting you get dragged into this disaster waiting to happen."

Sky crossed her arms and tilted her head, a defiant glint in her eye. "Too bad. I'm going whether you like it or not."

Ryan stared at her for a moment before breaking into a reluctant smile. "You know I can't say no to you," he said, his voice soft.

Sky smirked, turning to head back to class. "You know it."

Ryan watched her go, shaking his head with a mix of amusement and worry. The thought of Sky being anywhere near his father's workplace made his stomach churn, but he also knew there was no stopping her when she'd made up her mind.

Sky, on the other hand, was resolute. She wasn't about to let Ryan suffer through this alone. Besides, it was a public event. What could possibly go wrong?

That evening, the unease lingered in Sky's mind as she sat in her room, staring out the window. Snow flurries had begun to fall, dusting the streets and rooftops in a thin layer of white. Her wings shifted uncomfortably as she thought about what the career fair might entail. She'd heard plenty of stories about NisenX from Ryan—none of them good.

Her phone buzzed on the nightstand, pulling her from her thoughts. She picked it up to see a text from Ryan.

Ryan: You sure about tomorrow?

Sky: 100%. You?

Ryan: Not really. But at least I'll have you there.

Sky smiled faintly, her fingers hovering over the keyboard before she typed back.

Sky: I'll have your back. Always.

Ryan: I know you will. Thanks, Sky.

She set the phone down and exhaled deeply. Tomorrow would be a test—not just of their patience, but of their ability to face whatever secrets NisenX might hold. And though the storm brewing in the distance—both literal and figurative—seemed foreboding, Sky couldn't shake the feeling that this was just the beginning of something much bigger.

Thirty-One

Sky's stomach twisted with apprehension as she looked at the clock—4:36 pm. The NisenX career fair was scheduled to begin at 5 p.m., and she was still debating her outfit. Ryan had reassured her that casual attire would be fine, but Sky wanted to make a good impression—even if she wasn't thrilled about going. She eventually settled on her favorite jeans, a black shirt with white sparkles cascading down like tiny stars, and Ryan's homecoming suit jacket. The thought of him handing it to her with a grin made her smile.

Taking a deep breath, Sky stepped outside, letting the snowy December air sting her cheeks. Rather than waiting for a ride, she opted to fly. She launched herself into the sky, her wings cutting through the brisk wind as she soared over the quiet neighborhoods below. Flying had become her solace, a reminder of how far she'd come since her first shaky attempts at takeoff. After a while, the massive NisenX headquarters came into view. The building loomed like a fortress, its sleek, glass façade reflecting the dim light of the overcast evening. A glowing sign near the entrance read, "NisenX — Creating a Better Tomorrow."

Sky spotted Ryan waving at her from the rooftop. His emerald green button-down shirt and dark jeans stood out against the stark industrial background. She landed softly beside him and was immediately greeted by his warm embrace.

"I see you brought a jacket," Ryan teased, his hazel eyes crinkling with amusement.

"This is the best one I've got," Sky quipped with a grin.

"What about my varsity jacket?" he asked, feigning offense.

"Hmm," she teased, "this one's more formal."

Ryan laughed, his gaze lingering on her a moment longer than usual. Together, they descended a long staircase, their footsteps echoing off the concrete walls. The entertainment hall was bustling with activity when they arrived. The cavernous space felt overwhelming, with its towering ceilings, glittering chandeliers, and rows of massive windows that stretched nearly to the roof. Circular tables were scattered throughout the room, each draped in crisp white linens and surrounded by sleek chairs. Booths lined the edges of the hall, labeled with signs like "Robotics," "Genetic Research," and "Corporate Careers."

Sky's breath hitched as she took it all in. The room was alive with conversation, the buzz of curious students mingling with the measured tones of professionals in white lab coats. Her wings twitched involuntarily as she tried to process the scale of it all.

Ryan noticed her tension and placed his hands gently on her shoulders. "We can just hang out on the stage steps if this is too much."

Sky nodded, relieved. "That sounds perfect."

They made their way to the left corner of the stage, where they sat on the polished wooden steps. The stage itself was grand, with a shimmering red curtain framing its backdrop. Sky turned to Ryan; her voice low.

"How are you holding up?"

Ryan shrugged; his usual confidence dimmed. "Could be worse, I guess. I haven't seen my dad yet, so that's a plus."

Sky smiled gently. "We'll get through this."

Ryan leaned back, his expression softening as he looked at her. "You're good at that."

"At what?"

"Pulling me out of my head," he admitted, his voice barely above a whisper.

Sky blushed, looking away. "You do the same for me."

Their quiet moment was interrupted by the overhead speakers crackling to life. "Ladies and gentlemen, we will begin our main demonstration in 15 minutes. Please find your seats."

Ryan sighed. "Guess we should find my mom."

Karen Daniels was manning the healthcare booth, chatting animatedly about wound care to a pair of uninterested students. She lit up when she saw them approaching.

"Having fun yet?" she asked with a teasing smile.

Ryan rolled his eyes. "Not exactly."

Karen chuckled and turned to Sky. "At least Sky is here to keep you company. You're good for him, you know."

Sky blushed, and Ryan muttered something under his breath. Karen winked at him before excusing herself to help with the demonstration.

Before they could retreat to a quieter corner, Mr. Daniels appeared. His presence was as imposing as ever, his tailored suit and sharp gaze making him stand out in the crowd.

"Ryan," he said, his tone measured. "I'm glad to see you here."

Ryan's jaw tightened. "Not by choice."

Ignoring the comment, Mr. Daniels turned to Sky. "Ms. Treder, have you reconsidered my offer to tour the facility?"

Sky's feathers ruffled instinctively. "Thank you, but I'm not really interested."

Mr. Daniels raised an eyebrow. "You'd be a guest, not an employee."

Ryan stepped in, his voice firm. "She said she's not interested."

Mr. Daniels' lips thinned; his annoyance evident. "Well, enjoy the presentation," he said before walking away.

Sky's stomach churned as she watched him go. Ryan squeezed her hand. "Let's just get this over with."

Thirty-Two

They found seats at the very back of the room, nearest to the exit. A couple of rows ahead, Sky noticed two doctors dressed in royal blue scrubs. They seemed far more animated than the other professionals scattered throughout the auditorium. Their hushed voices carried just enough for Sky's sharp ears to pick up on their conversation. She leaned forward slightly, curiosity overpowering her apprehension.

The taller of the two had patches of red, irritated skin along his face and neck. His eyes gleamed with excitement as he spoke. "Did you hear about the girl with 'Leucism'?"

The second doctor, whose poorly secured toupee threatened to slip off his head at any moment, nodded eagerly. "Yes! Mr. Daniels spoke highly of her. He says she'll be vital in our research."

Sky felt her stomach twist into a knot. Her fingers trembled slightly as she fidgeted with the hem of her jacket.

The taller man's tone lowered, but his words were unmistakably sharp. "I don't see why they haven't brought her in already. Being able to identify the genetic codes for color expression in her unique mutation could be mind-blowing!"

The toupee-wearing doctor nodded again, his eyes narrowing. "It's not just about her mutation. She's the perfect candidate for the development of the 'SF' unit. Imagine an entire squadron with her kind of precision and adaptability. She'd be a prime example."

Sky's pulse quickened as an icy chill shot down her spine. She knew—deep down, without a doubt—that they were talking about her. She was the only Humanimal known to have leucism.

She bit her lip to keep herself steady and forced her hands to stay still, though her instinct was to run as far away as possible. Every word they said felt like a spotlight casting her deepest secret into the open.

The taller doctor's eyes lit up as he continued, his voice dripping with ambition. "Think bigger. If we can isolate those specific DNA strands, we could produce a serum—a specialized treatment for those suffering from the side effects of radiation. Do you know how many lives that could save?"

The other doctor adjusted his glasses, pushing them higher onto his nose. "And think of the financial backing we'd get. Corporations would line up for exclusive rights. But she's more than a genetic resource—she's a proof of concept."

Sky's heart was hammering now. She felt trapped in her chair, like the walls of the auditorium were closing in around her. The room had grown colder despite the crowd and the buzz of pre-presentation chatter.

She swallowed hard and forced herself to breathe slowly. *Keep calm*, she thought, though her mind was screaming. She glanced at Ryan; his face was pale. He had to be hearing the same things as her.

They can't know I'm here, she thought, trying to shrink further into her oversized jacket. She could feel the sweat gathering at the nape of her neck.

The taller doctor leaned closer to his colleague. "You know Mr. Daniels would have her in a lab tomorrow if it were up to him."

"But it's not," the other man muttered. "For now."

Sky felt her breath hitch at the word 'lab.' The image of sterile, white rooms and surgical tools flashed through her mind. The thought of being reduced to an experiment filled her with dread.

They don't know it's you, she reminded herself, but the thought offered little comfort.

The doctors' conversation continued, each sentence tightening the coil of fear in her chest.

"It's only a matter of time," the taller one said with a smirk. "We're closer than ever."

Sky stared straight ahead, her vision blurring with unshed tears. She gripped the seat, her knuckles white. *Breathe,* she told herself. *Stay calm.*

But no matter how many times she repeated it, she couldn't shake the gnawing fear. She wasn't just scared—she was terrified.

If they ever got her in the lab, she wasn't sure she'd ever see the sky again.

Thirty-Three

The lights dimmed, and a spotlight illuminated the stage. Karen stood at the center; her smile radiant as she addressed the crowd.

"Welcome, everyone! We are thrilled to have the students of Foreman Falls join us tonight. At NisenX, we are committed to creating a better tomorrow, and that starts with you—the future innovators and leaders of our world."

A projector screen lit up behind her, displaying images of the company's work. Karen explained the history of genetic mutations caused by the nuclear spill, detailing how it had led to sickness for some and remarkable abilities for others. Photos flashed on the screen—emaciated individuals in tattered clothing, followed by "after" images of healthy, smiling people.

Ryan leaned close to Sky. "Pretty sure those are photoshopped," he whispered.

Karen's voice grew more animated. "Humanimals are miracles of science. Their DNA holds the keys to evolution and innovation. With your help, we can change lives and create a brighter future."

She gestured to the side of the stage. "And now, please welcome Tyra and Youseff, two remarkable individuals who have benefited from our groundbreaking work."

The crowd applauded as Tyra and Youseff stepped onto the stage. Sky's breath hitched. Tyra's frail frame was unsettling. Her thin, leathery bat wings jutted awkwardly from her arms, and her dark skin seemed stretched over sharp bones. Her large, pointed ears twitched constantly, and her black, pupil-less eyes scanned the crowd with eerie precision. She wore a navy-blue polo shirt tucked into tight black leggings; her movements unnervingly swift. When she opened her mouth, two sharp fangs glinted in the stage lights.

Youseff was just as unnerving. He towered over everyone, his elongated neck spotted with brown and white patches reminiscent of a giraffe's. Two small, rounded antlers sprouted from his head, and his feet ended in cloven hooves instead of shoes. His arms were covered in short, bristly fur, and his fingers looked stiff and darkened, almost claw-like. He moved stiffly, his exhaustion evident.

Karen's voice brimmed with pride. "Tyra was once a frail, Humanimal child with partial mutations. With our treatments, she has developed incredible abilities."

Tyra demonstrated by launching herself into the rafters with uncanny agility. She let out a high-pitched screech, the sound piercing enough to make Humanimals in the crowd cover their ears.

"Isn't she marvelous?" Karen exclaimed, to scattered applause.

Next, she turned to Youseff. "Youseff was terminally ill, but with our help, we used DNA from his brother, who is part giraffe, to save his life and enhance his abilities."

Youseff walked stiffly across the stage, his tall frame casting long shadows. Sky's stomach churned as she watched. This wasn't a demonstration of triumph—it was a display of suffering.

Ryan leaned close; his voice tight. "Let's get out of here."

Sky nodded, tears stinging her eyes as they slipped out the back. They ran upstairs to the roof, she collapsed to her knees, trembling.

"What is going on?" she whispered.

Ryan paced, running his hands through his hair. "I didn't know. I swear I didn't know they were doing this to kids."

Sky looked up at him, her voice shaking. "What if that's what your dad wants from us?"

Ryan knelt beside her; his hazel eyes fierce. "They won't get near you. Ever."

"How can you be sure?" Sky asked, her voice barely audible. "Your mom works here. My parents might work here."

Ryan's voice softened. "I trust my mom. She's the reason I'm not still trapped here."

Sky stood, wrapping her wings around herself. "But your dad..."

Ryan pulled her into a tight hug, his wings encircling her. "I won't let anything happen to you. I promise."

Sky leaned into his embrace, her tears soaking his shirt. For a moment, the piercing air and their fears melted away. But in the back of their minds, the images of Tyra and Youseff lingered, haunting them like ghosts of a dark future.

Ryan texted his mom after the career fair, letting her know he would be staying at Bryant's house for the night. Karen responded with a cheerful, "Have fun!" But in reality, Ryan had no intention of going to Bryant's. Instead, he and Sky flew back to her house, seeking refuge from the night's revelations.

They landed softly on Sky's bedroom window. Ryan helped her climb inside before following right behind. As soon as they were both in, Sky collapsed onto her bed, her body wracked with silent sobs. Ryan's heart clenched. He couldn't bear to see her like this, nor could he fathom returning home to face his parents after what they'd witnessed. The weight of the night pressed down on him like a physical force.

Sky curled into herself on the bed, tears soaking her pillow. Ryan hesitated for only a moment before climbing onto the bed beside her. He wrapped himself around her, his chest against her back, his arms encircling her protectively. He fit against her perfectly, his face brushing the edge of her feathers. Holding her felt natural, like this was where he was meant to be. Her trembling gradually subsided as his warmth surrounded her.

Ryan's thoughts raced as he held her. Anger, guilt, and helplessness churned in his chest. How could his parents be involved in something so monstrous? His mother, who had always seemed so compassionate, and his father, who had never hidden his sternness but now appeared utterly numb. Ryan had always struggled to meet his father's impossible expectations, but tonight had cemented something darker.

"How could they do this?" he thought, his jaw tightening. "How could they look at those kids, suffering and transformed, and call it progress?"

He buried his face in Sky's hair, inhaling the faint scent of lavender. The warmth of her body anchored him, reminding him why he needed to stay strong. He couldn't allow anyone to hurt her.

"I'll protect her," he silently vowed. "No matter what it takes."

The steady rhythm of Sky's breathing eventually told him she had cried herself to sleep. Her soft, even breaths were a balm to his frayed nerves. Ryan let himself relax, though his thoughts remained heavy. Tears slipped from his eyes, silent but steady. He tightened his hold on Sky, finding solace in her presence as he drifted off to sleep.

Thirty-Four

Morning light filtered through the curtains, painting the room in soft hues of gold. Ryan stirred first; his hazel eyes cracking open to find Sky still nestled against his chest. Her head rested just below his chin, and her wings lay tucked neatly against her back. She looked so peaceful, her face free of the worry and pain that had consumed her the night before. For a brief moment, Ryan felt a glimmer of happiness, as if the world outside didn't exist.

Sky shifted, her eyelashes fluttering as she woke. She blinked sleepily, confusion crossing her face as she realized she was wrapped in a warm embrace. Her gaze traveled upward, landing on Ryan, who was watching her with a soft smile. He reached out, gently brushing a strand of hair from her face.

"You sure like to sleep in, don't you?" he teased quietly.

Reality hit Sky like a freight train. She had just spent the night snuggled up to Ryan. Panic rose in her chest, and she scrambled to push herself away. In her haste, she rolled right off the side of the bed, landing on the floor with a hard thud.

Ryan couldn't contain his laughter. "You're adorable in the morning," he said, his voice full of amusement.

Sky's cheeks burned red as she glared up at him from the floor. "Adorable?" she muttered, mortified.

Ryan slid off the bed and offered her a hand. "Come on, let me help you up."

Sky reached for his hand, but her socks slipped on the hardwood floor, and she yanked him down with her. Ryan landed on top of her with a soft "oof." Propping himself up on his elbows, he grinned down at her.

"You just wanted to snuggle again, huh?" he teased, his face mere inches from hers.

Sky's blush deepened, and she stammered incoherently. Ryan's grin widened, and he leaned down, pressing a gentle kiss to her lips. It was brief but sweet, leaving Sky speechless.

Standing, Ryan offered his hand again. This time, Sky managed to stand without incident. "How about breakfast?" he asked, his tone light.

Still dazed, Sky nodded, her words coming out as a jumble of nonsense. Ryan chuckled and headed downstairs, leaving her to compose herself. She closed her bedroom door, leaning against it for a moment to catch her breath. Her heart was pounding, not from fear, but from the warmth Ryan's presence brought.

After a quick shower, Sky threw on a pair of cheer joggers she'd borrowed from Nia and an oversized pajama top. The smell of bacon wafted through the air as she descended the stairs. Turning into the kitchen, she saw Ryan at the stove, still wearing his clothes from the night before. A pan of bacon sizzled in front of him.

Ryan glanced over his shoulder at her. "Pajamas today, huh?"

Sky crossed her arms. "At least I'm not still wearing last night's attire."

Ryan smirked, flipping the bacon. "Touché."

Sky sat at the kitchen island, watching as Ryan carefully piled burnt bacon, scrambled eggs, and pancakes onto a plate. He turned to her, looking sheepish. "I did my best with what you had in the fridge. Hope you like crispy bacon."

Sky picked up a piece of bacon and took an exaggeratedly loud crunching bite. "Perfect," she said with a grin.

They laughed as they ate, the tension from the night before easing with each bite. After breakfast, Ryan headed to the shower. When he returned, he was wearing her dad's oversized pajama pants and an old t-shirt. Sky burst into laughter at the sight.

"What's so funny?" Ryan asked, feigning offense.

Sky shook her head, still laughing. "You look ridiculous."

Ryan grinned and launched himself over the back of the couch, landing beside her. He immediately began tickling her sides, eliciting a fresh round of laughter. When they finally settled down, they turned on the TV, flipping to the news.

A segment on NisenX filled the screen, and the air grew heavy. The cheerful banter disappeared, replaced by the weight of unspoken fears. Ryan's arm tightened around Sky as they sat in silence, each lost in their thoughts.

Sky's mind replayed the night's events. The sight of Tyra and Youseff haunted her, their altered forms a cruel reminder of what NisenX was capable of. "Is this what they want for us?" she wondered, her stomach churning. "What if this is my parents' legacy?" The thought made her feel sick.

Ryan's thoughts were equally tumultuous. He couldn't shake the image of his mother smiling on that stage, speaking so proudly about the company. "How can she not see what they're doing?" he wondered. "And my dad..." The thought of his father's cold, calculating demeanor made Ryan's blood boil. But more than anything, he was determined to protect Sky. "No one is going to hurt her," he vowed silently. "Not while I'm here."

Thirty-Five

Ryan grabbed the remote and flipped through channels aimlessly, settling on a nature documentary to fill the silence. The soothing narration contrasted sharply with the tension between him and Sky. He turned to her, his face a mixture of concern and determination.

"Do you want to talk about...you know, last night?" he asked softly.

Sky hesitated, her gaze fixed on a spot on the floor. "We probably should," she murmured.

Ryan nodded. "Where do we even start?"

Sky's voice cracked as she said, "How could anyone think of that display as progress?" She turned to him, her expression a storm of emotions—anger, confusion, and hurt. "How could your parents be a part of something so...so horrible?"

Ryan ran a hand through his hair, his eyes clouded with guilt. "I had no idea what they were doing, Sky. I swear."

Sky's tone grew sharper, her anger spilling over. "And they wanted to do that to you?" Her voice wavered, and Ryan could see her hands trembling.

He stood up, trying to keep his voice steady. "I would have gotten out of there before they could even try," he said, though the words felt hollow even to him.

Sky's pupils suddenly expanded, a primal sign of her mounting rage. "But what if you didn't?" she demanded, her voice rising. The feral edge in her tone sent a shiver down Ryan's spine. He recognized this reaction. He'd read about it in anatomy class and seen it during their flying practice. Sky's protective instincts were kicking in, and they were dangerous—not to him, but to her own sense of control.

"Sky, look at me," Ryan said, his voice calm and grounding. He stepped closer, his hazel eyes steady and warm. "I'm here. I'm okay. With you."

Sky's breathing was shallow, the roar of her pulse drowning out everything else. But his words broke through, tethering her to reality. Her eyes met his, and she saw no fear, no panic—just unwavering calm. Slowly, her pupils began to shrink back to their normal size. The roaring in her mind faded to a murmur.

She exhaled shakily, brushing a hand through her hair. "That...that has to be how your dad knew about me," she said, her voice quieter now but still tinged with fear. "That company must have some kind of database. They're keeping track of us with those dumb health checks."

Ryan frowned, the pieces clicking into place. "That would make sense," he admitted. "Everyone takes those checks, especially during the years when our traits develop. They probably use the data to monitor growth, mutations, even illnesses."

Sky began pacing the room, her hands gripping her elbows as if trying to hold herself together. "Is that what he wanted me to come in for? To become their new guinea pig?" Her voice cracked on the last word, and Ryan could see the fear bubbling to the surface again.

He stepped forward and gently grabbed her shoulders, stopping her mid-step. "They'd have to go through me first," he said firmly. His eyes bore into hers, and the intensity of his words left no room for doubt.

A small, fragile smile tugged at the corners of Sky's lips. His presence was like ice to her burned nerves.

Ryan's expression softened as he continued. "I can't explain everything we saw back there. I can't even begin to imagine what they're planning. But I do know this, we can't stick around and let it get worse."

Sky's brow furrowed. "What are you saying?" she asked, her voice barely above a whisper.

Ryan took a deep breath. "Winter break is coming up. We'll spend Christmas with our families, and then...we'll leave. That night, we'll fly as far as we can. Maybe to Canada. Somewhere safe."

Sky's eyes widened. "Leave everything behind?" she asked, her voice tinged with disbelief.

Ryan nodded; his expression resolute. "We'll explain everything to Nia and Bryant. They're our best friends. They'll understand, and maybe they'll come with us. We have two weeks to plan this."

Sky shook her head, doubt clouding her face. "Ryan, this isn't going to work. Nia has her mom, and Bryant...I don't even know his situation."

Ryan interrupted her gently but firmly. "We'll figure something out. It's not impossible, Sky. We just have to try."

He pulled her into a hug, his arms wrapping around her protectively. Sky rested her head against his chest, her thoughts a whirlwind of fear and uncertainty. She wanted to believe him, to trust that everything would work out. But the enormity of what they were planning felt suffocating.

"What if this falls apart?" she thought. "What if we can't get far enough? What if they catch us?" Her mind spiraled with worst-case scenarios, but she forced herself to push them aside. Ryan needed her to be strong, and she couldn't afford to fall apart now.

She let out a shaky sigh, her arms tightening around him. "As long as we're together," she thought, "we'll find a way."

Thirty-Six

Sky couldn't focus all day. The decision to bring Nia and Bryant into the fold weighed heavily on her mind. As much as she trusted her friends, the risk of telling them the truth felt monumental. She could barely sit through her classes, her thoughts a constant swirl of "What if they think I'm crazy?" and "What if they don't believe us?"

When the final bell rang, she bolted to Ryan's locker. He was waiting for her, his face set in determination. Without exchanging words, they flew off to her house. They needed privacy for this conversation.

A little while later, Bryant's familiar jeep pulled up outside. Nia jumped out first, practically sprinting to the front door. She flung her arms around Sky in a tight hug, clearly concerned.

"What's going on, Sky? You're scaring me," Nia said, pulling back to look her in the eyes.

Sky offered a weak smile. "It's…complicated. Let's get inside. We need to talk."

Bryant joined them, his tall frame radiating curiosity and worry. They all settled in the living room, Nia and Bryant on the couch, with Ryan and Sky sitting across from them. Sky fidgeted with her hands, unsure how to begin.

"So," Nia said, breaking the silence. "What's the big emergency?"

Sky took a deep breath. "It's about NisenX."

Nia tilted her head. "The career fair? What about it?"

Sky glanced at Ryan, who nodded for her to continue. "It wasn't just a career fair. They were showcasing...things. People." Her voice faltered, and she looked down, unable to continue.

Ryan picked up where she left off. "They had these two kids on stage, Tyra and Youseff. Both of them...mutated. More animal than human. They said it was progress, but it looked more like torture."

Bryant's brows furrowed. "Wait, mutated? What do you mean?"

Ryan's voice grew heavier. "Tyra had bat wings and echolocation—she screamed so loud it hurt everyone's ears. Youseff...his body was twisted. His neck was abnormally long, covered in spots like a giraffe. They called it 'enhancement,' but they looked...broken."

Nia's eyes widened, her hand flying to her mouth. "Oh my gosh. That's...horrible."

Sky nodded, her voice barely above a whisper. "They're using the health checks to track us. They're collecting data, watching how we develop. It's not just about health...it's...experimentation."

Bryant's arm tightened around Nia's shoulder. "Are you sure about this? It sounds...unreal."

Ryan's jaw clenched. "I lived it, Bryant. When I was a kid, my dad took me to NisenX. They tested me—blood samples, scans, experiments. I...I thought it was normal, but looking back...it was anything but. They see us as lab rats."

Nia's eyes filled with tears. "This is terrifying. How could they do this?"

Sky's hands clenched into fists. "And now they want to do it to us. To me. That's why Mr. Daniels keeps trying to get me into their labs. He knows what I am."

Bryant shook his head in disbelief. "How can we stop them? What do we even do?"

Ryan's voice was firm. "We leave. Over winter break, we fly as far as we can. Canada, maybe further. We get out before they can find us."

Nia's tears fell freely now. "Leave? Just...leave everything? My parents, my home? I can't do that, Ryan. I can't leave my mom and dad."

Bryant looked down; his voice heavy with sorrow. "I can't leave either. I take care of my little sisters. They're sick, and they need me."

Ryan's shoulders sagged, but he nodded. "I get it. I'm asking a lot. I just wanted you to know what's going on. You deserve to know the truth."

Nia wiped her eyes. "We need time to think. This is...a lot."

Bryant nodded; his expression grim. "We'll let you know what we decide."

They stood to leave, Nia giving Sky one last hug before heading out the door. The sound of Bryant's jeep faded into the distance, leaving Ryan and Sky alone in the living room.

Ryan dropped his head into his hands, the weight of their situation pressing down on him. Guilt gnawed at him for asking so much of his friends, and fear for their safety consumed him. "What if I'm making the wrong call?" he thought. "What if I can't protect them?"

Sky sat beside him, her mind racing. She couldn't shake the image of Nia's tears or the weight in Bryant's voice. "How can I ask them to give up everything?" she thought. "But how can I leave them behind? What if they get hurt because we didn't try hard enough to convince them?"

The silence stretched between them, heavy with unspoken fears and doubts. For now, there were no answers—only the quiet thrum of their hearts and the uncertain path ahead.

Thirty-Seven

The last day of school before winter break arrived in a blur of tension and anticipation. Ryan had been staying at Sky's house, claiming to his mother that he was crashing at a friend's place until school let out. Karen, always trusting and hopeful, looked forward to her son's return home. But Ryan knew he couldn't face his parents—not after what they had seen at NisenX.

That morning, Ryan quietly packed his duffle bags. His face was grim, his movements methodical. Sky silently helped him, folding stray clothes and tucking them neatly into the bag. The weight of their plan loomed over them like a dark cloud. Sky couldn't ignore the knot in her stomach every time she thought about him going back to that house.

They loaded his things into the truck and drove to school. The plan was clear: Ryan would spend as little time at home as possible. They would spend the next week gathering supplies for their escape—camping kits, freeze-dried meals, tents, flashlights, and anything else they might need for a long, uncertain journey. Sky tried to focus on the practicality of it all, but her thoughts kept drifting to what they were leaving behind.

The school day passed in a haze. Sky struggled to concentrate; her mind preoccupied with the enormity of what was coming. Nia and Bryant had been acting normal for the past week, carefully avoiding any mention of their plan. But Sky could feel the tension beneath the surface. Nia, always so upbeat and cheerful, seemed distant. Sky knew she was wrestling with the decision, torn between loyalty to her family and the need to protect herself.

When the final bell rang, the group decided to grab lunch at the Sonic near school. They sat around a picnic table under the pale winter sun, the air thick with unspoken emotions. The boys tried to lighten the mood, talking about football.

"I still can't believe we won state this year," Bryant said, taking a bite of his burger. "Foreman Falls hasn't had a season like that in decades."

Ryan smirked. "You're welcome. Those game-winning touchdowns weren't easy, you know."

Bryant rolled his eyes. "Yeah, yeah, Mr. MVP. You'd be nothing without a good O-line."

"And you'd be nothing without me catching those lousy passes," Ryan shot back, earning a laugh from Bryant.

Nia tried to join in, forcing a smile. "Okay, football nerds, give it a rest. Prom committee starts planning in January, and I swear, if you guys show up in jeans, I will personally murder you."

Sky looked up, startled by the mention of prom. She'd forgotten it was coming up in March. It felt so distant and irrelevant now. She tried to smile but couldn't summon the energy to join the conversation.

Ryan noticed and reached over to rub her back gently. "Hey, you okay?" he asked softly.

Sky nodded but kept her eyes fixed on the ground. She couldn't bring herself to tell them what was on her mind: that in less than a week, she and Ryan would be gone, leaving behind everything and everyone they knew. The thought was suffocating.

Her mind drifted to a distant memory—her fifth birthday party. She could see herself at the kitchen table, sitting in front of a bright pink cake covered in frosted flowers. A large '5' candle sat in the center. To her left was her father, his face lit up with a broad smile. To her right was her mother, her shoulder-length dirty blonde hair framing her face as she beamed at Sky.

They were singing "Happy Birthday," their voices filling the room with warmth. Sky felt a surge of joy as she took a deep breath and blew out the candle, spitting all over the cake in the process.

Her parents burst into laughter, clapping their hands. Her father leaned in and asked, "Did you make a wish, kiddo?"

Sky hesitated, deep in thought. Her mother placed a gentle hand on her shoulder and said, "You don't have to tell us, sweetie. It's your birthday wish."

Sky smiled, her tiny hands reaching into the cake and grabbing a fistful of frosting and sponge. Her parents laughed even harder, pulling her into a group hug. She felt safe. Loved. Whole.

The memory faded, and Sky blinked back tears. She stared at her untouched food, feeling a pang of loss. "Why can't things just go back to being simple?" she thought.

The conversation around her continued, but it felt like background noise. Bryant was passionately arguing about who deserved the Heisman Trophy, while Ryan smirked and teased him about his terrible predictions. Nia chimed in occasionally, her laugh a little too forced. Sky sighed, trying to focus on the moment. These were her best friends, and this might be the last time they were all together.

Ryan glanced at her again, concern etched on his face. He leaned closer and whispered, "It'll work out. I just know it."

Sky nodded, offering a faint smile. She wanted to believe him, but the weight of the unknown was crushing. For now, all she could do was hold on to the present and hope they'd make it through what was coming.

Thirty-Eight

Christmas Eve had arrived, cloaked in cold, crisp air and the soft glow of holiday lights adorning every corner of the city. Sky and Ryan had spent the day preparing for their journey, their hearts weighed down by the knowledge of what they were about to leave behind. The finality of their decision loomed closer with each passing hour.

That evening, they took to the skies, gliding over neighborhoods where houses sparkled with strings of colorful lights and glowing ornaments. Sky, bundled in Ryan's varsity jacket, gazed down at the scene below with mixed emotions. It was beautiful, but bittersweet. Her thoughts were interrupted by the vibration of her phone. She pulled it out to see a text from Nia: "We need to talk. Meet us at the school parking lot."

Ryan noticed the tension in her expression. "What is it?" he asked, his voice soft but tinged with concern.

Sky held out the phone for him to see. His brows furrowed as he read the message. Without a word, they adjusted their course toward the school, the glow of the lights below fading as they focused on the dark outline of the building ahead.

Ryan's mind raced with possibilities as they flew. "Are they going to tell us they're staying?" he wondered. The thought sent a pang through his chest. He didn't want to blame them if they chose to stay; the life they were leaving behind was a lot to give up. Still, the idea of leaving without their best friends made the already daunting journey feel even lonelier.

He glanced at Sky, who was silent beside him, her face illuminated by the faint moonlight. She looked tense, her wings beating in a steady rhythm but her posture rigid. Ryan could see the worry etched on her features, and it mirrored his own. He wished he could reassure her, but the truth was, he didn't know what was coming.

Ryan was also grateful to be away from his house, even if only for a short while. NisenX was holding a company Christmas party at the local botanical gardens, and his parents had left earlier that evening to attend. Watching them drive away had filled him with a mix of relief and resentment. The second their car disappeared down the long driveway, he had bolted to the treehouse where Sky was waiting for him. When she had asked if he was ready, he had replied, "Yeah, I have to be." Now, flying through the icy air, he clung to that determination.

The school parking lot came into view, and in the far corner, they spotted Bryant's black jeep. They descended gracefully, their wings folding as they landed beside the vehicle. Nia was the first to emerge, running to Sky and enveloping her in a tight hug. Bryant followed, greeting Ryan with a firm hug of his own. There was a somber energy in the air as they all gathered in a small circle.

Bryant was the first to speak. "We've been doing a lot of thinking," he said, his voice heavy with emotion. "And we just…we can't."

Nia's eyes filled with tears as she added, "Our families need us. If things get crazy, we need to be here to protect them." Her voice broke, and she clung to Bryant's arm for support.

Sky felt her heart shatter. She had suspected this was coming, but hearing it out loud made it real. She forced herself to nod, even as her throat tightened. "I understand," she said quietly.

Bryant's voice cracked as he looked at Ryan. "We'll miss you, man. School won't be the same without you guys."

Ryan nodded; his jaw clenched. "Don't let the team slack off without me," he said, forcing a small smile.

Bryant chuckled weakly. "Never. If anything, they'll probably play better without you hogging all the glory."

Ryan laughed and feigned a punch to Bryant's arm. "Yeah, right."

Nia turned to Sky, tears streaming down her face. She pulled her into another hug, holding on for what felt like forever. "You better come visit us when this is all over," she whispered. "Promise me, Sky."

Sky's voice trembled as she whispered back, "I promise." She clung to Nia, wishing she could freeze this moment, knowing it might be their last together.

The group stood in silence for a moment, the weight of their goodbyes settling over them. Finally, Ryan and Sky unfolded their wings, ready to take off. Bryant and Nia watched as their friends rose into the air, their silhouettes fading into the dark blue sky.

Ryan glanced at Sky as they flew, his heart aching at the sight of her tears. Tiny crystals formed in the cold as they fell from her eyes, glinting like stars before disappearing into the night. He reached out and took her hand, their wings moving in perfect harmony. When she turned to look at him, he gave her a small, reassuring nod. She managed a fleeting smile before her expression turned somber again.

The city lights twinkled below them as they flew in silence, the wintry air sharp against their skin. Suddenly, a deafening boom shattered the quiet, followed by a screeching sound that seemed to tear through the atmosphere. They froze mid-flight, scanning the horizon for the source.

"What was that?" Ryan asked, his voice tense.

Sky's eyes locked on a distant plume of flames rising into the sky. The fire danced in her reflection as she whispered, "The gardens."

The explosion sent waves of heat and light into the air, illuminating the night with a fiery glow. Smoke billowed upward, black and ominous, twisting into the star-speckled sky. The shockwave rippled outward, rattling nearby windows and shaking the air around them. The acrid smell of burning wood and chemicals filled the air as the distant wail of sirens grew louder.

Ryan's chest tightened as he processed the sight. "Something's not right," he thought, gripping Sky's hand tighter as they turned toward the source of the chaos.

Thirty-Nine

Christmas Eve's iciness was biting as Sky and Ryan raced toward the botanical gardens, the ominous glow of flames lighting their way. The air was thick with the acrid smell of smoke, and the distant shriek of sirens grew louder as they approached. When they arrived, the scene before them was a chaotic nightmare.

The gardens, once a lush and tranquil haven, were now a hellscape of fire and destruction. Flames licked at the bushes and trees, consuming them with relentless hunger. Smoke billowed into the night sky, swirling in dark clouds that obscured the stars. The glow of the fire painted the area in shades of orange and red, casting long, flickering shadows across the ground. Firefighters were scattered throughout the area, battling the blaze with hoses and axes, their faces strained with determination. Ambulances lined the outer edge of the gardens, their lights flashing red and blue.

The air was filled with cries of pain and despair. People lay sprawled across the grounds, some clutching at injuries, others eerily still. Blood stained the cobblestone paths, pooling near victims who hadn't yet been reached. The heat was oppressive, radiating out from the flames and forcing Ryan and Sky to shield their faces. Ryan's heart pounded as his eyes scanned the devastation.

"We have to find my mom," he said, his voice trembling with urgency. Sky could see the fear in his eyes, his usual calm replaced by raw panic.

"We'll find her," Sky said, her voice steady despite her own rising fear. "Let's split up."

Ryan nodded, and they launched into the chaos, going in opposite directions.

Sky flew low, weaving through the smoke-filled air. The heat was unbearable, stinging her eyes and making her throat burn. Her wings felt heavy, weighed down by ash and soot as she maneuvered around fiery branches falling from above. Each flap sent waves of smoke swirling around her, obscuring her vision.

The gardens were unrecognizable. Flames climbed trellises and wrapped around ornamental statues, reducing once-beautiful structures to smoldering ruins. The flowers, once vibrant and colorful, were now blackened, charred remnants of their former beauty. Sky's heart ached as she took in the devastation, but she forced herself to focus. Karen Daniels' face was all that mattered now.

People were scattered throughout the paths. Some were limping toward the exits, clutching at burns and injuries, their faces twisted in pain. Others lay motionless, their bodies covered in soot and blood. Sky's stomach churned, but she pressed on, calling out Karen's name as she searched. Her voice was hoarse, the smoke stealing her breath.

Finally, from behind a toppled table, a hand shot up into the air. Sky's heart leapt as she dove down, shoving the table aside. There, crumpled on the ground, was Karen. Her red dress was scorched and torn, and her left side was marred by a severe burn that stretched from her shoulder to her knee. Her skin was blistered and raw, and her breathing was labored.

"Karen!" Sky exclaimed, kneeling beside her.

Karen's eyes fluttered open. "Sky?" she croaked, her voice barely audible over the chaos.

"I'm here," Sky said, wrapping an arm around Karen's good shoulder. "I've got you."

Karen winced in pain as Sky tried to lift her. "Ryan," Sky shouted, her voice breaking. "Ryan!"

Moments later, Ryan appeared, his face a mask of fear and determination. He landed beside them and took in the scene with wide eyes. Without a word, he scooped Karen up into his arms, lifting her as though she weighed nothing.

"Let's get her out of here," he said, his voice steady despite the turmoil around them.

Sky nodded, coughing hard as smoke filled her lungs. She followed Ryan as he carried his mother toward the exit, her wings brushing against fiery foliage as she went. Each step felt like an eternity, the smoke growing thicker and heavier with every passing second.

When they finally reached the edge of the gardens, EMTs rushed to meet them. Ryan gently laid Karen on a stretcher, his hands trembling as he stepped back to let the medics work. Karen's eyes fluttered open, and she reached out weakly toward Ryan, her lips moving as though she wanted to speak. But the pain was too much, and she let her arm fall back to her side.

The medics worked quickly, securing IVs and monitoring her vitals before loading her into the ambulance. Ryan watched as the vehicle sped away, its sirens piercing the night. He stood frozen, his mind racing with worry and guilt.

"Ryan," Sky's voice broke through his thoughts. He turned to see her coughing violently, her face streaked with soot. Her steps were unsteady as she approached him, and he rushed to her side, wrapping an arm around her shoulders.

"You inhaled too much smoke," he said, his voice thick with concern. "Come on, let's get you some air."

He guided her to the back of a fire truck, where a firefighter handed him an oxygen mask. Ryan carefully placed it over Sky's nose and mouth, his hands gentle as he adjusted the straps. "Take deep breaths," he said softly, his eyes never leaving hers.

Sky nodded, the cool oxygen soothing her burning lungs. She closed her eyes, leaning into Ryan's side as he wrapped an arm around her. "You're always getting hurt somehow, huh?" he teased, trying to lighten the mood.

Sky managed a weak smile. "Guess I like keeping you on your toes."

Ryan laughed, holding her closer. "Thank you for finding my mom," he said, his voice sincere.

"Of course," Sky replied, her voice muffled by the mask. She reached up to touch his hand, her eyes shining with gratitude.

As the fire began to die down and the chaos subsided, a familiar voice cut through the night. "What are you doing here, Ryan?"

They turned to see Mr. Daniels approaching, his expression as stern and cold as ever. Ryan stiffened, his body tensing as his father's gaze fell on him.

"Where were you?" Ryan demanded, his voice rising. "Mom was seriously burned! She needed you!"

Mr. Daniels' expression didn't waver. "I was meeting with shareholders on the west end of the gardens. The explosion was on the east side. I had no idea."

Ryan's anger boiled over. "You didn't even bother to look for her! What kind of husband does that?"

Mr. Daniels puffed out his chest, his tone icy. "You will respect me, son."

"Respect?" Ryan spat. "I can't respect a man who doesn't protect his own family."

Sky squeezed Ryan's hand; her voice soft but firm. "He's not worth it, Ryan."

Ryan looked down at her, his breathing heavy as he tried to calm himself. Mr. Daniels, sensing his son's restraint, smirked. "A real man controls his emotions," he said, his voice dripping with condescension. "You have much maturing to do."

With that, he turned and walked away, leaving Ryan and Sky alone on the curb. Ryan's shoulders sagged as tears welled up in his eyes. Sky pulled him into a tight hug, holding him as he broke down. Her own anger simmered just below the surface, but for now, all that mattered was being there for him.

"I've got you," she whispered, her voice steady. Ryan buried his face in her shoulder, clinging to her as the weight of the night finally crashed over him. Side by side, they sat in silence, finding solace in each other's presence amidst the chaos.

Forty

The night was heavy with tension and the sterile scent of the hospital as Ryan and Sky sat beside Karen's bed. The fluorescent lights above cast a pale glow over the room, illuminating Karen's still form beneath the crisp white sheets. Her breathing was steady but shallow, her face pale against the bruises and burns that marred her arms and shoulders. The rhythmic beep of the heart monitor was the only sound breaking the stillness.

Sky sat slumped in a chair near the corner of the room, her head nodding as she struggled against the pull of exhaustion. Ryan was positioned closer, his head resting on the edge of the bed, his right hand firmly holding his mother's. The weight of the past twenty-four hours pressed on him, and though his eyes were closed, his mind was far from at ease.

A soft stirring from Karen brought both of them to alertness. Her hand, weak but deliberate, reached out to gently comb through Ryan's hair. "My baby boy," she murmured, her voice rasping but filled with love.

Ryan's head shot up, his hazel eyes locking onto hers. "Mom, you're awake," he said, relief flooding his voice as he leaned closer, his grip on her hand tightening.

Sky rubbed her eyes and straightened in her chair, a smile spreading across her face as she saw Karen's eyes open. Karen's gaze shifted to Sky, her expression softening further. "Thank you for saving me," Karen said, her voice strained but sincere.

Sky shook her head, her voice catching in her throat. "It wasn't just me. Ryan carried you to the medics. We just... we had to get you out."

Karen's lips curled into a faint smile. "Both of you," she said, looking between them. "Thank you. You're my heroes."

Before either could respond, the door opened with a soft knock. A doctor stepped in, his demeanor calm and professional. He was tall and lean, with short black hair and a tanned complexion. His white coat swished slightly as he approached the bed. "Mrs. Daniels," he said, a warm yet composed smile on his face, "it's good to see you awake."

Karen attempted a nod, but it turned into a grimace of pain. The doctor moved to her side, checking her vitals and adjusting the IV bag. "You're very lucky," he continued. "The explosion last night was catastrophic. Many weren't as fortunate."

Ryan's brow furrowed. "How bad was it?" he asked, his voice tight.

The doctor's expression turned somber. "Fifteen confirmed fatalities," he said, "and thirty-six injured, many of them critically. We're still treating some of the worst cases."

Sky's breath hitched, her hand flying to her mouth as she processed the enormity of the disaster. Ryan's grip on his mother's hand tightened, his knuckles turning white.

"What about my mom?" Ryan asked, his voice trembling. "How long before she can come home?"

The doctor's face softened with empathy. "Her burns are severe," he said. "The damage goes deep beneath the skin, and she'll need extensive care and rehabilitation. We're estimating three to four months before she's well enough to leave."

Ryan's shoulders sagged, his head bowing as he absorbed the news. "Months?" he whispered, his voice breaking.

The doctor placed a reassuring hand on Ryan's shoulder. "She's stable and in good hands. We'll move her to a specialized burn unit shortly, where she'll receive the best care possible. You'll be able to visit her there, though communication will be through a glass partition to prevent infection."

Ryan nodded reluctantly; his throat too tight to speak. Sky placed a comforting hand on his arm, her touch grounding him. "Thank you, Doctor," she said softly.

The doctor gave a small nod. "She'll be just fine with time. Focus on keeping her spirits up during her recovery." With that, he turned and exited the room, leaving the three of them alone once more.

Nurses entered a moment later, preparing Karen for transport. Ryan stayed at her side, his eyes glistening with unshed tears. "I'll be okay, honey," Karen said weakly, reaching up with her uninjured hand to stroke his cheek. "Don't you worry about me."

Ryan's lip quivered as he tried to smile. "I'll visit you every day," he promised, his voice barely above a whisper.

Karen's smile wavered as tears pooled in her own eyes. "You're such a good boy, Ryan," she said, her voice filled with love and pride.

As the nurses wheeled Karen out of the room, Ryan and Sky followed her to the elevator. Karen blew a kiss to Ryan just before the doors slid shut, leaving the two of them staring at the closed metal elevator.

Ryan's composure finally cracked. He turned to Sky, his shoulders shaking as he buried his face in her neck. She wrapped her arms around him, holding him tightly as he let out the emotions he'd been holding back. Her hand gently stroked his hair as she whispered, "She'll be okay, Ryan. She's strong, just like you."

Ryan lifted his head, his hazel eyes red-rimmed and filled with gratitude. "Thank you for being here," he said, his voice raw. "I don't know what I'd do without you."

Sky smiled softly, her own eyes glistening. "You'll never have to find out," she said firmly. Together, they turned and walked down the hallway, finding solace in each other as they faced the uncertain days ahead.

Forty-One

Christmas Day arrived with a sense of heaviness in the air. The morning sunlight filtered weakly through the hospital room's blinds, casting soft streaks across Karen's pale face. Sky sat quietly in a chair near the window, her phone in her lap, while Ryan leaned over his mother's bedside, holding her hand as they talked softly.

Karen, though weak, tried her best to sound cheerful. "So, Ryan, tell me about school. How's football? Have they started looking for a new receiver yet?"

Ryan chuckled; his voice warm despite the circumstances. "They're going to have a tough time finding someone as good as me," he teased, earning a small laugh from his mother.

Sky smiled faintly, listening to their exchange while her thoughts drifted. Earlier that morning, she'd received an email from her parents. Her heart had leapt at first, hoping for a Christmas surprise. Instead, the message was a familiar disappointment.

Subject: Christmas

Dear Sky,

We wanted to wish you a Merry Christmas. Unfortunately, we won't be able to visit today as work has kept us in Georgia longer than expected. We'll try to come up for New Year's if our schedules allow. Stay safe, sweetheart, and know that we're thinking of you.

Love, Mom and Dad.

Sky's grip on her phone tightened as she read and reread the email. Her parents always canceled, always chose their careers over her. She shook her head, pushing the disappointment aside. What else was new? She tucked her phone away and focused on the people in front of her—the family that, even in chaos, was there.

By lunchtime, Karen's strength waned, and she drifted off to sleep. The heart monitor's steady beep was the only sound in the room. Ryan and Sky exchanged a glance, silently agreeing it was time to leave. They quietly gathered their things, taking care not to wake Karen, and slipped out of the hospital.

The air outside was frigid, the kind of cold that bit through layers and made breaths visible. They took to the skies, flying back to Sky's house in silence. When they landed, Ryan's exhaustion became evident. He collapsed just inside the doorway, sitting against the wall with his head in his hands.

Sky knelt beside him; worry etched on her face. "Ryan, come on. You need rest."

He didn't respond, his body heavy with the weight of the past few days. Sky managed to coax him onto the couch, draping a blanket over him. He lay there motionless, his eyes staring blankly at the ceiling. She wanted to say something, to comfort him, but no words felt adequate.

Instead, she stepped back, turned off the lights, and retreated to her room. As she closed the door behind her, the silence of the house enveloped her. It was a solemn, lonely quiet, the kind that made the emptiness of Christmas without family all the more pronounced.

Sky sank onto her bed, her knees drawing up to her chest. The weight of everything came crashing down. She grabbed her pillow and screamed into it, the muffled sound barely breaking the stillness. She screamed until her throat burned and voice gave out, until she had no energy left to do anything but cry.

Her mind was a whirlwind of thoughts and emotions. How could everything have gone so wrong? The botanical gardens, Karen's injuries, the looming threat of NisenX—it was all too much. Why was she in the middle of this nightmare? Why did Ryan have to suffer so much? He didn't deserve this, none of them did.

The image of Ryan's tear-streaked face from the hospital flashed in her mind. He'd been so strong for his mother, but she knew how fragile he felt inside. Sky's chest tightened, the overwhelming urge to protect him surging through her. But how could she protect him when she didn't even know what the future held?

Her thoughts turned to her parents. She pictured them in some sterile lab, far away in Georgia, too busy to think about their only child.

Sky clutched her pillow as fresh tears streamed down her face. Where had that love gone? When had her parents' become strangers who only reached out through hollow emails and broken promises?

She stared at the ceiling, her vision blurred by tears. The future felt so uncertain, so terrifying. NisenX was still a looming threat, Ryan's father was a constant source of fear, and their plan to escape felt like a distant dream. She didn't know what would happen next. For now, all she could do was let herself cry, her sobs echoing in the empty, cold house until sleep finally claimed her.

Forty-Two

The week between Christmas and New Year's was dark and frigid. Snow had settled over the mountains, blanketing the world in a pristine white layer, but the beauty of the landscape did little to lift the spirits of those within it. The air was harsh, a biting wind tearing through the trees and rattling the windows. Smoke from chimneys curled up into the steel-gray sky, blending into the low-hanging clouds that promised more snow. The town seemed quieter than usual, muffled by the thick snow and the weight of recent events.

Ryan and Sky spent their days visiting Karen at the hospital. Each morning, they bundled up against the frigid air and flew to the hospital. The smell of antiseptic and the constant beeping of machines greeted them as they entered the burn unit. Some days, Karen was awake and cheerful, asking about their lives and laughing at Ryan's jokes. Other days, she slept, her face pale, her body wrapped in gauze that seemed to consume her. Despite her weakened state, Karen always lit up when she saw Sky and Ryan together, often commenting on how lucky her son was to have someone so kind by his side.

As New Year's Eve approached, Karen called Ryan closer during one of their visits. Her voice was still hoarse, but her determination was clear. "Ryan, I need you to do something for me," she said, gripping his hand tightly.

Ryan frowned, already sensing he wouldn't like what she was about to ask. "What is it, Mom?"

Karen's lips curved into a weak smile. "NisenX is hosting a New Year's Gala at headquarters. I can't go, obviously, but I want you to attend in my place. Your father will be there, and it would mean a lot to him."

Ryan's stomach churned at the thought. He turned his head away, his jaw clenching. "Mom, I... I don't think I can do that."

Karen's grip tightened. "Please, Ryan. I know how you feel about your father and that place, but just make a quick appearance. For me?"

Sky, sitting on the other side of the bed, noticed Ryan's internal battle. She reached out, placing her hand over his. When he met her gaze, she gave him a small nod of encouragement. "You'll only be there for a little while," she said softly. "I'll go with you."

Ryan sighed, his shoulders sagging in defeat. "Okay, Mom. But only for a bit."

Karen's face lit up, a brief flicker of joy cutting through the pain. "Thank you, honey. That means so much to me."

That night, Ryan and Sky prepared for the gala with little enthusiasm. Ryan purposefully ignored the formal dress code, opting for casual clothes to irk his father. Sky matched his energy, choosing a simple outfit that prioritized comfort over style. They piled into Ryan's truck and drove through the icy streets to the towering NisenX headquarters.

The building loomed over them, its sleek glass façade reflecting the cold, pale light of the streetlamps. Above the entrance, the company's slogan glowed in stark white: *"Creating a Better Tomorrow."* Sky shivered, though not from the wind.

Inside, the entertainment hall had been transformed into an opulent ballroom. Gold and white decorations adorned every surface. Streamers hung gracefully from the high ceilings, and balloons sparkled in the soft glow of the chandeliers. A long buffet table lined one wall, laden with elaborate dishes, while a bar offering champagne and sparkling cider stood at the opposite end. In the center of the room, couples danced to the soft strains of a live band, their laughter mingling with the music.

Sky's anxiety spiked as they entered. The grandeur of the room made her feel small and out of place. Her wings tensed under her coat, and she fidgeted with the hem of her sleeve. Ryan noticed her unease and led her to a quiet table in a far corner.

"We'll stay for ten, maybe fifteen minutes," he promised, squeezing her hand. "Then we're out of here."

Sky nodded, trying to steady her breathing. As Ryan left to grab drinks, she sat alone, her gaze darting around the room. The adults seemed so carefree, sipping champagne and laughing as if the world outside didn't exist. To her left, a nearby table caught her attention. Four well-dressed people were deep in conversation, their voices low but urgent.

"Can you believe that was the sixth attack this month?" a woman in a sharp black business suit said, her tone incredulous.

"I'm not surprised," replied a man in a vest and tie. "They're getting more cocky."

Sky's heart skipped a beat. Were they talking about the ReFramers?

"The ReFramers will get what's coming to them," the woman continued. "No way they'll get away with killing seventeen of our own, especially not at Christmas."

Sky's stomach churned. Seventeen dead? Her mind raced as she listened intently.

"I still can't believe they managed to sneak a bomb into the botanical gardens," another man said, shaking his head. "The smell of gasoline was everywhere."

The woman leaned forward, a sinister smile on her lips. "Just wait until they see what we have cooking downstairs. If they think we're monsters now, wait until they meet the MFHP."

The group chuckled, raising their glasses in a toast. Sky's blood ran still. *What is the MFHP?* she wondered, her heart pounding. Her thoughts spiraled as she tried to piece together the fragments of their conversation. Whatever it was, it couldn't be good.

Ryan returned, setting two cups of water on the table. "Sorry, that took a while. The line was crazy." He paused, noticing Sky's distant expression. "Sky? What's wrong?"

She hesitated, glancing at the group nearby. "We'll talk about it later," she said quietly, not wanting to draw attention.

Ryan frowned but didn't press. Instead, he followed her gaze, his eyes landing on his father across the room. Mr. Daniels stood in a circle of men, laughing and gesturing animatedly. Ryan's jaw tightened. "The man can't even visit his wife in the hospital," he muttered, his voice laced with bitterness.

Sensing his growing anger, Sky reached out and placed a hand on his. "Hey," he said softly. "Let's go dance."

Sky's expression softened. "You sure?"

Ryan nodded, a small smile tugging at his lips. "Just one song."

He led her to the dance floor, pulling her close as a slow song began to play. His hands rested gently on her waist, and her arms looped around his neck. For a moment, the world around them faded. Ryan's hazel eyes locked onto hers, and he leaned his forehead against hers.

"I've been dying to do this since homecoming," he admitted, his voice barely above a whisper.

Sky's cheeks flushed. "Oh, really? Then why'd you wait so long?"

He grinned. "Had to wait for the right moment."

She arched an eyebrow. "And a NisenX gala is the right moment?"

Ryan chuckled; his breath warm against her skin. "If I'm with you, it's always the right moment."

Sky's heart fluttered at his words. She leaned into him, letting his presence drown out her fears. For a few precious minutes, they were just two teenagers, lost in the magic of a dance.

As the song ended, they lingered on the dance floor, their foreheads still touching. Ryan was about to speak when a voice behind them broke the moment.

"Sky? Is that you?"

Forty-Three

Sky knew that voice. It sent shivers down her spine, her heart skipping a beat as she turned around to see a familiar face. Standing just a few feet away was a woman wearing a deep purple knit pantsuit. Her skin was pale and fair, her brown eyes wide with shock. Dirty blonde hair framed her face, stopping neatly at her shoulders. Sky couldn't ignore the look of surprise and disbelief etched into the woman's features.

Sky's lips trembled as the word escaped her mouth, "Mom?"

Dr. Denise Treder, world-renowned veterinarian and Sky's estranged mother, stared back at her, seemingly at a loss for words. Her gaze shifted over Sky, lingering as if trying to make sense of the girl in front of her with the one she had left behind so long ago.

"Sky," her mother finally said, her voice trembling. "What are you doing here?"

Sky's chest tightened, her emotions swirling between anger and disbelief. "What am *I* doing here? What about you?" she snapped. "Why are you here?"

Her mother's expression softened as she answered, "We told you we got jobs with NisenX. William mentioned a gala at the Tennessee headquarters, and he personally invited us."

Sky's mind raced. William—Ryan's father. Of course, he would've extended the invitation to her parents. It felt like a cruel twist of fate. Before Sky could respond, a large figure stepped up beside her mother.

"Denise, what's going on?" the man asked. He was tall and broad, dressed in a perfectly pressed black suit. His polished dress shoes reflected the overhead lights, adorned with the same NX pin Sky had seen on Mr. Daniels. A long tie with the letters "NX" repeated in white patterns adorned his chest. His clean-shaven head gleamed under the lights, and his piercing eyes locked onto Sky.

Her father. Brad Treder.

"Sky," he said, his voice firm and commanding. "What are you doing here?"

Sky struggled to find words, her mouth opening and closing as her emotions battled for control. Before she could speak, Ryan stepped forward, placing a hand protectively on her shoulder. "She's here with me," he said firmly. "She's my plus one." Dr. Denise Treder's eyes widened further, darting between Sky and Ryan.

"Your plus one?" she echoed, her tone filled with a mix of confusion and something else Sky couldn't quite place.

Sky's mother stepped forward, her hands trembling as she reached out. "Sweetheart, we've missed you so much."

Sky recoiled, stepping back. "Missed me?" she said bitterly. "You've never had time for me. You're always too busy."

Her mother's hand froze mid-air before dropping to her side. Her father joined her, his face hardening as he said, "Sky, you know our work is important. We've been trying to build a better future—for you and for everyone."

Sky's anger flared. "A better future? By abandoning your family? By abandoning *me*?"

Ryan's grip on her shoulder tightened, a silent reminder to stay calm, but Sky could feel her control slipping. Her mother's expression faltered, and she tried again. "Sky, we were planning to surprise you for New Year's. We—"

"Sure you were," Sky interrupted, her voice sharp. "You've been planning to surprise me my entire life. Except you never show up."

"Sweetheart, that's not fair," her father said, his tone growing stern. "You know how demanding our work is. We've always tried to make time for you."

"Tried?" Sky spat. "Do you even know anything about me anymore? Do you know what my life has been like? What I've been through?"

Her father's eyes darkened, and his voice lowered. "Sky Treder, lower your voice. You're causing a scene."

But Sky didn't care. The heat of her rage boiled over, and she felt an unfamiliar sensation building within her. Her wings, tightly tucked under her coat, began to press against the fabric, and her breathing quickened. Her vision blurred for a moment before sharpening, her surroundings taking on an almost surreal clarity. Ryan stepped closer, whispering, "Sky, breathe. Calm down."

Her parents' faces changed. Shock turned to something akin to fear as they stared at her. "Sky, what's happening?" her mother asked, her voice trembling.

Sky's rage surged. "What's happening? I'm finally telling you how I feel. How you've made me feel since I was six years old. Like I don't matter!"

The gasps from the surrounding crowd broke through her fury, and she realized all eyes were on her. Her parents weren't just staring at her—they were staring at her eyes. Sky blinked, noticing her reflection in a nearby window. Her pupils had expanded, the whites of her eyes darkened, giving her an almost feral appearance.

"Sky, sweetie," her mother began, stepping forward again. "You'll be okay. We can fix this."

That was the breaking point. Sky's wings burst from her coat, unfurling to their full span. The crowd gasped audibly, some stepping back, while others leaned in with fascination. Her mother covered her mouth, her father took a step back, and Sky's voice trembled with emotion as she shouted, "I'm not a problem you can fix!"

Ryan grabbed her hand, his voice urgent. "Sky, we need to go. Now."

She barely registered his words, her instincts taking over. She bolted for the exit, pushing past the stunned crowd. The cold air hit her like a slap, but it wasn't enough to quell the storm inside. Without a second thought, she launched herself into the sky, her wings slicing through the freezing wind. Snow pelted her face, stinging her eyes, but she didn't care. She needed to get away—from her parents, from NisenX, from everything.

Behind her, Ryan followed, his wings beating furiously as he tried to keep up. The icy air bit at his skin, but his focus remained on Sky's white wings ahead of him. She was fast—faster than he'd ever seen her fly before. His heart pounded, both from exertion and fear. He couldn't lose her. Not like this.

"Sky!" he called out, his voice nearly drowned by the roaring wind.

Sky didn't respond, her mind clouded by a primal rage she couldn't fully control. The world below blurred into streaks of white and gray as she pushed herself faster, higher. But the farther she flew, the heavier her chest felt. The icy air burned her lungs, and her vision started to blur.

Ryan surged forward, finally closing the gap between them. He reached out, grabbing her wrist gently but firmly. "Sky, stop! It's me!"

The sound of his voice broke through the haze. She slowed, her wings faltering as exhaustion caught up with her. The two of them hovered in the air, snow swirling around them. Sky's breathing was ragged, her eyes shimmering with unshed tears. Ryan pulled her close, wrapping his arms around her as she began to sob into his chest.

"It's okay," he murmured, his voice steady and calm. "I've got you. It's going to be okay."

Sky clung to him, her wings folding in as she let herself cry. Ryan held her tightly, shielding her from the biting wind as they drifted slowly back toward the ground. Neither spoke, the silence between them filled with unspoken words and shared pain.

Forty-Four

Ryan and Sky had made their way to Bryant's house through the bitter cold. The snow-laden wind howled around them, the world a blur of white and gray. Ryan practically carried Sky, her body weak and trembling as the adrenaline drained from her system. Each step he took crunched against the icy ground, his arms steady despite his own exhaustion.

Bryant opened the door, his eyes widening in shock. "What the heck? I thought you two were gone by now!" he exclaimed, stepping aside to let them in.

Ryan didn't respond, guiding Sky over to the hearth where a roaring fire cast flickering shadows across the walls. He sat her down gently, wrapping his arms around her as she shivered. Her fingers felt like ice, her tears frozen into tiny crystals on her cheeks, and her wings quivered uncontrollably.

Bryant wasted no time, gathering every blanket he could find and piling them onto the couple. He wrapped Sky in layers of warmth, his movements frantic yet caring. "What happened?" he demanded, sitting on the couch behind them and watching Ryan closely.

Ryan held Sky close, positioning her between himself and the fire. His own hands shook, not from the weather, but from the weight of everything that had happened. His crystallized hair began to thaw, the water dripping onto the blanket as he tightened his hold on Sky.

"I couldn't let her stay out there in this," Ryan finally said, his voice thick with emotion. "She needed to get warm."

Bryant leaned forward, his elbows resting on his knees. "I get that, but why are you two still here? What's going on?"

Ryan glanced down at Sky, her eyes barely open, before turning back to Bryant. He took a deep breath, his voice low and steady as he began to explain. "The botanical gardens exploded the night of Christmas Eve. It was bad. My mom was there. She got caught in the fire." His voice cracked slightly as he continued. "She's in the hospital now, burned so badly she'll be there for months."

Bryant's face fell. "Dang, man. I'm sorry. Is she going to be okay?"

Ryan nodded faintly. "Yeah. She's tough, but... it's going to take a while." He hesitated, then added, "Sky and I decided to stay until the school year ends. I can't leave her like that."

Bryant didn't push further, waiting as Ryan gathered his thoughts. Finally, Ryan continued, "Last night, we went to this stupid New Year's Gala at my dad's work. It was my mom's idea—she wanted me to go in her place, to keep up appearances for my dad."

Bryant, while quickly texting Nia what happened, scoffed. "Sounds like a nightmare."

Ryan's jaw tightened. "It was. And then Sky's parents showed up—completely unannounced."

Bryant's eyebrows shot up. "Her parents? They're back?"

Ryan nodded grimly. "It wasn't a good reunion. They didn't even recognize how upset she was. It... it drove her over the edge."

Bryant handed Ryan a mug of hot chocolate, which he set down on the brick ledge of the fireplace without drinking. "She bolted," Ryan said, his voice quieter now. "Flew out of there as fast as I've ever seen. I couldn't leave her. I had to follow."

Bryant sighed, leaning back against the couch. "Man, you two have been through it." He looked down at Sky, wrapped in the blankets, her breathing now calm and steady. "She's lucky to have you."

Before Ryan could respond, a knock echoed through the house. Bryant rose to his feet, peering through the window before opening the door. Nia burst in, dressed in mismatched pajamas under a thick jacket, her face pale with worry.

"What happened?" she demanded, rushing to Sky's side. She crouched down, brushing stray strands of hair from Sky's face. "Is she okay? What's going on?"

Bryant quickly recounted everything Ryan had just said, his voice quiet but urgent. Nia listened, her eyes wide and brimming with concern.

"Oh, Sky," she whispered, her voice trembling. "You've been through so much." She turned to Ryan. "What's the plan now?"

Ryan didn't respond immediately, his gaze fixed on Sky. Her face looked peaceful now, but he knew the storm was still brewing inside her. "I don't know," he admitted, his voice heavy with uncertainty. "I just... I need to make sure she's okay."

Nia placed a gentle hand on his arm. "She's strong, Ryan. She'll pull through this."

Ryan nodded, but his thoughts were far from certain. *What if she doesn't? What if I can't protect her?* His mind raced with every worst-case scenario, each one more terrifying than the last. He felt the weight of their situation pressing down on him, the responsibility of keeping her safe and the uncertainty of what the future held.

For now, all he could do was hold her close, hoping his warmth and presence would be enough to give her strength. As the fire crackled beside them, he whispered quietly, "I'm not going anywhere. Not without you."

Sky stirred slightly at his words, a faint smile gracing her lips before she drifted back to sleep. Ryan leaned his head back against the couch, his thoughts swirling but his resolve unshaken. No matter what came next, he knew one thing for certain: he wouldn't let her face it alone.

Forty-Five

That morning after the event was hard. Sky didn't speak a word as her friends did their best to help her. Nia made her eat a few bites of breakfast, coaxing her gently while Bryant prepared plates for everyone. Ryan sat close by, his watchful eyes never leaving Sky. She stared blankly into nothingness, her plate untouched except for the few bites Nia had practically begged her to eat.

"Come on, Sky," Nia said, kneeling beside her and forcing a smile. "We're all here for you. Besides, you wouldn't want me to embarrass myself trying to tell jokes, would you? Remember the last time? Ryan's face turned so red he looked like a tomato!"

Nia laughed lightly, hoping to spark some kind of reaction. But her words fell flat, her smiles met only with silence. Sky's expression didn't change, her gaze fixed somewhere in the distance, her body unmoving. Nia's laughter faded into a sigh as she sat back, glancing at Ryan with helplessness in her eyes.

Sky's mind felt clouded, her thoughts swirling in a dull grey fog. The world around her seemed darker than before, every sound muffled, every sensation muted. Her whole body ached—not from physical pain, but from an emotional weight she couldn't shake. She could feel the heavy cloud resting upon her head, blocking out the words and pleas of her friends.

She lay on Bryant's couch for the next few days, barely moving. Her friends stayed close, unwilling to leave her alone. Bryant balanced caring for his sisters and ensuring his friends had what they needed. Ryan and Nia were constantly nearby, trying to find ways to reach her. But nothing worked.

Nia tried everything she could think of: comforting words, soft music, and even her notoriously bad jokes. But nothing pierced the thick barrier Sky had built around herself. Ryan sat silently; his jaw clenched tight as he watched her slip deeper into her own mind. He ignored the constant buzzing of his phone, text after text from his mom asking where he was. He couldn't bring himself to respond. Every message reminded him that Karen's suggestion had led them to the gala and the disaster that followed. He couldn't face her right now.

Sky's phone sat on the coffee table, untouched. Unlike Ryan's, it had no missed calls, no concerned texts from family—just one email. When the screen lit up with a notification, Ryan's curiosity got the better of him. He opened the email, his expression hardening as he read:

Subject: Our Apologies

Dear Sky,

We want to start by saying how sorry we are for what happened at the gala. It was not our intention to upset you, and we deeply regret the pain our presence caused. For too many years, we've let our work come first, and we see now how much that has hurt you. There's no excuse for the distance we've allowed to grow between us.

We realize now that our being here only seems to bring you more pain. Because of this, we've decided to return to Georgia immediately. We hope that giving you space will help you work through your feelings without our interference.

We wish you nothing but the best and hope you find happiness and peace in your life. You deserve it.

With love,
Mom and Dad

Ryan stared at the screen, his jaw tightening with every word. *That's it?* he thought. *That's all they have to say for themselves?* His grip on the phone heavy as he handed it to Nia, who read the message with growing fury.

"Are you kidding me?" she exclaimed, standing abruptly. She began pacing, her voice rising. "That's it? Years of ignoring her, abandoning her, and this is all they can manage? 'Sorry we're terrible parents, but here's a generic apology before we run away again!' Unbelievable! What kind of parents just give up like that? They should be on their knees begging her forgiveness, not running off to Georgia like cowards!"

Nia's rant continued, filled with colorful language and cutting remarks about Sky's parents' lack of empathy. Bryant glanced up from across the room, nodding in agreement but wisely choosing to stay silent.

Ryan barely heard her. His attention remained fixed on Sky, who hadn't reacted to the email or Nia's outburst. She was still staring at the fireplace, her eyes reflecting the flickering flames. Her face was pale, her body still wrapped in blankets. Ryan felt his heart twist. He wanted so desperately to fix this, to pull her back from the void she was sinking into. But he didn't know how.

As the days passed, the new semester loomed closer. They all knew they would soon have to return to their own homes and routines. The thought weighed heavily on Ryan. Nia noticed his distant expression and asked softly, "Have you come up with something?"

Bryant joined the conversation, his voice steady. "Ryan, you're more than welcome to stay here. Better here than at your parents' place."

Nia added, "And Sky can stay with me. She shouldn't be left alone right now."

Ryan opened his mouth to protest. "I can stay with Sky. She's my—"

Bryant cut him off with a firm tone. "Ryan, you've been through hell too. You can't take care of her if you're falling apart yourself. Let us help. You need support as much as she does."

Ryan stared at Bryant, his protest fading. He looked down at his hands, gripping the edge of the blanket he had tucked around Sky. Bryant's words were true, and deep down, he knew it.

"Thank you," Ryan said quietly, his voice heavy with emotion.

Nia leaned forward, placing a hand on Sky's shoulder. "We'll take care of her. You'll still see her every day at school. We'll get through this."

Ryan nodded, his gaze returning to Sky. She hadn't moved; her eyes still fixed on the fire. His mind raced with thoughts of their future, of how to pull her out of this darkness. He couldn't bear to see her like this. The vibrant, fierce girl he loved was buried somewhere beneath the layers of grief and hopelessness. He vowed to find her, to bring her back.

I'll do whatever it takes, he thought, his jaw set with determination. We'll get through this.

Forty-Six

It had been a week since school started back, and Sky found herself retreating into the quiet solitude of the library almost daily. She sat at her usual spot beside the chilly window, the cool glass radiating a frosty air that matched the numbness inside her. Her notebook was her only companion, its pages filling with her thoughts and feelings. Journaling had been Nia's idea— "It'll help you process everything," she'd said with her usual brightness. Reluctantly, Sky had agreed. For the last week, her words spilled out in the form of poetry, scribbles, and fragments of thoughts. Writing seemed to be the only way she could express the storm within her.

Nia had become Sky's lifeline, dragging her out of bed every morning and insisting she get dressed for the day. "You can't stay in pajamas forever, Sky," Nia would tease, trying to coax a smile from her friend. Sky often managed a weak one, but it never quite reached her eyes. Still, she followed Nia's lead, going through the motions of the school day.

Ryan, too, was never far. He would meet Sky and Nia in the mornings, walking them to class and checking in. Bryant, ever watchful, kept a close eye on Ryan, ensuring he wasn't left alone with his thoughts. Ryan spent hours in the team's workout room with Bryant, pushing himself harder and harder. He channeled his frustration and pain into the weights, lifting more than he ever had before. But even Ryan's newfound strength couldn't completely mask the haunted look in his eyes—a look Bryant caught each time he had to remind him not to push too far.

After school, the four friends would gather at Nia's house. They'd watch movies or play games, but Sky would often sit off to the side, furiously journaling. Ryan tried to pull her closer, sometimes wrapping her in his arms as they sat on the couch. She'd let him hold her, feeling the warmth of his embrace, but her mind remained distant, wrapped in a fog of guilt and despair.

The bitter January days passed slowly, each one feeling heavier than the last. Sky and Ryan both fought their battles in different ways. Sky, through her writing and reluctant exercise sessions with Nia, and Ryan, through grueling workouts and quiet determination. By early February, Ryan was beginning to resemble his old self again. He stood taller, his laughter returned, and he found himself joking with his friends more often. But Sky still struggled. Her nights were plagued with recurring nightmares.

Each dream was the same: she would watch helplessly as the people she cared about were hurt or killed. Sometimes it was Nia, other times Bryant, and more often than not, Ryan. She'd see his pained expression, his body crumpling as she reached out to save him. Her wings would always ache in these dreams, as if they were being torn or weighed down by an invisible force. The pain was so vivid it would wake her in the middle of the night, leaving her gasping for air and drenched in sweat.

During the days, the guilt she felt toward Ryan ate away at her. She convinced herself that she had brought so much trouble into his life. Causing a deeper rift between him and his parents, football friends, and plans for the future. Her journal became a confessional of her self-blame, each page filled with words she could never say aloud. But as the days passed, she began to notice small changes. She caught herself smiling at Nia's silly jokes or laughing quietly at Bryant's exaggerated stories. Ryan's presence, his unwavering support, started to chip away at the wall she'd built around her heart. Slowly, she felt warmth returning to her life.

By Valentine's Day, the shift within Sky was undeniable. That morning, she stood by her locker, pacing the halls and wondering if Ryan had plans for the day. She felt nervous, unsure if he'd want to do anything special. But when she turned, there he was—leaning against the wall, his hazel eyes gleaming as they locked onto hers. His smile sent a flutter through her chest, and she couldn't help but smile back.

Ryan was holding something behind his back as she approached him. "What are you up to?" she asked, tilting her head curiously.

"You'll see," he teased, his grin widening.

Sky turned to open her locker, and as the door swung open, a cascade of flower petals spilled out. She gasped, her hands flying to her mouth as she turned back to Ryan, who now held a single daisy in front of her.

"You remembered daisies are my favorite," she said, her voice soft with surprise.

"How could I forget?" he replied, his voice just as soft. He held the daisy out to her, and she took it, her fingers brushing against his.

Ryan leaned in slightly, his eyes meeting hers. "I was thinking we could hang out at your place tonight," he said. "Unless you have plans?"

Sky couldn't tear her gaze away from him. His smile, the way he looked at her—it was as if he saw only her, even in a crowded hallway. "No plans for me," she said, her voice steady but her heart racing.

"Perfect," he said, his grin growing. "I'll cook something, and you can pick the movie."

As he walked off to his next class, Sky stood there, holding the daisy and staring after him. For the first time in what felt like forever, she felt a spark of hope. The fog in her mind was lifting, replaced by something warm and familiar. Ryan's kindness, his patience, his unwavering belief in her—it was as if his light was defrosting the frozen pieces of her heart.

She clutched the daisy close, letting herself savor the moment. For the first time in weeks, she felt like herself again, and it felt good.

Forty-Seven

Sky was home, staring into her floor-length mirror. Ryan had texted to say he was on his way, and her heart raced with excitement. She wanted to look her best for their first Valentine's Day together. Rifling through her closet, she groaned at every outfit she pulled out. Nothing felt right. Frustrated, she dropped onto her bed, her eyes catching a glimpse of a sweatshirt lying crumpled on the floor. It was Ryan's—the one he'd given her the morning after the championship party when her own sweater had been torn to shreds.

She picked it up and held it close, inhaling deeply. It still faintly smelled like him: pine trees and forest air, a scent she'd come to associate with his comforting presence. Smiling, she slid it on, its oversized warmth wrapping around her like a hug. Pairing it with her gray cheer joggers, she looked in the mirror and decided it was perfect. The casual, cozy look felt right—like her and Ryan.

She spent a few minutes on her makeup, carefully blending blush onto her cheeks before pulling her hair into a high ponytail, braiding it down her back. Staring at her reflection, she felt a flicker of confidence. She had changed so much since she'd transferred schools. She smiled faintly, her reflection showing a girl who was starting to heal.

The doorbell rang, and she practically flew down the stairs. Opening the door, she found Ryan standing there, his hair catching the winter wind. He wore a dark blue V-neck shirt that highlighted his hazel eyes and a pair of distressed jeans that had seen better days. His smile—the one that always made her heart stutter—lit up his face.

"Hey, beautiful," he said, his voice warm.

Sky was momentarily dazed, her cheeks flushing. Ryan chuckled softly. "Earth to Sky? Are you okay?"

Shaking herself from her trance, she stammered, "Wait, what?"

Leaning down, he kissed her forehead. "You're too cute," he said, stepping inside with a bag of groceries. Sky shut the door, still feeling embarrassed by her reaction, and followed him to the kitchen.

"What are you planning to make?" she asked, watching him unload the bag onto the counter.

Ryan grinned, pulling out a pan. "You'll see."

Sky perched on a stool at the kitchen island, her chin resting in her hands as she watched him work. He moved with ease, chopping vegetables and sautéing chicken in a garlic butter sauce that filled the air with an irresistible aroma, he was starting to become a much better cook. She didn't realize she'd been staring until Ryan glanced at her and laughed.

"What's so funny?" she asked, her cheeks warming again.

"I like your shirt," he said, nodding toward the sweatshirt she was wearing.

Sky smiled. "It's the best I've got."

"Oh, really?" he teased, flipping the chicken in the pan.

"I like your shirt too," she shot back. "Navy is probably your best color."

"Is it my best color, or is it your favorite?" he asked, smirking as he plated the food.

Sky looked away, pretending to be busy examining her nails. "Gotcha," he said softly, setting down two plates in front of her.

The food looked amazing: golden-breaded chicken atop a bed of slightly burnt vegetables. Sky's eyes lit up. "Sesame chicken! I'm impressed!"

Ryan laughed, taking a seat beside her. "Yeah, me too. Only the vegetables had to suffer."

They dug in, Sky finishing her plate long before Ryan. She eyed the chicken left on his plate, reaching over with her fork.

"What makes you think you can have mine?" he asked, blocking her fork with his own.

"Because this meal is my Valentine's present," she said, grinning. "Therefore, it's all mine."

Ryan shook his head, laughing as he let her steal a piece. "You're unbelievable." He watched her chew, a mischievous glint in his eyes. "What makes you think that was your only Valentine's present?"

Sky choked on her bite, her face turning bright red while she rushed to the living room. Ryan laughed harder, finishing his food as she sat on the couch flustered. "You're cute when you're embarrassed," he said, standing to join her.

She scrolled through movies, finally landing on her favorite chick flick, *The Notebook*.

"Why?" Ryan groaned, leaning back against the cushions.

Sky grinned. "We always watch your favorite movies. It's my turn."

Ryan sighed but smiled. "Fine." He pulled her closer, draping a blanket over them.

As the movie played, they couldn't stop teasing each other. Sky poked his side during emotional scenes, and he retaliated by tickling her until she squealed. By the end, they were both lying on the couch, tangled in each other's arms, laughing at their antics.

When the movie ended, Sky suddenly remembered something. "Oh! I almost forgot your present!" She jumped up, running upstairs.

Ryan watched her go, smiling to himself. When she returned with an envelope, he sat up, curious. "What do you have there?"

She handed it to him, looking away shyly. Ryan opened it carefully, unfolding the paper inside. Written on it was a poem:

A bird, small and unsure, in a new and frightening place,
Its wings trembling, afraid to fly in open space.
Then came another, bold and strong,
Whispering courage in its song.
They soared together, high and free,
Through skies of endless possibility.
And though the winds may test and try,
Together, they'll forever fly.

Ryan's eyes glistened as he looked at her. "This is beautiful, Sky. Thank you."

She smiled; her cheeks warm. "I figured it was the best way to say how I feel."

Ryan reached into his pocket, pulling out a delicate gold chain with a wooden charm shaped like wings in the form of a heart. "I carved this for you," he said softly.

Sky's eyes widened. "You made this?"

"Remember the old mansion from homecoming?" he asked, fastening the necklace around her neck. "The wood is from there. I thought it was fitting."

He turns Skys' shoulder away and gathers her hair to the side, his fingers brushing against her skin. He can feel goosebumps along her neck, reaching to place the necklace on her.

Tears welled in her eyes as she looked at him. "You'd do all this for me?"

Ryan grabs her hands, admiring the chain that rests along her collarbone. He notices the wings resting lower on her chest. He feels excitement rush through him saying, "I'd do anything for you, Sky."

She hugged him tightly, their hearts beating in sync. They embrace for a moment as his hands find their way to the sides of her face. She pulls back, only to be drawn into a kiss. She is lost as his lips press against hers, their warmth spreading across her skin. When their lips met, the world around them melted away. The kiss was passionate and consuming, leaving them both breathless and longing for more.

She wraps her arms around his neck as the kiss continues. Sky feels overwhelmed, nervous, excited. Slowly, Ryan's hands travel down to her waist with a firm grasp. She doesn't even flinch, feeling the need to be closer. Sky and Ryan separate abruptly, breathing heavy and in sync. She whispers "We should probably stop before we can't stop". Ryan smiles saying, "Dang it". They look at the time and see 10:05 pm. Ryan shrugs, "Bryant will kill me if I come back too late". Ryan and Sky stand up, walking towards the door, both still reeling from that kiss. He stands in the door way before turning to give her one last peck on the cheek. He holds her head close in his hands, taking in the warmth of her breath.

He looks into her eyes, "Happy Valentine's Day".

She can barely whisper back "Happy Valentine's Day". Ryan turns around and takes off into the air.

Sky closes the door, and sinks down, clasping her necklace. She was feeling something stronger than any time before. Electricity seemed to rush through her, the feeling of him kissing her, holding her close, was intense. She hated to cut it off so quickly. Her body ached to kiss him again.

Sky found herself walking up the stairs to her room, ready to crash from an amazing night. She enters her room pushing past the doorway clogged with clothes.

Sky sat down on the edge of her bed still in a daze when she heard the door creak. She looked up, not having time to react, Ryan appeared, pulling her in for another kiss.

They separate for a moment as she says, "You came back through my window?"

Their hearts racing, he says, "I couldn't leave you, not yet."

With that he pulls Sky in close, feeling her heartbeat through the sweatshirt. His grip on her grew firmer as he lowered them down to the edge of her bed. He could feel his right-hand trace along her waist while one hand cradled her face. They kissed. Each one deeper than the last. Sky could feel the pull return, she wanted him, more of him. She kissed back, falling into a rhythm. She kept her arms wrapped around his strong neck, feeling his heart pounding with force. One of her hands lowered in front, tracing down his neck to the collar of his shirt. She grabbed onto his V-neck, pulling him closer, falling onto the bed. Ryan fell right in sync and lowered her head slowly to the bedding below. They kissed for what felt like a lifetime. His hold on her grew, pulling her waist to his as he laid on top of her. Sky tugged on his shirt, keeping his lips pressed against hers. Neither of them could think of anything else but the other. Ryan was drawn into her face as Sky welcomed his embrace.

After a while of kissing, they stared at each other's faces, reveling in the amazing moment they just experienced. Sky lay there, her lips happily aching. Ryan was the same, locking eyes with her. They smiled, Sky tucking her head into his chest, feeling complete. Ryan held her close, using one arm to grab at the blanket that lay crumpled to the side of the bed, pulling it over them. Their warmth quickly filled the covers. Sky's breath, ever so softly, brushing against his shirt.

Ryan was at a loss for words. Nothing could describe the emotional, mental, and physical connection he had with her. With Sky he felt joy, he felt at home, with her, he felt complete. He let his mind wander off as sleep drew near.

Before they knew it, the soft morning light was spilling through the curtains. The memory of the previous night lingered in Sky's mind as a dream. Instead of panicking like she might have before, she found herself sinking deeper into the warmth of Ryan's embrace. His arm was draped securely around her, and her head was tucked into the curve of his chest, where she could hear the steady rhythm of his heartbeat. She smiled faintly, savoring the rare sense of calm that filled the air.

Little did Sky know; Ryan had woken up moments before and was silently admiring her. His hand gently brushed through her hair, the strands slipping like silk between his fingers. Her presence felt magnetic, grounding him in a way he hadn't fully understood before. Watching her breathe softly, her lips curled into a faint smile even in sleep, he couldn't help but feel an overwhelming sense of gratitude for her being there with him.

Her eyes fluttered open, and she tilted her face up to meet his gaze. "Good morning," she said softly, her voice warm and tender.

Ryan's lips curved into a lazy grin. "Good morning, beautiful."

For a while, neither of them moved. The silence was filled with unspoken words, with shared glances and subtle shifts that brought them closer. Eventually, they rose with each other, making their way downstairs for breakfast. It was a simple meal—toast and eggs—but the lighthearted banter and lingering touches made it feel like much more.

When Ryan finally left to return to Bryant's house, they lingered at the door, neither wanting to say goodbye. Their bond felt deeper, like they'd crossed a threshold into something more profound. Sky watched as he disappeared into the sky, a small ache in her chest reminding her of how much he meant to her.

Forty-Eight

The rest of February drifted by, carrying the last of the winter's sting with it. By the time March arrived, the air felt lighter, and prom planning consumed much of their time. Nia, ever the perfectionist, had corralled Sky, Ryan, and Bryant into her decorating committee. The theme, "A Midnight Summer's Dream" was ambitious, but Nia was determined to make it magical—even if it meant bossing around her friends.

With news of ReFramers targeting Humanimal schools and community centers, the school administration had decided to keep prom in the gym for safety. Though the venue lacked glamour, Nia was adamant about transforming it into an enchanted wonderland. During study halls, the group was tasked with crafting intricate decorations: paper flowers, ivy strands, and shimmering stars. The gym's drab walls would soon be covered in layers of green and gold, twinkling lights, and whimsical props.

Ryan and Sky worked side by side at a corner table, sharing scissors and glue while sneaking glances and giggling over inside jokes. Nia, armed with a ruler like a drill sergeant, wasn't having it. She slammed the ruler down in front of them, making both jump.

"Back to work!" she barked, glaring at them with exaggerated seriousness.

Sky grinned. "Man, Nia takes her job seriously."

Ryan smirked, glancing over at Bryant, who was hunched over his station, meticulously cutting out delicate patterns while Nia hovered like a hawk. "I'm scared for Bryant. I can't imagine what their arguments are like."

They both chuckled, watching as Bryant shot them a desperate look, silently begging for rescue. But Nia's sharp eye caught him slacking, and she was quick to snap him back into focus.

Finally, after an intense week of preparation, the day before prom arrived. The school buzzed with anticipation as students finalized plans for the big night. After the last bell, Nia found Sky and Ryan at their lockers. She stepped between them with her usual assertiveness, much to Ryan's annoyance.

"Sorry, Ryan, but I'm taking Sky for the rest of the day," Nia announced matter-of-factly.

Sky blinked, surprised. "What for?"

Nia grinned. "We're going dress shopping, of course. Can't have my best friend showing up to prom in something basic."

Ryan crossed his arms, frowning playfully. "What about me? Who's going to make sure I'm not basic?"

Bryant sauntered up just in time to hear the exchange. "Relax, man. I need to get my tux anyway. We'll make it a bro trip."

Nia raised an eyebrow at him. "Fine," she said reluctantly, pointing a finger at Ryan. "But no peeking at us while we're shopping. Got it?"

Ryan laughed, holding up his hands in surrender. "Scout's honor."

As the final bell rang, Nia grabbed Sky's wrist and pulled her down the hall. "Let's go!" she commanded, her excitement evident.

Sky glanced over her shoulder to see Ryan shaking his head and grinning. Her heart felt lighter, knowing that whatever lay ahead, they'd all face it together.

Nia drove like a madwoman to the mall, her hands gripping the steering wheel with a ferocity that left Sky clinging to the door handle. The car swerved around corners and zipped past slower vehicles, leaving Sky's stomach churning with motion sickness. By the time they arrived, she stumbled out of the car, taking deep breaths to steady herself.

"It wasn't that bad," Nia said dismissively, tossing her keys into her bag.

Sky shot her a look. "Remind me to never let you drive again."

Nia only laughed, already leading the way toward the mall entrance. They navigated through the bustling crowds, heading straight to the same boutique where they had found Sky's homecoming dress months earlier. Nia's determination was noticeable; she immediately began grabbing dress after dress, mumbling about how the perfect one had to be hidden somewhere.

Meanwhile, Sky decided to explore the store on her own. She wasn't one for bold colors or extravagant designs, so she carefully scanned the racks for something that felt like her. Across the way, her eyes caught sight of Ryan and Bryant in the men's store. Ryan stood stiffly as a tailor measured his shoulders and chest, looking visibly uncomfortable.

Sky giggled, amused by his awkwardness. He must have sensed her watching because he turned his head sharply, catching her gaze. His glare was playful yet pointed, and he shook his head as if to say, "Don't even start." She laughed to herself and returned to her search.

The store felt overwhelming, each rack bursting with vibrant gowns. Sky's fingers brushed against the fabrics as she wandered, feeling a little hopeless. Nothing seemed right. Then, she saw it. A mannequin near the back of the store was adorned in a gown that stole her breath.

The dress was a vision of understated elegance. Its sleeveless, sweetheart design was perfect for her wings, allowing them to move freely without restriction. The snow-white satin fabric draped gracefully from the hips, falling down to form a soft, flowing train. The bodice was adorned with tiny, glistening crystals that caught the light like a constellation of stars. They were intricately woven, forming a pattern that resembled the twinkling night sky. The dress's clean, bright white hue felt ethereal, almost otherworldly.

Sky stared at it, captivated. It was flawless—delicate yet bold, simple yet breathtaking.

"That would look perfect on you!" Nia's voice suddenly piped up behind her, making Sky jump.

"You've got to stop doing that," Sky muttered, clutching her chest.

But Nia was already waving down a sales associate, her excitement taking over. "We need to try this one," she declared, pointing at the dress.

The associate began the meticulous process of disassembling the mannequin, carefully removing the gown. Sky felt awkward. "You really don't have to go through all this trouble," she said, but Nia waved her off, practically shoving Sky toward the fitting room.

Inside, Sky treated the gown like a piece of art, carefully stepping into it and sliding it over her hips. She zipped up the back and turned to face the mirror. The girl staring back at her didn't look like the Sky she knew. This girl was radiant, regal even. The dress hugged her figure perfectly, accentuating her silhouette without feeling overdone. The shimmering crystals on the bodice seemed to dance with every slight movement, and the flowing satin gave her an exquisite grace. She felt like a princess in a fairytale.

For a moment, she just stood there, dumbstruck. Could this really be her?

"Let me see!" Nia called from outside the fitting room, her voice impatient.

Sky hesitated, glancing at her reflection once more. "I think I'll keep this one to myself for now," she replied, a small smile tugging at her lips.

Nia groaned but didn't press, following Sky to the register. Both girls carried their garment bags out to the parking garage, the buzz of their successful shopping trip filling the air. As they walked, Nia threw an arm around Sky's shoulders.

"So, what are you and Ryan's plans after school lets out?" she asked.

Sky shrugged. "We still want to get away, but we haven't settled on anything concrete."

Nia squeezed her shoulder. "Well, let's make the most of it while you're still here, okay?"

Sky smiled, warmed by Nia's optimism. "Okay."

The sound of footsteps behind them made both girls turn around. Ryan and Bryant were walking toward them, each carrying black garment bags. Nia crossed her arms. "You weren't supposed to follow us," she said, narrowing her eyes at Bryant.

Bryant smirked. "No, you said not to look while you were shopping. Meeting you after the fact is fair game."

Nia rolled her eyes, though she couldn't hide her smile as Bryant draped an arm around her shoulders. Meanwhile, Ryan walked up beside Sky, his gaze softening as it landed on her.

"Did you find what you were looking for?" he asked.

Sky shyly looked away. "I think so."

Ryan reached for her garment bag, his hand teasingly moving toward the zipper. "Can I see?"

Sky pulled it away, clutching it tightly. "No looking until prom."

He shrugged; his smile playful. "So close."

The group continued to their cars, laughter and lighthearted banter filling the cool evening air. The excitement for tomorrow was palpable, the anticipation of prom sparking a shared sense of joy and possibility.

Forty-Nine

Prom day had finally arrived, and the school had sent out mass texts reminding students to be safe and have fun—but not too much fun. Sky and Nia had been preparing since the early morning hours. Nia had declared it a mission to achieve perfection, which meant makeup, hair, and outfit coordination had to be flawless. Sky found herself seated in front of Nia's vanity mirror, her reflection showing a mix of excitement and nerves as Nia fussed over her curls.

In the background, the faint sound of a news broadcast droned on from the living room.

"WARNING HAS BEEN ISSUED TO HUMANIMALS IN THE CITY! BE ON ALERT! CLINICS AND SCHOOLS HAVE BEEN THE CENTERS FOR REFRAMER ATTACKS OVER THE LAST FEW DAYS! PROCEED WITH CAUTION!"

The words sent a twinge of worry through Sky, a dark cloud over what was supposed to be a joyous day. She clenched her hands in her lap, hoping that, after the garden incident, no one would dare try something like that again. As her thoughts spiraled, a sudden heat grazed her scalp, making her flinch.

"Hold still!" Nia snapped, her fingers steadying Sky's shoulder. "You keep moving, and I'll never finish."

"Sorry," Sky murmured, forcing herself to stay still as Nia worked the curling iron with precision. With each strand that fell into place, Sky's hair began to transform into a cascade of soft, wispy curls that framed her face. The lightness of the style complemented her features, giving her a heavenly glow.

Nia stepped back, admiring her handiwork. "Perfect," she declared with satisfaction. "You're going to turn every head at prom."

Sky gave a small smile. "Thanks, Nia. You've really outdone yourself."

By the time 5:30 rolled around, Nia was running frantically around the house, making sure she hadn't forgotten anything. "Perfume, dress, corsage...what else? What am I missing?"

Sky chuckled, sitting on the edge of the bed. "Don't the guys usually bring the corsages?"

Nia stopped mid-spin, realizing Sky was right. "Fair point," she admitted, before rushing off to finish her own preparations.

Sky stood and walked to the mirror, taking in her reflection. The white gown, with its shimmering crystal bodice and flowing satin skirt, made her feel like royalty. She had never felt so beautiful in her life. She turned to catch the light bouncing off the crystals, which looked like tiny stars woven into the fabric. Her wings rested gently against her back, their softness complementing the dress's delicate elegance.

Before she could dwell too long, Nia's voice echoed down the hall. "They're here!"

Sky's heart skipped a beat. She followed Nia's hurried footsteps to the living room, where Nia's mom had already opened the door for Bryant and Ryan. Both boys stepped inside, looking sharp and confident. Bryant wore a sleek black tuxedo with a bold red tie that perfectly matched Nia's dress, while Ryan—Sky's breath caught for a moment. Ryan was dressed in a fitted white tuxedo, the crisp lines of the suit emphasizing his broad shoulders. His hair was slicked back and he carried himself with a strong demeanor. Everything about him—from his suit to his warm smile—radiated charm.

Nia's mom offered them water, which they politely declined. Nia ran back to Sky, grabbing her hand. "You ready to show them what we've got?"

Sky hesitated but nodded, following Nia into the living room.

"Bryant, are you ready to see me?" Nia called, striking a pose as she entered.

Bryant's jaw dropped. "Wow, babe. You look...amazing."

Nia's red sequin dress hugged her body tightly, the glitter catching every bit of light. She had styled her hair in a bob of elegant waves that framed her face, giving her a classic, glamorous look. She smiled proudly, and Bryant walked up to her, clearly mesmerized.

Sky lingered in the hallway, nerves bubbling in her chest. She heard Ryan's voice call out, "Are you still back there, Sky?"

Taking a deep breath, she stepped into the living room, careful not to trip in her heels. Ryan turned to see her, and for a moment, the room seemed to stand still. His eyes widened, and a faint red crept across his cheeks. He was completely speechless.

"What do you think?" Sky asked, a hint of teasing in her voice.

Ryan finally blinked, shaking his head as if snapping out of a trance. "Wow," he said softly. "You look…you look incredible."

Sky blushed under his gaze. The way he was looking at her, like she was the only person in the room, filled her with a warmth that spread through her chest. She walked closer, noticing that her silver heels brought her eye level with him. "Are you ready to go?" she asked, her voice gentle.

"Definitely," he said, his tone filled with admiration.

Reaching into his pocket, Ryan pulled out a delicate white corsage adorned with tiny crystals. "I almost forgot this," he said, carefully slipping it onto her wrist. His fingers brushed against her skin, and Sky felt her cheeks flush again.

"It's beautiful," she whispered, admiring the corsage.

Ryan took her hand, leading her outside to join Nia and Bryant, who were posing for photos. Nia's mom insisted on taking pictures of all four of them, and soon the group was laughing and goofing around in front of the camera. After what felt like a hundred photos, they finally piled into Bryant's jeep, ready to head to the school.

As they drove, Nia glanced at Ryan and Sky. "Wait a second," she said. "Ryan, your suit matches Sky's dress perfectly. Did you plan that?"

Bryant looked like he wanted to disappear. "Uh...well..."

Ryan smirked. "We may have asked the boutique for some hints after you two left."

Nia's eyes narrowed, her face turning red. "You what? I told you not to peek!"

Bryant held up his hands defensively. "You said not to peek. You didn't say we couldn't ask."

Nia glared at him for a moment before sighing. "Fine. I guess it's sweet that you wanted to match us." She placed a hand on Bryant's arm, and he visibly relaxed.

Ryan and Sky exchanged a knowing glance, holding back their laughter as they pulled into the school parking lot. The gym's faint glow was visible through the large windows, and streams of students dressed in their best were heading inside.

Sky paused, her hand tightening around Ryan's arm as they approached the entrance. The thought of being in such a crowded room filled her with anxiety, but Ryan's reassuring squeeze steadied her. She looked up at him, and his warm smile melted her fears away. Together, they stepped through the doors, ready for an unforgettable night.

Fifty

The group of friends stepped into the gym, their hard work on full display. The transformation was nothing short of extraordinary. Along the walls, cutouts of lush greenery and trees intertwined with paper flowers, creating the illusion of a dense, enchanted forest. Overhead, string lights wrapped in faux vines glimmered, casting a soft, magical glow across the room. The ceiling was adorned with a large moon, its pale white light reflected on hundreds of delicate star cutouts suspended from above. At the far end of the gym, a massive artificial tree stood as the centerpiece, its branches stretching wide, twinkling with golden fairy lights. The DJ booth nestled beneath the tree looked like it had grown from the forest itself.

Sky stood in awe; her eyes wide as she took in the breathtaking scene. "It's perfect," she whispered. The beauty of the gym made her forget, if only briefly, the worries she'd been holding onto.

Nia's voice rang out beside her, filled with pride. "Now this is how you do prom!" She spotted a group of cheer friends waving at her from across the room. "Catch you guys later!" she said, pulling Bryant along with her.

Sky and Ryan stayed close to the wall, observing the lively scene around them. Teens danced, mingled, and laughed, the air buzzing with excitement. Ryan nudged her shoulder. "You know, maybe Nia's dictatorship was worth it after all."

Sky giggled, nudging him back. "Just don't let her hear you say that."

They wandered towards the refreshment table, eyeing the assortment of snacks and punch. Ryan grabbed a cup of the questionable pink liquid and took a sip, immediately wincing. "I think this is just sugar and food coloring."

Sky laughed, taking a sip of her own cup. She wrinkled her nose. "And it's warm. Great." They both set their cups down, opting to steer clear of the refreshments for the rest of the night.

The upbeat music shifted to a familiar pop tune, and Ryan's face lit up. "Come on, let's dance."

"I'm not much of a dancer," Sky protested, but Ryan was already pulling her toward the center of the gym.

"Just follow my lead," he said confidently. He started with the macarena, moving with exaggerated precision. Sky burst out laughing as he transitioned into the robot, his movements stiff and hilariously bad.

"You're terrible!" she said through her laughter, but soon she joined in, mimicking his moves. Together, they looked ridiculous, but neither of them cared.

"Okay, okay," Ryan said, pausing to catch his breath. "You're way better at this than I am."

Sky grinned. "That's not saying much."

They continued to dance through a few more songs until the music slowed. The opening notes of Ed Sheeran's "Perfect" filled the room, and Sky's face lit up. "This is one of my favorites," she said softly.

Ryan extended his hand. "Then I guess we better dance to it."

He pulled her closer, his hand resting gently on her waist while their fingers intertwined. Sky placed her free hand on his shoulder, and they swayed to the rhythm. Ryan couldn't take his eyes off her. The soft lights reflected off the crystals on her dress, making it look like she was glowing. Her wings shimmered faintly in the gaze of the moon, and her expression was serene.

Sky, meanwhile, was keenly aware of how safe she felt in his arms. His touch was warm, steady, and comforting. She rested her head against his chest, letting herself relax fully for the first time in weeks.

Neither of them spoke; they didn't need to. The music carried them, creating a moment that felt entirely their own. As the song came to an end, Ryan kissed her forehead gently. "Dancing with you is the best," he murmured.

Sky tilted her head up to meet his gaze. "Same. But your freestyle dancing? That's hard to beat."

Ryan laughed. "Hey, I'm just trying to keep you entertained."

Sky smiled but her attention was drawn to a group of students near the gym doors. They weren't familiar faces, and their behavior seemed off. They were glancing around nervously, speaking in hushed tones. Sky's brow furrowed as she watched them shuffle into the hallway.

"What's wrong?" Ryan asked, noticing her distracted look.

Sky hesitated. "I think I'll be right back."

"Sky—" Ryan started, but she had already moved toward the doors. She slipped into the hallway, glancing around for the group. She turned down the right corridor and caught faint whispers. The voices grew distant, accompanied by the sound of hurried footsteps.

She followed the sounds, her curiosity growing with each step. The whispers stopped, and Sky turned a corner, only to find the hallway empty. She sighed in frustration, returning to the gym. But just as she reached the doors, she saw a figure dart outside toward a maintenance room. Sky froze for a moment before quietly following them.

Outside, she peeked around the corner and saw two teens inside the maintenance room. One of them, a boy, was untangling green hoses and attaching them to a wall outlet. The other, a girl in a flowing purple tulle dress, was helping him, her brown hair neatly tied in a bun. Sky's heart sank. She recognized that voice—it couldn't be.

The boy sighed, wiping his forehead and smearing something red across his skin. "All good on my end," he said.

"Should be good to go," the girl replied with a smile.

They hurried further into the school, leaving the maintenance room behind. Sky's stomach churned. Was that...Lydia?

She returned to the gym, scanning the crowd for Ryan. She found him near the DJ booth, chatting with Bryant and Nia. "Something's going on," she said, her voice urgent.

Ryan frowned. "What do you mean?"

"I think I saw Lydia," Sky said. "And she's up to something."

Ryan's expression darkened. "Are you sure?"

Sky nodded. "She was with some guy, and they were setting something up outside. It looked...off."

Ryan placed a hand on her shoulder. "It's prom. Try not to worry too much. I'm sure everything's fine."

Sky forced a smile, but her unease lingered. As the DJ hyped up the crowd with a high-energy remix, Sky's ears picked up a faint screeching noise. She winced, her hands instinctively covering her ears.

Ryan noticed, his brow furrowing. "You hear that too?"

Sky nodded. "It's...weird. And it's not coming from the speakers."

They both looked around, trying to pinpoint the source of the sound. Sky's gaze traveled upward, and she noticed a small drip falling from the sprinkler system. She leaned down to inspect it, watching as a thick red droplet landed in her palm. Her stomach dropped.

"Ryan," she said, her voice trembling. "This isn't water."

Ryan looked up just as the screeching sound intensified. The sprinklers erupted, dousing the room in a torrent of red fluid. Teens screamed as the liquid rained down, soaking everything and everyone. Sky stared in horror as the thick, crimson substance covered her once-pristine dress.

"It's blood," she whispered.

Ryan pulled her close, trying to shield her with his jacket. The gym descended into chaos as students fled for the exits. Sky's eyes darted around, searching for answers, until she spotted the purple dress slipping out of the gym doors.

Before Ryan could stop her, Sky bolted after the figure, determined to get to the bottom of it.

Fifty-One

Sky raced through the hallway; her heels abandoned somewhere along the way, and Ryan presumably close behind. Her bare feet slapped against the cold tiles as she chased the figure in the flowing purple dress. Her heart pounded, and her mind raced with questions. Why would Lydia do something like this? What could she possibly gain?

The chase ended abruptly at the double doors leading to the school's front lawn. The figure stopped, her hand on the door handle. Sky, breathless but determined, shouted, "Stop!"

The girl froze before slowly turning around. Sky's suspicions were confirmed. Lydia stood there, her makeup slightly smeared, but her face was calm—too calm. The contrast between the chaos in the gym and Lydia's composed demeanor sent a chill down Sky's spine.

Sky's voice trembled as she spoke. "Lydia, tell me you didn't have anything to do with this."

Lydia's expression shifted into a smirk. "Actually, I planned the whole thing."

Sky felt like the air had been knocked out of her. She stared at her former friend, searching for some sign of remorse, but found none. "Why? Why would you do something like this? Don't you remember what happened at the party in the fall?"

Lydia's smirk faded, replaced by a look of bitter anger. "That's exactly why I did it," she snapped. "You and your friends thought it was funny to threaten me, to taunt me. They locked me in a room with a…with a monster."

Sky's heart clenched at the venom in Lydia's voice. "Lydia, I never would have let anyone hurt you. You have to know that."

"But you did!" Lydia's voice cracked. Her composure was slipping, and tears welled in her eyes. "You don't understand what that night did to me. I was terrified. My best friend became my worst nightmare."

Sky stepped closer, her own tears threatening to fall. "I'm still the same person. I'm still me. Please, Lydia, you can trust me."

"Trust you?" Lydia laughed bitterly, shaking her head. "How can I trust someone who could have killed me? How can I trust someone who…who isn't even fully human?"

The words hit Sky like a punch to the gut. She felt tears streaming down her cheeks as she stared at the girl she had once considered a sister. "I never wanted to hurt you. I never wanted to hurt anyone."

Lydia's expression softened for a fleeting moment, but then she looked away. Her hand went to her wrist, where a small beaded bracelet rested. It was the friendship bracelet Sky had made for her years ago. Lydia hesitated before pulling it off and holding it up.

"You gave me this," Lydia said, her voice trembling. "It used to mean everything to me. But now...now it's just a reminder of how blind I was." She tossed the bracelet to the ground, where it landed with a soft clink.

Sky stared at the bracelet; her vision blurred by tears. When she looked back up, Lydia was crying too, though her face was hard with resolve. In the distance, the sounds of sirens and shouting grew louder. The police were arriving.

Sky took a shaky breath. "Lydia, you don't have to run. We can fix this. We can talk to the police and make it right."

Lydia shook her head. "There's no fixing this, Sky. Not for me. Not for us."

Sky bent down, picking up the bracelet. She clutched it tightly in her hand, the beads pressing into her skin. When she looked up again, Lydia was already pushing through the doors. Sky's voice caught in her throat. She wanted to call out, to stop her, but the weight of their shattered friendship held her back.

"Go," Sky whispered, her voice barely audible.

Lydia hesitated for a fraction of a second before disappearing into the night. Sky stood there, the bracelet in her hand, as tears streamed down her face. The sound of approaching footsteps brought her back to reality.

Ryan appeared, his face a mix of concern and relief. "Sky! Why did you run off?"

Sky didn't respond. She couldn't. Her thoughts were a whirlwind of pain, anger, and heartbreak. She stared down at the bracelet, her grip tightening as she replayed Lydia's words in her mind. How could Lydia think she was a monster? How could she throw away years of friendship like it meant nothing?

Ryan stepped closer, gently placing his hands on her shoulders. "Sky, what happened?"

Still, she couldn't speak. Her tears fell silently, mixing with the remnants of blood that still clung to her dress. Ryan didn't press her for answers. Instead, he wrapped his arms around her, pulling her into a firm embrace. Sky buried her face in his chest, her sobs muffled by his shirt. He held her tightly, his own heart breaking at the sight of her pain.

"It's okay," Ryan whispered, his voice steady despite the chaos around them. "I've got you."

Sky clung to him; the bracelet still clutched in her hand. As the sirens grew louder and the world outside spun on, she allowed herself to be held, finding solace in the only person who could make her feel whole again.

Fifty-Two

It was all over the news. The "Foreman Falls Prom Disaster" blared across every television screen. Reporters spoke with urgency as dramatic footage replayed: teens drenched in red, sprinting from the gym, their faces twisted in shock and horror. Some screamed, others sobbed. The gruesome imagery and chaos had not only captivated local media but had spread across the state, even gaining some national attention.

Newscasters detailed the incident, emphasizing that several suspects were already in custody. All of them were teenagers from a neighboring high school, Norman High. The revelation that these students were affiliated with the ReFramers, a notorious anti-Humanimal organization, only added fuel to the fire. The suspects all bore the telltale black tattoo of the group, a mark that sent waves of anger and fear through the community. Parents from both schools were now at war, each blaming the other. Heated debates raged online and in the streets, dividing the town further.

Foreman Falls High decided to close its doors for the following week. The administration sent daily email updates to parents, offering support resources and providing information about the ongoing investigation. The messages included details about counseling services for traumatized students, updates on the cleanup efforts at the gym, and assurances that measures were being taken to ensure a safe return to school. They also informed parents that some suspects were still at large, but authorities were working tirelessly to track them down.

The gym's cleanup crew worked in eerie silence. The thick, congealed animal blood—a horrifying mix of cow, pig, and chicken—had soaked into every crevice. Workers scrubbed relentlessly, but the metallic tang lingered in the air. The sprinklers, which had sprayed the blood onto unsuspecting students, were being dismantled and replaced. For now, the school stood empty, its halls quiet and its classrooms dark.

Outside, however, the town was anything but silent. Protesters lined the streets near Humanimal schools and clinics, their chants echoing through the humid spring air. "Humanimals are a plague!" "Exterminate the hybrids!" "Send them out of our country!" Their signs bore similar messages, scrawled in angry red paint. "Keep Our Children Safe," "No More Abominations," and "Pure Blood Forever" were among the most common. The protesters, a mix of fervent ReFramers and fearful locals, stood defiantly in the late winter breeze, their voices unyielding.

The town itself felt heavier, burdened by fear and division. Conversations at grocery stores, coffee shops, and church gatherings revolved around the prom disaster. Parents whispered about the gym incident with hushed voices, their expressions a mixture of anger and dread. Teens who had attended the prom shared their stories; each testimony more harrowing than the last. Some described the sheer terror of being drenched in blood, while others spoke of the panic that erupted when the sprinklers went off. "It was like a horror movie," one girl said, her voice shaky during a televised interview. "The blood was everywhere—on my dress, in my hair. It's something I'll never forget." Another student added, "I remember slipping in it, trying to get out. It was so thick, and the smell..." He trailed off, visibly distressed.

Back at Bryant's house, the group of friends stayed together, finding solace in each other's company. They watched the news in uneasy silence, the sensationalized coverage replaying over and over. Nia sat perched on Bryant's lap, her arms crossed tightly. Sky and Ryan sat side by side on the couch, her head resting on his shoulder. Every word from the TV felt like a stab to their hearts, a reminder of the night that had gone so horribly wrong.

Finally, Nia had enough. She stood abruptly, grabbing the remote and switching off the television. "This is ridiculous!" she shouted, pacing the room. "The one night I poured my heart and soul into, the one night that was supposed to be perfect, ruined by a bunch of normal jerks!" Her voice cracked with frustration. "Do you know how many hours I spent planning every detail? All for what? For those...those monsters to turn it into a nightmare?"

Bryant reached out a hand, trying to calm her. "Nia, it wasn't your fault."

"It feels like it is!" she snapped back. "If we hadn't worked so hard on this stupid prom, maybe they wouldn't have had such a perfect stage for their sick joke!"

Sky's voice was soft but filled with guilt. "It's my fault."

All eyes turned to her. Ryan's brow furrowed. "Sky, no. You didn't know what they were planning."

Sky shook her head, tears brimming in her eyes. "If I had just stayed hidden, didn't expose my wings to the world, maybe Lydia wouldn't have felt the need to do this."

Nia knelt down in front of Sky, her tone firm but compassionate. "Sky, listen to me. Lydia was never a true friend if she could treat you like this. This isn't your fault. It's hers. She made this choice, not you."

Sky nodded slightly, but the guilt didn't dissipate. Bryant's voice broke the silence. "Did they ever catch her? Lydia?"

Ryan shook his head. "I don't think so. She ran before the cops could find her."

Sky looked away, unable to meet their gazes. She knew she could have stopped Lydia. She had the chance to turn her in, to end it all. But she couldn't do it. Despite everything, she couldn't betray the girl who had once been her closest friend, her sister in all but blood.

Her thoughts spiraled. She felt torn between loyalty and betrayal, guilt and anger. She thought about Lydia's words, the pain in her eyes, the way she had thrown their friendship away like it meant nothing. How could Lydia see her as a monster? How could she plan something so vile?

Sky's chest ached as the weight of it all settled on her shoulders. She clutched the small beaded bracelet in her pocket, the one Lydia had thrown at her feet. It felt heavier than it should, like it carried the burden of their broken bond.

Ryan gently placed a hand on her knee, grounding her. She looked up at him, his hazel eyes filled with concern and understanding. "We'll get through this," he said softly.

Sky nodded, though her heart still felt heavy. As her friends continued to discuss the events of prom night, she sat in silence, lost in a whirlwind of emotions she wasn't sure she'd ever fully untangle.

Fifty-Three

Finally, Monday arrived, and Foreman Falls High reopened its doors. As Ryan and Sky drove into the school parking lot, they were met with an unsettling scene. Protesters lined the front steps, their voices rising in a cacophony of anger and defiance. Signs with bold, hateful messages bobbed above the crowd: "Keep Our Children Safe!" "Humanimals are a plague!"

A line of police officers stood as a barrier between the protesters and the school entrance. Their faces were grim, their presence adding to the tension in the air. Sky felt a wave of nausea churn in her stomach. It was impossible to ignore the venomous insults being hurled their way.

Ryan parked the car and stepped out, scanning the scene. "This is insane," he muttered.

Sky followed, clutching her backpack tightly. As they approached the building, her eyes caught sight of additional security—burly men in black uniforms stationed near the doors. The emblem on their shirts read "NisenX" in small, white letters. A shiver ran down Sky's spine.

Ryan noticed her reaction and whispered sarcastically, "I didn't know NisenX cared so much about us." His tone was dry, but Sky could sense the bitterness behind it.

The first few days back at school were tense. Protesters remained outside, and the presence of NisenX security felt suffocating. The students themselves seemed quieter, subdued by the weight of recent events. Many of Sky and Ryan's peers avoided public places altogether, as arguments and fights about humanimal rights had become commonplace around town. The divide between humanimals and normals had never felt wider.

By Friday, the tension reached its peak. Parents were demanding answers, safety, and swift action. Principal Henderson had been in constant discussions with the school board and state officials, trying to navigate the chaos.

During Sky's Avian Anatomy class, the overhead speakers crackled to life. **"All students are to report to the auditorium immediately,"** a voice announced. **"Again, all students and teachers, please head to the auditorium at once."**

Sky exchanged a glance with Ryan. "What's going on?" she asked.

Ryan shrugged. "Guess we're about to find out."

Together, they joined the throng of students filing toward the auditorium. Nia and Bryant caught up with them in the hallway, sticking close as they entered the large space. The atmosphere was buzzing with confusion and whispers. Some students seemed anxious, while others looked relieved to escape class.

They found seats near the back, far from the stage. The room gradually filled, and the noise of murmuring voices grew louder. Once the last students were seated, the lights dimmed, and bright floodlights illuminated the stage. Several chairs had been arranged in a neat row, occupied by Principal Henderson and a group of officials.

Principal Henderson stood and approached the microphone. His face was pale, his brow glistening with sweat. He adjusted the microphone with trembling hands and cleared his throat before speaking.

"Good morning, students," he began, his voice cracking slightly. "We hope your day has been kind to you."

The room fell silent as he continued. "As many of you know, we have been doing everything in our power to protect this school and its students. The events of prom night were... unprecedented, and our town has been grappling with the aftermath ever since."

Sky shook her head. "Understatement of the year," she muttered under her breath.

"Your safety is our top priority," Principal Henderson went on. "So, after careful consideration and lengthy discussions with the school board and local authorities, we have decided it is in the best interest of everyone to close the school for the remainder of the year."

Gasps rippled through the crowd. A few students cheered quietly, high-fiving each other. Others exchanged worried looks.

"We will resume classes in the fall as planned," Henderson explained. "During this time, we will work closely with law enforcement to secure the school grounds. Additionally, we are grateful to have the support of NisenX, which has pledged significant funding and resources to help us rebuild and ensure the safety of our students."

Ryan's expression darkened. His jaw clenched as he muttered, "This is exactly what my dad wants."

Sky placed a comforting hand on his. She could see the frustration and discomfort etched on his face.

The principal continued, "For our seniors, diplomas will be mailed to you. For the rest of you, we urge you to stay safe and vigilant during this time. Thank you for your understanding." He stepped back, his shoulders slumping as he returned to his seat.

Students began to file out of the auditorium, some still whispering excitedly about the unexpected break. Ryan and Sky remained seated, joined by Nia and Bryant.

Nia broke the silence. "I guess summer break starts early?" Her cheerful tone faded when she noticed Ryan's grim expression.

"This can't be happening," Ryan muttered.

Sky squeezed his shoulder. "We'll figure it out."

Bryant offered a suggestion. "How about we grab some food and talk things over?"

The group nodded in agreement and headed to their lockers to clear them out. Sky quickly emptied hers and helped Ryan with his, noticing how slowly he moved. He seemed lost in thought, each movement mechanical.

"Are you ready?" she asked gently after closing his locker.

Ryan gave her a faint smile. "Sure."

Fifty-Four

The drive to Nia's favorite Chinese restaurant was quiet. When they arrived, Bryant and Nia were already seated with heaping plates of food. Nia was mid-rant, waving her chopsticks animatedly.

"...and now my parents don't even want me leaving the house!" she exclaimed. "They're scared something will happen every time I step outside. How am I supposed to go to cheer camp if they won't even let me out of their sight?"

Sky and Ryan sat down, and Sky held onto Ryan's hand. Nia turned to them; her frustration evident. "This whole thing is just stupid! And NisenX being involved? I don't trust them as far as I can throw them."

"It's messed up," Bryant agreed between bites of orange chicken.

Ryan's grip on Sky's hand tightened. "My dad had something to do with this. I know it." His voice was low, simmering with anger. "I've had it with him controlling my life."

Sky thought back to the many conversations she and Ryan had shared about his father. He had opened up to her about the pressure, the manipulation, the way his dad saw him as nothing more than a trophy son. She remembered the pain in his voice, the way his shoulders tensed whenever he talked about the man who had shaped so much of his life.

Nia sighed, placing a hand on Bryant's. "I can't imagine having such a jerk for a dad."

Ryan shook his head. "It's worse than you think."

The conversation shifted to summer plans. Bryant talked about college tours and football scholarships, while Nia gushed about cheer camp and her hopes for a scholarship of her own. When Nia turned to Ryan and Sky, her tone grew teasing. "So, what about you two? Still planning on running off to Canada?"

Ryan's jaw tightened. "Still working on it," he said curtly.

Sensing the tension, Nia quickly changed the subject, chatting about Bryant visiting her over the summer. Sky excused herself to grab food for her and Ryan. As she stood in line, she overheard the conversation of two boys behind her. They spoke in hushed tones about a "safer place" and a hidden location off the grid.

Sky's curiosity piqued. She couldn't help but listen closely, her mind racing with possibilities. Could this be the answer they were looking for?

When she returned with the food, her mind was spinning. Bryant and Nia were still deep in conversation, and she placed the tray down gently, trying not to interrupt.

She leaned close to Ryan, her voice low. "I think I overheard something... something important."

Ryan raised an eyebrow, his frustration melting into curiosity. "What is it?"

Sky hesitated, glancing back at the table where the two boys sat. They were still there, hunched over their plates, whispering between bites. She lowered her voice further. "Those guys back there—they were talking about some place off the grid. A safe place. They didn't say much, but... it sounded like somewhere we could go."

Ryan's eyes narrowed as he followed her gaze. "You think it's legit?"

"I don't know," Sky admitted. "But if there's even a chance..."

Ryan nodded slowly, the gears in his mind turning. Nia caught wind of their hushed conversation and leaned in. "What are you two whispering about?"

Sky filled her in, recounting the snippets of conversation she had overheard. Nia's face lit up with interest. "If this is a real place, it could be exactly what you guys need."

Bryant chimed in; his tone cautious. "But how do you know it's not some kind of trap? What if these guys are connected to... you know, the wrong people?"

Sky bit her lip, the thought gnawing at her. "I don't know. But I feel like we have to at least find out more."

Ryan placed a reassuring hand on hers. "Then we'll find out together."

The group exchanged a determined look, their earlier conversation forgotten. Whatever this lead was, it might be the break they were desperately seeking. Sky felt a flicker of hope in her chest, fragile but growing. For the first time in what felt like weeks, the future didn't seem so bleak.

Fifty-Five

Sky walked up to the guys slowly, careful to keep her excitement in check so she wouldn't scare them off. Every part of her wanted to sprint toward them, but she forced herself to take measured steps. Her heart pounded in her chest as if it were already halfway to freedom. As she approached the table, the whispers between the two boys faded. The guy in the black hoodie glanced up, his sharp brown eyes narrowing with suspicion. He had a rather lean and athletic build. His chestnut skin was smooth, reaching up to his braided black hair.

"Hi, I'm Sky," she greeted with a bright smile that she hoped came across as friendly rather than desperate.

Both boys looked at her, confusion evident in their expressions. The hoodie guy raised an eyebrow. "I'm Daren," he replied warily.

The second boy, dressed in a green jersey and mid-bite with a mouth full of rice, mumbled something unintelligible.

Sky tilted her head. "Sten?" she repeated.

Daren rolled his eyes and muttered, "His name is Stan."

Sky let out a soft laugh despite the tension. "Nice to meet you both," she said, still trying to put them at ease.

Daren's eyes stayed wary as he asked, "Do you want something?"

Sky shifted on her feet, suddenly aware of how vulnerable this all felt. "Well, sort of," she admitted. She took a steadying breath. "I was in line... right in front of you guys." She hesitated, then pushed forward. "I kind of overheard your conversation about a place. A safe spot in the middle of nowhere."

The reaction was immediate. Daren's hand shot out, gently but firmly grabbing her wrist. His grip wasn't tight enough to hurt, but it sent a clear message.

"Sit," he said, his voice low.

Sky slid into the seat between them, her wings pressing lightly against the chair's back. The boys exchanged a worried glance.

Daren leaned in closer. "How much did you hear?"

Sky swallowed and fidgeted slightly under their scrutinizing stares. "Not everything," she said quickly. "Just that you're leaving tomorrow morning, heading somewhere safe."

Stan groaned and punched Daren's arm. "I told you not to talk about it in public!"

Daren shook his head and returned his focus to Sky. "Why should we tell you anything?"

Sky glanced back at her friends across the room. Ryan's piercing gaze was fixed on her, a mix of concern and protectiveness in his eyes. She turned back to Daren and spoke softly, hoping he'd see the sincerity in her words. "Because I think we have more in common than you realize."

She smiled gently and, with a small rustle, unfurled her wings slightly, wrapping them partway around her shoulders. The soft, white feathers reflecting the restaurant's lights.

Stan, mid-bite, choked on his chicken. His face turned red as he struggled to swallow. "She's got wings!" he sputtered.

Daren's eyes widened slightly, though his expression remained guarded. "Wow… you're really something, huh?"

Sky's smile stayed, but her voice was softer. "I think you're something too," she said, tilting her head toward his forehead, where small antler nubs were visible under his hoodie.

Daren rubbed at the nubs with an almost embarrassed motion. "They're just starting to grow back. They shed every winter."

Stan let out a frustrated huff. "Dude, just tell her already."

Daren hesitated, studying her face. His shoulders relaxed slightly, but his voice remained cautious. "Fine. But not here." He glanced around the restaurant, his eyes flicking toward nearby tables. "Meet us in the parking lot— far corner, blue minivan, five minutes."

Sky's heart leapt with excitement. "Thank you!" she whispered.

Daren winced and pressed a finger to his lips. "Not so loud. You never know who is listening."

He stood and walked to the trash can, tossing his tray. Stan followed after shoveling the last of his food into his mouth.

Sky walked back to her friends, her grin threatening to burst from her face.

Nia leaned forward eagerly. "Well? What happened?"

Sky's eyes sparkled. "It's real! There's a place just like we hoped!"

Ryan, however, wasn't smiling. His jaw clenched as he asked, "Are you sure? Because when that guy grabbed your arm, I was about ready to go over there and deck him."

Sky chuckled and placed a reassuring hand on his. "I promise, they're not dangerous. They're just... scared, like us." She paused before adding, "They want to help. I know they do."

Ryan's expression softened a bit, though the tension in his shoulders remained. "Where are you meeting them?"

"The parking lot," Sky replied. "In five minutes."

Ryan straightened. "Not without me."

Sky smiled. "Of course not."

The four friends gathered their things and exited the restaurant. The cool evening air met them as they stepped outside. Sky's eyes scanned the lot until she spotted the blue minivan near the back corner.

"There," she said, pointing.

Daren was sitting in the open side door with Stan beside him, swinging his legs. As Sky led her friends over, Ryan leaned in and whispered, "If this goes sideways, we're flying out of here. Got it?"

Sky nodded, appreciating his protective nature. She waved to Daren and Stan. Stan waved back eagerly until Daren elbowed him. "Stop drawing attention," Daren muttered.

"Sorry," Stan replied, ducking his head.

Sky approached cautiously. "I brought my friends, if that's okay."

Daren's gaze shifted from Sky to Ryan, Nia, and Bryant. His lips pursed. "As long as they're not snitches."

"They're not," Sky assured him. "We're all in this together."

Ryan folded his arms, standing tall. His eyes never left Daren.

Daren reached into his back pocket and pulled out a large, paper map. "This," he said, unfolding it, "is the key to freedom."

The map was covered with hand-drawn notes and arrows spanning from Tennessee to northern Idaho. At the top of Idaho was a large, red star.

Sky's breath caught. "Is that it?" she asked.

Daren nodded. "Yeah. It's deep in the forest. Miles of trees surround it."

Stan's voice grew quieter but more excited. "It used to be an old college campus. Humanimals rebuilt it after it was abandoned. It's a refuge—a sanctuary."

Sky felt a rush of hope so strong it made her knees weak. Ryan placed a steadying hand on her shoulder.

"How do we know you're not making this up?" Ryan asked.

Daren's face darkened. "You don't. But I'm not." His voice softened. "I heard it from my sister, Delilah." He paused; his voice thick with emotion. "She was doing an internship at NisenX's Nebraska facility. It wasn't a normal internship. She told me about the experiments—the pain. Every day was worse than the last." He swallowed hard. "Then one day, there was a boom. A truck rammed through the gym wall during a training session. They weren't NisenX. They rescued her."

Daren's eyes shimmered. "They took her miles away. She said they drove until the roads ended, then walked until the forest swallowed them. That's where she found the campus." His voice cracked. "She's safe now. She told me to come. She said I'd finally be free."

Sky's heart broke for him. "She sounds amazing," she whispered.

Daren smiled faintly. "Yeah. She is."

Ryan's gaze softened. "So can we come with you?"

Daren shook his head, regret clouding his eyes. "My van's full. Friends, family... you'll have to find your own way."

Sky's excitement dimmed for a second. "Can I copy your map?"

Daren blinked, surprised. "Sure. But by hand—no photos or scanners."

Sky nodded eagerly and tugged Ryan's sleeve. He sighed but relented, retrieving a blank map from his truck.

Sky raised an eyebrow. "You carry maps?"

Ryan smirked. "You never know when you'll get lost—especially when flying."

They placed the maps side by side, and Ryan copied the notes with careful precision. When he finished, he folded the map and slipped it into his pocket.

"Thanks," Ryan said.

Daren nodded. "Good luck. You're gonna need it."

The van door slid shut, and the engine roared to life. Sky and her friends watched as it pulled away and disappeared into the distance.

Sky exhaled and clasped her hands together. "I can't believe it—we found it!"

Ryan chuckled and placed his hands on her shoulders. "Well, technically, you eavesdropped. But good work."

Sky laughed, feeling warmth spread through her chest. Nia stepped closer; her eyes wide with excitement. "So is that the plan?"

Sky and Ryan exchanged a look, a silent understanding passing between them. The map in Ryan's pocket wasn't just paper—it was their key to a new beginning.

Fifty-Six

The next few days were a whirlwind of excitement and planning. Sky and Ryan spent every available minute poring over maps, jotting notes, and ironing out every detail of their journey. Sky's living room was covered with open notebooks, scraps of paper, bowls of half-eaten popcorn, and highlighters in a rainbow of colors. The coffee table had become their makeshift command center.

Ryan lounged on the couch, tossing pieces of popcorn into his mouth—and occasionally aiming them at Sky with a mischievous grin. "Alright," he said, brushing stray kernels off his shirt, "you've got everything written down, right?"

Sky caught a piece of popcorn mid-air with her mouth and smiled triumphantly. "Of course!" she said proudly, holding up her notebook like a trophy. The cover was decorated with doodles of birds, stars, and bold lettering that read: *Escape Plan: Take 2.*

Ryan sat up and leaned forward. "Alright," he said, his voice taking on a mock-serious tone, "let's go over it one more time."

Sky groaned and flopped back onto the couch dramatically. "Do we have to?" she teased, her head lolling over the armrest. "We've been through this a hundred times."

Ryan gave her a look, tossing another piece of popcorn at her. "Indulge me."

Sky giggled as she sat back up and flipped to the first page of her notes. She cleared her throat theatrically. "Step one: check everything on our packing list to make sure we don't forget anything essential. This includes sleeping bags, clothes, emergency supplies, food, water, and plenty of cash."

Ryan nodded, grabbing the list she handed him. "Got it. What's next?"

Sky glanced at her notes. "Step two: destroy our current phones and buy burner phones." She looked up at him with a serious expression. "In case anyone—especially our parents—enabled location tracking."

Ryan's face darkened slightly. "My mom probably checks my location every day," he muttered. "She's never outright said it, but I know she does."

Sky reached out and squeezed his hand. "That's why we have to be careful."

He exhaled and gave her a small nod before she continued.

"Step three: load everything into your truck and swap out the license plate with the temporary one we got from the junkyard." Sky's eyes gleamed with pride at their resourcefulness. "I don't want anyone finding us because of something as dumb as a license plate."

Ryan smirked. "Agreed. I'd rather not lead anyone on a breadcrumb trail to our new home."

Sky flipped to the next page. "Step four: say goodbye to Nia and Bryant." Her voice softened. "We'll give them our new phone numbers in case they really need to reach out."

Ryan's face grew somber as he stared at the page. "That's going to be hard."

Sky closed the notebook for a moment and looked at him. "I know. But they're our friends—they'll understand."

Ryan nodded but looked away as if trying to process the thought of leaving his friends behind.

Sky gave him a moment before flipping to the next step. "Step five: follow our detailed route from here to the sanctuary." She waved the map. "Every rest stop, every gas station, every turn—it's all written down."

Ryan chuckled and leaned his head back against the couch. "Good thing it's written down. Otherwise, we'd get lost halfway there."

Sky nudged him playfully. "Hey, I'm great with directions!"

Ryan grinned and wrapped his arm around her. "I know you are. You're the navigator."

She leaned into his shoulder, feeling the steady rhythm of his heartbeat. "I really hope this place is everything Daren said it was."

Ryan's voice softened. "Yeah... me too."

They sat in silence for a moment, wrapped in each other's warmth. Then Ryan pulled out his phone and opened the calendar app. "Okay," he began, his tone more serious. "Today's Thursday, March 30th. If we pack everything tonight and tomorrow, I can visit my mom one last time and tell her I'm going on a late spring break trip with Bryant."

Sky nodded. "She's going to miss you."

Ryan's face grew more serious, his jaw tightening. "Yeah. She's probably the only one other than Bryant who'd notice I'm gone." His voice cracked slightly at the end.

Sky pressed closer to him. "I'm grateful we don't have to say goodbye."

Ryan's arm tightened around her shoulders. "Yeah. There's no way that's ever happening." He leaned down and kissed the top of her head, his lips warm and reassuring.

He glanced at his phone again. "Alright... so, the plan: tomorrow, we pack everything and tie up any loose ends. I'll say goodbye to my mom, then we'll head to Bryant's place to see them one last time. Then, Saturday morning, at the crack of dawn—we're gone."

Sky felt her heart flutter with a mix of nerves and excitement. This was it. They were finally doing it. Every step, every detail—they were making their escape real.

Ryan stared ahead, his mind spinning as the weight of their decision settled over him. He pictured every possible scenario—the good, the bad, and the worst. He thought of Sky, who had just started to feel like she belonged somewhere, and how she was about to give it all up again. He knew the road ahead would be long and hard, and he promised himself that he'd be her strength when she needed it. He'd crack lame jokes and sing terrible songs if it kept her smiling.

A small chuckle escaped his lips.

Sky tilted her head up, curious. "What's so funny?"

Ryan hugged her tighter, resting his chin on her head. "Nothing," he whispered. "Nothing at all."

His words trailed off as they sat side by side, their thoughts filled with dreams of forests, freedom, and a new life where they could finally be safe.

Fifty-Seven

Sky sat in her room, surrounded by the mess she had created in an attempt to pack her life away. The largest suitcase she could find from her parents' closet lay open on her bed, filled with clothes shoved in with little regard for order. The drawers of her dresser hung open, spilling their contents onto the floor in heaps. Shirts and sweaters draped over the edge of her desk chair. Books were stacked precariously by the window. Her toothbrush, deodorant, and shampoo sat tucked into the side pocket of the suitcase, alongside less practical items like her journal and a few poetry books. Each piece she added felt like boxing up fragments of her life.

The silence of her room wrapped around her as she continued packing, her movements slow and deliberate. She pressed her pen sets and notebooks deep into the pockets of the suitcase, pushing until the zippers strained against the seams. When she finally tugged the zipper shut with a victorious smile, she let out a long breath.

Her eyes drifted to her nightstand, where a familiar frame caught the light. She walked over and gently picked it up, brushing her fingers along the glass. The surface was dusty, the photograph within slightly faded but still precious. It was from her sixth birthday—a snapshot of the last time her family had felt whole.

The memory rushed back in vivid detail. Her mom and dad had thrown her a party in the backyard, decorating everything with balloons shaped like birds and stars. She could still remember the way her mom's laughter rang out as Sky tore through wrapping paper, her father holding up the camera and calling, "Say cheese!" It was one of the rare days when work calls and research papers were forgotten. The three of them had danced barefoot in the grass until sunset.

But soon after that day, everything changed. Her mom had won an award for her groundbreaking achievements in animal medicine, and her father's reputation as a medical innovator only grew. The spotlight found them both, and suddenly, Sky was an afterthought in their world of accolades.

She remembered the first grade; how nervous she had been on her first day of school. Her parents had taken turns dropping her off, filling the car ride with songs and silly jokes to make her laugh. On the way home, they'd stop for ice cream if she had a tough day. But by the middle of the year, the car rides became quiet, her parents answering emails and taking calls instead of singing. Ice cream trips faded away, replaced by rushed drives to the office. Homework help turned into brief nods from across the kitchen table as they buried themselves in their work.

Sky felt the familiar sting of sadness as she remembered the gala. Her fists tightened around the photo frame as she thought about how she had waited and hoped they'd come home to her—only to realize that they never really would. That night, she had finally understood that her parents weren't her heroes anymore. They were strangers who had once loved her but had moved on to a different life.

A faint cracking sound made her freeze. She glanced down to see her white-knuckled grip had broken the glass of the frame. Slowly, she set it back down, watching the fractured lines splinter out like spiderwebs. She wouldn't bring these things with her—the weight of painful memories had no place in the life she was about to build.

Her gaze shifted to the walls of her room, where framed certificates of academic and art achievements hung in neat rows. Art projects from elementary school adorned the corkboard above her desk, surrounded by pinned photographs of the past. She stepped closer and stared at the board, her heart clenching as her eyes landed on a series of snapshots with Lydia.

One photo showed them on the playground in third grade. Lydia had a wide grin despite her scraped knees from a failed attempt at launching off the swing. Another was from the sixth-grade dance. Neither of them had dates, so they dressed up in ridiculous outfits and declared themselves each other's dates. Sky smiled faintly, remembering how they'd stolen the spotlight on the dance floor, spinning in circles and laughing until their sides hurt.

Her fingers trembled as they brushed over the most meaningful photo—one from their freshman year. Lydia was holding the camera up to take a selfie, her glasses reflecting the sunlit hallway behind them. Sky stood beside her in a pale blue trench coat, her eyes puffy from crying but smiling anyway.

The memory of that day hit her like a wave.

It was their first day of high school. Sky had felt like her heart was going to beat out of her chest as she walked to school, the morning breeze nipping at her skin. The golden leaves crunched beneath her feet, filling the air with the scent of autumn. The school loomed ahead, a maze of brick and glass that felt more like a fortress than a place for learning. As she stepped through the front doors, the noise engulfed her—students talking, lockers slamming, the PA system blaring announcements. The walls seemed to close in. Panic bubbled up until she turned on her heel and fled outside, sinking to the ground near the entrance.

She had hugged her knees to her chest, tracing circles in the grass with her finger as tears blurred her vision. The world felt too loud, too big, and too overwhelming.

"Sky! You're supposed to be inside, not hiding out here!"

Sky had looked up to see Lydia's familiar face beaming at her, clad in her signature floral overalls and a sunflower pin in her hair. Her glasses reflected the morning light as she held out her hand.

Sky had wiped at her eyes and muttered, "It's just... a lot."

Lydia's smile softened as she sat down beside her. "Yeah, high school's pretty crazy. But you're not doing this alone." She held up her friendship bracelet—the same one they had made at summer camp when they were 9—and said, "I can't leave my best friend out here in the woods."

With that, she grabbed Sky's hand and pulled her up. "Come on," Lydia said brightly. "We've got lockers to decorate!"

Sky had let herself be led inside, her heart feeling a little lighter as they walked through the crowded hallway. Lydia chattered away about their classes and teachers, effortlessly filling the silence with laughter. When they reached their lockers, Lydia gasped with excitement. "Look! Our lockers are side by side!"

Sky's lips had curved into a small smile despite herself.

Lydia had pulled out a roll of decorative tape and a stack of photos. "Almost forgot!" she said, digging through her bag until she pulled out her beloved camera. "First day of high school selfie!"

Sky had hesitated. "Do we have to?"

"It's tradition," Lydia said with a playful pout.

Sky had sighed but relented, standing beside her as Lydia threw an arm around her shoulder and raised the camera. "Say Norman High!"

Sky didn't say anything, but she managed a soft smile as the camera clicked.

Back in the present, Sky felt tears stream down her face as she stared at the photo. Memories of that day merged with the painful ones—Lydia's angry words, her betrayal at prom, the way she had ripped away years of friendship like it was nothing.

The photo blurred as tears soaked the edges. Sky crumpled the picture in her hand, feeling her heart crack along with the paper. She let it fall to the floor and watched as it fluttered down, landing softly on the carpet.

She sat there for a long time, her breath uneven, her chest tight with grief. All the moments she had loved—the family hugs, the late-night talks with Lydia, the shared library escapes—felt like ghosts she would never touch again.

A knock at the front door pulled her from her spiral. She inhaled deeply, wiping her face with the sleeve of her shirt. She grabbed her suitcases and took one last look around the room.

Her eyes lingered on the cracked frame, the crumpled photo, and her bed where she had once felt safe, wrapped in Ryan's arms. A bittersweet smile formed on her lips as fresh tears traced her skin.

"Goodbye," she whispered, her voice steady but soft.

She closed the door behind her, leaving the fragments of her old life behind.

Fifty-Eight

Ryan was sitting on Bryant's couch, his duffle bags spilling out onto the floor like a chaotic reminder of his impending journey. He didn't have much with him—most of his belongings were still back at his parents' house, untouched since the day he left. His life there had become a distant memory he wasn't eager to revisit. He stared at the scattered clothes around him: shirts, shorts, pants—all tossed into the bag without much care. Unlike Sky's methodical packing, Ryan's was haphazard and impatient, as if he could will himself out of town by stuffing everything into a bag faster.

Once everything was crammed inside, he zipped the bag shut and leaned it against the door. Then, with a long sigh, he sank to the floor, leaning his back against the couch. The silence of the house wrapped around him, interrupted only by the faint ticking of the kitchen clock.

His eyes wandered to the fireplace—the same place where, not too long ago, Sky had been curled up in his arms, trembling from exhaustion and grief. He remembered the way her fragile frame had felt against him, how he had held her as tightly as he could, wishing he could take away all her pain. The fire had crackled in front of them, but the coldness in her eyes that night was something he'd never forget.

The memory tightened his chest, but then another, softer one emerged—a memory from when he was small and carefree.

He was three or four, racing around the living room with his arms spread wide. "Airplane!" he had shouted, zooming from the couch to the kitchen. His dad was right behind him, his arms outstretched, making engine noises as they zigzagged through the house.

"Crash landing!" his dad called out before tackling him onto the bed upstairs and tickling him until Ryan's laughter turned into breathless hiccups. His dad's face had been pure joy back then—free of the stress and sternness that came later.

"Lunch is ready, my silly boys!" his mom had called from the kitchen.

Ryan had raced downstairs, skidding into the kitchen to find the table full of ham and cheese sandwiches. He had reached for one, but his dad had swept him up into the air.

"Time for takeoff!" his dad had announced with a grin, hoisting Ryan above his head.

Ryan had squealed with delight, stretching his arms out again. "Higher, Daddy! Faster!"

His mom had laughed, wiping her hands on a towel. "No plane can fly without fuel," she had teased as she placed a plate in front of him.

Ryan had scarfed down his sandwich, eager to get back to playing. But just as he finished, his dad's phone rang. The joy on his face dimmed as he answered it.

"When will Dad be back?" Ryan had asked as his dad stepped into the next room.

His mom's smile faltered. "I don't know, honey. He's busy with his new job."

The new job—NisenX. The name that would come to haunt Ryan.

He had waited and waited, but his dad didn't return to play with him. Finally, Ryan had wandered down the hall and peeked into his dad's office. Papers and books covered the desk. His dad was scribbling notes, lost in thought.

"Daddy, can you play with me?" Ryan's small voice broke the silence.

His dad barely glanced up. "Not now, Ryan."

"Please, Daddy?" Ryan had asked again, his voice hopeful.

His dad's gaze hardened as he snapped, "I said not now! Leave, Ryan."

The sharpness in his dad's voice had felt like a slap. Ryan's heart sank as he ran down the hallway, tears streaming down his cheeks. He buried his face in his pillow until he heard his mom's soft knock on the door.

She knelt beside him, brushing his hair back gently. "What happened, sweetheart?"

"Dad was mean to me," Ryan sobbed.

She wrapped her arms around him. "I'm so sorry, honey. He's just stressed. He didn't mean it."

Ryan shook his head. "He did mean it. I hate his stupid job."

Her voice softened. "He works hard to take care of us, Ryan."

"I don't care about the house or toys!" Ryan cried. "I just want Dad to play with me."

She kissed his forehead and whispered, "It's going to be okay."

But it hadn't been okay. Sitting on the floor of Bryant's living room, Ryan muttered, "She was wrong." Everything had only gotten worse. His dad's absence became distance, and distance became disdain. Ryan had gone from being his dad's pride to a disappointment.

The quiet crackle of the empty fireplace pulled Ryan back to the present, but another memory pushed in—the day he met Bryant.

Ryan had been seven, nervous as his mom dropped him off at the new school for gifted students—children who had already shown signs of animal traits. His wings had grown in but were small and delicate. His mom had kissed his forehead and waved as she drove away.

A teacher led him down a hallway decorated with bright, colorful art. Finger-painted birds, macaroni frogs, and glitter-covered fish lined the walls. They stopped at a door decorated with paper cutouts of animals.

"This is your classroom," the teacher had said, opening the door.

A woman in a bright yellow dress greeted him with a beaming smile. "You must be Ryan!" Her red curls bounced as she knelt to his level. "I'm Mrs. Jennings. We're so excited to have you!"

She led him to a craft table surrounded by other kids. Some had tails, scales, or fur.

"Hi!" a boy next to him said, holding out a blue marker. He had dark skin, curly hair, and a round face that lit up when he smiled.

Ryan tilted his head. "What are you?"

The boy grinned proudly. "I'm Bryant! I'm a bear!"

Ryan blinked. "A bear? Like... a real one?"

"An American grizzly," Bryant said with a nod. "But you have wings? That's so cool!"

Ryan laughed for the first time that day. "Yeah. I'm a golden eagle."

"Can I touch them?" Bryant asked, his eyes wide.

Ryan hesitated but nodded. Bryant ran his fingers over the feathers with awe. "Wow. They're soft!"

Ryan smiled. "Thanks. What's that on your head?"

Bryant puffed out his chest. "These are my bear ears!" He wiggled them proudly.

Ryan giggled. "They look funny."

Bryant laughed too. "Yeah, but they're good for hearing things. I can hear when someone opens a bag of snacks from the other side of the room!"

Ryan's eyes widened. "No way!"

Bryant nodded seriously. "Way! And I bet your wings let you do cool things, too."

Ryan grinned. "I can glide if I jump from something high!"

Bryant's jaw dropped. "That's awesome! We should try it on the playground!"

Ryan laughed nervously. "Only if we don't get in trouble."

Bryant leaned in and whispered conspiratorially, "We'll make sure the teachers don't see."

The two boys shared a mischievous grin, their friendship cemented in that moment.

The sound of the front door opening brought Ryan back.

"Hey, man. Can you help me with the groceries?" Bryant called.

Ryan stood and followed him outside, grabbing two bags from the Jeep. They hauled the bags to the kitchen, and Bryant grabbed one as it slipped from Ryan's arms.

"Careful, man! You almost cracked my eggs!" Bryant laughed.

Ryan smirked. "You'd have cracked them yourself with those bear paws."

Bryant chuckled as they set the groceries down. But as Ryan watched Bryant put things away, his heart ached. This was home—his best friend, their inside jokes, the way Bryant made everything lighter.

"Try not to miss me too much when I leave," Ryan said, his voice quieter than he intended.

Bryant scoffed. "Why would I miss you? You leave your socks everywhere, you never refill the soap, and now you're crushing my eggs."

Ryan smiled, but he felt the weight of what was coming. Bryant was his brother in every way that mattered. Leaving him felt like cutting away a piece of himself.

As they finished, Ryan set the last can in the pantry and leaned against the counter. His thoughts drifted to Sky—her laughter, her quiet strength, and the way her wings caught the light. She was his reason for everything.

"I won't let anyone take her away," Ryan thought, his resolve hardening.

The kitchen felt quiet as the reality of his journey set in.

Bryant glanced at him. "You okay, man?"

Ryan nodded, pushing away the lump in his throat. "Yeah. Just... getting ready."

Bryant gave a knowing smile. "You've got this."

Ryan smiled back. "Yeah. I know." But even as he spoke, he felt the bittersweet weight of goodbye settle deep in his chest.

As the afternoon sunlight filtered through the window, they stood there, two brothers savoring the calm before everything changed.

Fifty-Nine

Friday morning marked a bittersweet day for Ryan and Sky. By 10 a.m., they were set to meet Nia and Bryant at the Foreman Falls Elementary School playground. The plan was simple but heavy—a final goodbye at a place packed with memories.

Ryan and Sky pulled into the gravel lot, the crunch of tires filling the still air. Ryan shut off the engine and sat for a moment, staring at the large fenced-in field that had been his kingdom as a child. The morning breeze carried the familiar scent of pine and dust, tugging at his heartstrings.

The playground sprawled out before them like a relic of their past adventures. There was the wide, emerald-green jungle gym, shaped like an alligator with its mouth open wide—a perfect spot for daring jumps. The blue slide tower stood tall like a sentry, its eight twisting slides cascading down like the tentacles of an octopus. Once bright and vibrant, the paint had faded to a soft baby blue, chipped at the edges by years of playful hands.

Basketball hoops lined one side of the field, their nets long gone, swaying slightly in the wind. Tetherball poles dotted the field like lonely sentries, missing their iconic balls. And at the far end stood the swing set—a worn rainbow of colors: red, orange, yellow, green, blue, indigo, and violet. The swings moved lazily in the breeze, creaking with each sway, like echoes of laughter long since passed.

Ryan stepped out of the truck, staring at the playground with a mix of nostalgia and grief. Sky followed, pulling her jacket tighter against the breeze as she took it all in.

"So, this is where you went to school?" Sky asked, glancing at the jungle gym.

Ryan nodded, his smile faint but genuine. "Yeah, this is where Bryant and I caused all kinds of trouble."

He walked forward and hopped the fence with ease, a move practiced from countless childhood summers. Sky followed, landing lightly beside him.

"What exactly did you guys do?" Sky asked, curiosity lighting her eyes as she brushed a strand of hair behind her ear.

Ryan grinned and headed toward the indigo swing, his favorite. "Just about everything you can think of." He sat down and began to sway gently.

Sky took the worn blue swing next to him. "Really? Anything?"

Ryan nodded. "Ask me anything."

Sky tilted her head, already swinging slightly. "Jumping off the swings?"

"Yep," Ryan replied, kicking off the ground and building momentum.

"Shoving Bryant off the monkey bars?" Sky's voice held a playful edge.

Ryan chuckled. "Oh, definitely."

Sky smiled as she swung higher. "Throwing the tetherball into other kids' faces?"

Ryan laughed. "Way too many times. I'm pretty sure we started a few tetherball wars."

Sky raised an eyebrow. "Recess detention?"

Ryan's grin widened. "Multiple times. Mrs. Jennings made us stand against the brick wall for the whole recess, but she never realized we loved it."

Sky slowed her swing. "You loved detention?"

"On hot days, that wall was cool and shady. We'd thank her for making us stand there," Ryan said with a laugh. "She was furious."

Sky laughed, shaking her head. "You two were ridiculous."

Ryan jumped off the swing at the peak of his arc, soaring through the air and landing with a soft thud. He turned back with a satisfied grin. "What can I say? We loved causing chaos."

Sky slowed her swing, pushing herself off with a graceful leap. Her wings spread wide, catching the air and letting her drift gently to the ground.

"Okay, you've heard my stories," Ryan said as he walked over to her. "Now it's your turn."

Sky bit her lip, hesitating. "Well... there was this one time in fifth grade."

Ryan's eyes lit up with curiosity. "Go on."

He stepped behind her, gently pushing her swing as she built momentum again.

"I wanted to make some extra money," Sky began. "I thought if I earned enough, maybe my parents would notice me more. I could buy my own colored pencils."

Ryan stayed quiet, listening intently.

"So, I took two empty soap bottles and filled them with a mix of hand soap, shampoo, conditioner, and my mom's floral body wash." Sky chuckled at the memory. "Lydia helped me. We told Mrs. Bennett we were selling homemade soap to raise funds for our scout group camping trip."

Ryan stopped pushing her swing and stared. "You tried to scam your teacher with fake soap?"

Sky laughed. "Yep. We almost got away with it too—until Lydia's mom came to pick her up the next day. Mrs. Bennett was so proud of herself for supporting our 'troop,' but Lydia's mom shut it down fast. She said, 'They're not in Girl Scouts.'"

Ryan shook his head, amazed. "What happened after that?"

Sky's swing soared higher. "I burst into tears. Mrs. Bennett felt so bad she let us off with a promise never to do it again."

Ryan scoffed. "You got away with it because you cried?"

Sky smirked. "Not my fault I knew how to work the system."

Ryan stepped closer, wrapping his arms around her waist as she came to a stop. "I get it. No one wants to punish a cute girl."

Sky's heart fluttered as she turned to face him. He leaned in, their faces inches apart.

"Save the PDA for later!" a familiar voice called.

Sky and Ryan turned to see Nia and Bryant striding toward them, their hands waving dramatically.

Bryant grinned. "We're still here, you know!"

Nia crossed her arms and shook her head with a playful smirk. "Come on, lovebirds. We have a farewell to do right."

Ryan and Sky shared a small, knowing smile before walking hand in hand toward their friends. Their time at the playground was more than just a goodbye—it was a reminder of where they came from and a promise of what lay ahead.

Sixty

The next couple of hours were filled with laughter and memories as the four friends ran around the playground like children. Ryan and Bryant led the charge, racing to the tetherball poles with a familiar competitive spark in their eyes. The tetherball spun wildly as Bryant gave it a powerful smack, sending it careening around in a blur.

"Dude, slow down!" Ryan yelled, dodging as the ball whooshed past his head.

Bryant grinned and hit it again, harder this time. "You call that dodging? I thought you were supposed to be an eagle!"

Ryan retaliated with a swing, but the ball was still spinning too fast, causing him to stumble. Nia and Sky watched from the sidelines, shaking their heads as the boys acted like elementary schoolers again.

Next, they wandered over to the slides. The towering blue octopus stood tall, though its paint had faded. Sky zipped down one of the curly tentacle-shaped slides with a loud cheer, landing gracefully at the bottom. Nia followed closely, her hair streaming behind her as she laughed.

The guys, however, had a tougher time. Ryan barely fit inside the winding slide and ended up wedged in the middle.

"I'm stuck!" Ryan called out, his voice echoing inside the slide.

Bryant stood at the top; arms crossed. "Yeah, I'm not even going to try. That's a death trap for guys our size."

Ryan finally wiggled his way free, sliding out with an ungraceful thud at the bottom. Sky clapped her hands, trying not to laugh too loudly. "I told you it wasn't built for grown men."

Bryant shrugged. "The monkey bars are more my speed."

They all made their way to the massive jungle gym, Ryan jumped up and grabbed the first metal bar, swinging easily from one to the next like he had done a hundred times before. Sky followed, though she struggled with the distance between the bars.

"Want a hand?" Ryan asked, pausing to look back.

Sky huffed. "Nope. I've got this."

She pushed through, reaching the end and landing with an out-of-breath grin. "See?"

Ryan gave her an impressed nod. "I stand corrected."

Behind them, Bryant was taking a different approach. Instead of using the bars, he had lifted Nia onto the alligator's head.

"Seriously?" Ryan called out, laughing. "You're supposed to swing to the end, not cheat."

Bryant leaned back with a lazy smile. "Too much work. Besides, my babe deserves the scenic route."

Nia smiled as she dangled her legs between the bars. "I'm perfectly fine up here."

Ryan shook his head, then leapt up to rest on the alligator's back. He held out his hand to help Sky up, but she used her wings to hover and land gracefully.

Ryan wrapped an arm around her shoulders and whispered, "Show-off."

Sky grinned. "You love it."

They spent the next few hours reminiscing and talking, the conversations flowing as easily as the breeze that rustled the grass. Eventually, Sky glanced at her phone and realized it was already past 1 p.m.

Nia stretched her arms above her head. "I'm starving."

Bryant nodded, his stomach growling audibly. "Seconded."

Ryan chuckled. "You're always hungry."

Sky thought for a moment. "I could kill for some Chinese food."

Ryan nudged her playfully. "You're always craving Chinese."

Sky shrugged with a grin. "It never gets old."

Nia perked up. "How about that Arby's on Fifth? That's where Bryant and I went on our first date."

Sky raised an eyebrow. "I thought we were going to places that relate to everyone."

Nia crossed her arms. "It's a special place for half of us, so I vote yes."

No one wanted to argue with her, so they piled into their cars and headed to Arby's. Inside, they ordered a ridiculous amount of food: Fourteen beef 'n' cheddars, 6 large curly fries, and two chocolate milkshakes to share between the couples.

The meal quickly turned into a competition. The guys were timed to see who could finish their sandwiches first. Bryant barely beat Ryan, who groaned and demanded a rematch. Next, Nia and Sky had a condiment challenge, doing shots of Arby's sauce. Sky downed all five cups in record time, while Nia barely made it through her second.

Nia winced, fanning her mouth. "It's way too spicy! How do you handle this stuff?"

Sky shrugged, wiping her mouth with a napkin. "Talent."

They sat across from each other, sipping their milkshakes through straws. Ryan locked eyes with Sky, turning it into an unspoken staring contest.

Sky narrowed her eyes playfully. "You're going down."

Ryan smirked and didn't blink, though he started sipping the milkshake faster. Suddenly, Sky gave him a small, well-placed kick under the table. Ryan blinked in surprise, and Sky burst into laughter.

"Cheater!" Ryan protested.

Sky leaned forward, victorious. "Winner, fair and square."

Ryan looked to Bryant for support. "Back me up here."

Bryant shook his head. "Didn't see a thing."

Nia winked at Sky. "Neither did I."

Sixty-One

After their meal, the group drove to Sky's house to set up a bonfire in the backyard. Earlier it was decided to have a serious moment together, to burn away the troubles of the past in preparation for the new chapter in their lives. They collected tree branches and stones, arranging them in a circle while Bryant dug a wide pit.

Sky ran inside and came back with a candle and a lighter.

Nia raised an eyebrow. "You want to start a bonfire with a candle?"

Sky rolled her eyes. "It helps get the flames started. Small flames grow into big ones."

She buried the candle under the wood and lit the wick. The flame flickered weakly, refusing to catch. Ryan ran back inside and returned with a can of hairspray.

Sky crossed her arms. "Where did you find that?"

Ryan grinned. "Your mom's bathroom. I've been here enough times to know where everything is."

He sprayed the candle, and the flames roared to life, the wood crackling as the fire grew into a beautiful display of orange and red.

Nia clapped her hands together. "Okay, who's going first?"

Everyone grabbed their mementos from their cars and returned to the fire.

Nia went first. She tossed in a purple hairbrush with green gum tangled in the bristles. "Mini cheer camp, third grade. Some friends thought it'd be funny to put gum in my hair. Not so funny when I had to cut it out."

Next, she held up a crystal-blue snow globe. Inside was a tiny snowman. "Fifth grade, a gift from my first boyfriend, Markus. He was cute but a cheater."

Bryant gave her a sideways look, and Nia tossed the snow globe into the fire with a grin. "Good riddance."

Her last item was a flyer for the Foreman Falls Prom. She angrily crumpled the paper and threw it in. "I don't think I need to explain this one."

Bryant stepped forward, holding a small, pink, flower-covered notebook. "This was my mom's hospital journal. She wrote down every procedure and every pain during her chemo treatments. I don't want to hold onto those memories anymore."

He placed the notebook gently into the fire, watching the cover curl as it burned.

His second item was a tiny brown football, the pigskin peeling. "This was the only gift my dad ever sent me—for my second birthday. He left it with a note on the table and never came back."

Bryant set the football down at the edge of the flames and stepped back.

Ryan took a deep breath and stepped forward with a small, colorful backpack. The green triceratops on the front smiled back at him, its eyes cartoonishly large. He unzipped it and pulled out a handful of crumpled papers.

"Family pictures, old test papers I failed on purpose, drawings of my dad and me playing airplanes, drawings of me crying in bed—everything that ever made me feel small."

He zipped the bag back up and placed it on the fire. The flames consumed it, warping the cartoon face as it burned.

Sky stepped forward, her hands trembling as she held up a tarnished silver heart locket. The chain was discolored with greenish stains, and the heart itself bore scratches from years of being handled.

She stared at the small piece of jewelry, her chest tightening with memories. She ran her thumb over the heart-shaped sticker on top that had faded from pink to gray. "This locket held everyone I ever loved."

Sky's voice was barely a whisper as she opened it. On one side was a photo of her parents, smiling and holding each other. On the other was a picture of Lydia, her face smeared with blue paint, her tongue sticking out as she laughed.

Tears welled in Sky's eyes. "They were my everything. But I wasn't anything to them."

Her fingers tightened around the locket, and for a moment, she hesitated. She remembered the hugs from her mom after school, Lydia pulling her out of panic attacks with silly jokes, her dad spinning her in the kitchen while music played.

Then she remembered the empty chairs at school events, the broken promises, and the way Lydia's friendship shattered at prom.

Ryan placed a hand on her back, grounding her. Sky took a deep breath and stepped closer to the fire. "It's time to let go."

She released the locket into the flames and watched as the silver heart darkened, the photos inside curling and dissolving. Her tears fell freely now, shimmering in the firelight.

They all sat quietly as the fire crackled and danced, turning their struggles and pains into ash that floated toward the sky.

As the stars began to peek through the darkness, Ryan stretched and spoke softly. "It's getting late. We wouldn't want to keep you guys."

Bryant nodded but hesitated. "I should probably check on my sisters."

Nia shot up, grinning. "Not yet! There's one more thing I've been dying to do!"

Sky blinked. "Something you can do in the middle of the night?"

Nia's grin widened as she bolted toward Bryant's jeep. Bryant groaned. "Babe, this is *my* car."

Nia hopped into the driver's seat. "And you're my boyfriend. So, it's *our* car."

Bryant shook his head but climbed into the passenger seat. Ryan and Sky exchanged amused looks as they got into Ryan's truck.

Sky leaned over. "What do you think she's planning?"

Ryan shrugged. "With Nia? Could be anything."

They followed the jeep down the quiet, empty driveway, the firelight still glowing faintly behind them as they drove into the unknown night.

Sixty-Two

Nia took them smack dab into the middle of town. The streets were eerily quiet, a stark contrast to the vibrant memories they had just shared at the playground and around the bonfire. Sky watched as buildings lay empty, their dark windows reflecting the glow of the streetlights like watchful eyes. The red parking meters stood like lonely protectors along the curbs, chipped and worn from years of service. The lampposts cast soft, golden halos of light that gently illuminated the cracked sidewalks and quiet streets, as though careful not to wake the slumbering town. Everything was still, save for the occasional whisper of the breeze, rustling the leaves of a nearby tree.

Sky rolled down the window and closed her eyes, letting the gusts of night air wash over her. The wind tangled her hair into soft curls as she savored the fleeting sensation of weightlessness, as if the night itself was cradling her. The hum of the engine was the only sound in the stillness until they approached a brightly lit building that glowed like a beacon.

The jeep slowed, and Sky sat up, blinking at the sight before her. The rectangle-shaped building was small and modest, but its glowing yellow sign boldly declared: "WAFFLE HOUSE." Black letters stood proudly on the neon backdrop, a stark contrast to the sleepy town. Inside, the warm light poured through the large windows, revealing the small, homey booths lining the walls.

Nia hopped out of the jeep, throwing her arms in the air. "We're here!" she announced, her grin wide.

Sky stared in disbelief. "You brought us to Waffle House?"

Ryan, Sky, and Bryant exchanged bewildered glances as they stepped out of their cars.

Nia placed her hands on her hips. "Yes! I've always wanted to make a midnight run to Waffle House with my friends. It's been on my bucket list forever."

Ryan chuckled as he held the door open. "Well, you sure know how to keep things interesting."

Inside, the air was filled with the unmistakable scent of frying bacon, buttered waffles, and brewed coffee. The white-tiled floor was worn but clean, and the walls were painted a neon yellow that matched the sign outside. A long counter ran along one side of the restaurant, with padded bar stools lined up in front of the griddle. Each booth was set with laminated menus and syrup bottles that glistened under the light.

They squeezed into a small booth near the front, laughing as they adjusted to fit.

Nia flipped open her menu. "Alright, guys, what are we getting?"

A server approached, wearing a blue apron and a crumpled paper hat. She smiled warmly and pulled out a notepad.

Nia ordered a chocolate chip waffle with scrambled eggs.

Bryant, ever the overachiever, ordered a double stack of chocolate chip waffles with a mountain of bacon.

Ryan opted for blueberry waffles and cheesy grits.

Sky smiled and asked for blueberry waffles with bacon and eggs.

Nia grinned mischievously after the server walked away. "Y'all's orders are so ridiculous. I'm the only one here with style."

Bryant raised an eyebrow. "Style? You ordered a waffle."

Ryan leaned back and smirked. "At least she didn't order a pig's worth of bacon."

Bryant shrugged. "I'm eighteen. I've earned it."

Sky giggled. "Bryant, you're done growing."

"My appetite isn't," Bryant retorted with a grin.

The smell of sizzling bacon and sweet waffle batter made their stomachs growl as they waited. When the food arrived, they dug in enthusiastically. Ryan reached over to steal a piece of Sky's bacon, but she caught his hand mid-air.

"Maybe Bryant will share," Sky teased.

Ryan sighed dramatically. "Just one piece?"

Sky shook her head, popping the last strip into her mouth. "Bacon is sacred."

Meanwhile, Nia had already swiped several pieces of Bryant's bacon.

"Babe," Bryant groaned, eyeing his near-empty plate. "You ordered your own food."

Nia gave an innocent smile. "Yours tastes better."

Ryan laughed and pointed at Bryant. "Figured that would happen."

They spent the next hour chatting, telling stories, and finishing their meal. Once their plates were cleared, they made their way outside and sat around the truck bed.

Ryan stretched out, leaning against the tailgate. "I never thought midnight waffles could be this much fun."

Nia clapped her hands triumphantly. "Told you!"

Bryant wrapped his arm around her and kissed her temple. "You're always right."

Nia smiled smugly. "I know."

Ryan leaned into Sky, resting his chin on the top of her head. "So... this is goodbye?"

Bryant stood up and extended his hand to Ryan. Ryan didn't hesitate. He pulled Bryant into a hug, and Bryant wrapped his arms tightly around him. The hug was fierce, brotherly, and unspoken in its depth.

"Gonna miss you, man," Ryan muttered, his voice cracking.

Bryant's voice was thick. "You're my brother, Ryan. Always."

Ryan felt the air leave his lungs as Bryant squeezed harder, and he laughed even as his eyes burned with tears. "Okay, okay, you win. Can't breathe!"

They pulled apart, wiping their faces with sheepish grins. Sky watched, her heart aching at the sight of their brotherly goodbye.

Nia was already in tears as she walked over to Sky. Sky tried to hold back her own emotions, but the moment they embraced, the dam broke.

Nia hugged her tightly, whispering, "Thanks for being the best sister I never knew I needed."

Sky's sobs muffled her words, but she managed to whisper back, "Thanks for being my first real friend."

Nia pulled back, brushing tears from Sky's cheeks. "You're the most beautiful person I know—inside and out. Don't you ever forget that."

Sky's chest felt tight as she nodded. "I won't."

They hugged again, holding on as though letting go would shatter them. The sound of the guys wrestling off to the side broke the moment. The girls laughed through their tears.

Finally, Bryant and Nia climbed into the jeep. Sky called out, "Until next time?"

Nia's tear-streaked face lit up with a smile as she waved. "Until next time."

The jeep rumbled to life, and Bryant nodded to Ryan before driving away. The headlights cut through the darkness as the jeep disappeared down the midnight street.

Ryan wrapped an arm around Sky's shoulders and kissed the top of her head. "We'll see them again. I promise."

Sky clung to him, nodding against his chest. "I know. Nia will hunt us down if we don't."

They chuckled softly before climbing into the truck. As they drove back to Sky's house, silence settled between them like a comforting blanket. Sky watched the streetlights blur into amber streaks, her tears tracing slow paths down her cheeks. Each light felt like a memory slipping past—glowing, fleeting, and gone.

Ryan reached over and intertwined his fingers with hers, his grip steady and warm. She turned to him and saw the shimmer of unshed tears in his eyes, but his smile was calm, reassuring.

In that quiet moment, words were unnecessary. The weight of what lay ahead was heavy, but they both knew that as long as they were together, they would be okay. Whatever came next, they would face it side by side.

Sixty-Three

4 a.m. came quickly for Ryan and Sky. The few hours of sleep they managed were spent snuggled together on the couch. Sky had refused to go into her room after saying her emotional goodbye. She wanted to stay close, savoring their last few moments in the home she was leaving behind.

Ryan stirred first, blinking groggily as the soft chime of his phone alarm filled the quiet space. He reached over to turn it off, but his hand missed, and the phone tumbled to the floor with a soft thud. He cursed under his breath and leaned over Sky, trying not to wake her as he reached down.

Sky mumbled in her sleep and instinctively burrowed deeper into Ryan's chest. He paused, a smile tugging at his lips as he breathed in the familiar lavender scent of her hair.

"It's time to get up," he whispered gently.

Sky groaned, wrapping her arms tighter around him. "Can't I just stay right here?"

Ryan's chest warmed at her words. He loved how she clung to him, as though he was her anchor. "I wish we could," he said softly, brushing a strand of hair from her face. "But we've got a long road ahead of us."

Sky cracked one eye open, staring at him sleepily. "Dang it... let's hurry up and get there then."

She rolled off the couch, stretching as she walked toward the kitchen. Ryan followed, watching her as she shuffled around to make a quick pancake breakfast. She attempted to flip a pancake without a spatula and struggled, making the batter fold awkwardly in the pan.

Ryan laughed and walked up behind her. "Here, let me show you how it's done." He placed his hands over hers, guiding the pan with a practiced motion. The pancake landed perfectly on the plate.

"Show-off," Sky muttered playfully.

In no time, they had plates piled high with pancakes and glasses of cold milk. They ate quietly, savoring the moment. When they finished, Sky washed the plates while Ryan grabbed their bags.

Ryan pulled off his shirt in the middle of the living room to change into his favorite red football jersey. Sky turned around just in time to see him, and her face flushed a deep crimson.

"Hey! Wait for me to leave the room!" she exclaimed.

Ryan smirked, knowing full well she was staring. "Why? You don't seem to mind."

Sky stammered, then bolted to her parents' room to get dressed for the day. Her heart raced as she shook her head, muttering to herself, "Focus, Sky."

She slipped into a royal blue athletic shirt with a small bird emblem stitched on the front, a reminder of that fun day she and Nia had at the Gear Bound store. She paired it with the grey cheer joggers Nia had given her during that embarrassing day when she was soaked in Gatorade. Her ombre tennis shoes shimmered with bold purple fading into teal blue.

She paused at the mirror, brushing her long hair that now reached just above her waist. She hadn't realized how much it had grown. For so long, she had tucked it away in ponytails and braids, too busy to notice.

Sky straightened her posture, staring at her reflection. Her wings, white and bold, rested behind her, unapologetically out for the world to see. A wave of pride swelled within her as she tied her hair into a high ponytail with her favorite scrunchie—the one with the white ribbons that framed her face.

She thought about everything that had led her here: the moments of fear, joy, heartbreak, and growth. She felt stronger now, more herself than she'd ever been.

Ryan's voice called from the living room. "You ready to go?"

Sky took a deep breath and stepped out. Ryan stood there in his red t-shirt with the number '19' printed in bold white. It hung loosely on his frame, complementing his grey sweatpants and worn red sneakers. He smiled at her, his eyes sparkling.

"So," he teased, "did you like me better with or without the shirt?"

Sky's face heated again. "I'm not answering that." She turned away, flustered.

Ryan laughed. "Don't worry. I already know the answer." He winked and gestured toward the door. "Ladies first."

Sky stepped into the doorway but hesitated. She turned back, taking one last look at the house she had called home. The scent of sweet pancakes still lingered in the air. The dim lights cast a soft glow across the dulled kitchen island. She felt the weight of the silence.

Memories flooded her mind: nights spent curled up with books, mornings watching the sunrise alone, and every quiet moment that had made this place both a sanctuary and a prison. But the emotions rising within her weren't sad. They were peaceful. She felt ready to leave.

Ryan stepped into her view and leaned close, his face inches from hers. "Why'd you stop?" he asked, grinning.

Sky's heart swelled as she closed the distance between them, pressing her lips to his. The warmth of their kiss melted everything else away.

When they parted, Ryan's smile was as wide as ever. "You could've just said you wanted a kiss."

Sky laughed, her eyes shining. "I like surprising you."

Hand in hand, they walked to the truck. The morning air was crisp, filled with the faint chirping of early birds. The back of the truck bed was covered by a tarp, concealing their bags. Sky glanced at it, feeling a twinge of anxiety. Everything she owned, everything that mattered, was packed in those bags.

Ryan opened the passenger door, and Sky climbed in, glancing at the empty back seat. She thought of homecoming night, when she and Ryan had shared the back of Bryant's jeep, laughing and dreaming. Now, the backseat held nothing but snacks and travel supplies. She chuckled at the sight of chips spilling out of Ryan's overstuffed backpack.

Ryan slid into the driver's seat and handed Sky his varsity football jacket. "Here," he said. "You might wanna use it as a pillow."

Sky didn't hesitate to put it on. It was warm and comforting, the familiar scent of pine and fresh air surrounding her.

They buckled in, and Ryan glanced at her with a soft smile. "Thank you, Sky."

Sky tilted her head. "Thank me? For what?"

Ryan's eyes softened. "For everything. For being the reason I could stand up to my dad. For making me believe I could leave all of that behind. You're my person, Sky."

Sky felt her heart swell. "You could've done that on your own," she whispered.

Ryan reached for her hand, holding it tightly. "No. You saved me from a life I hated. You gave me a reason to fight for something better."

Tears welled in Sky's eyes. "And you're my person, Ryan Daniels."

They shared a quiet kiss before Ryan started the engine. The rumble of the truck reverberated through the stillness as they pulled away from the house. Sky stared out the window, watching the familiar streets roll past. But this time felt different.

She wasn't coming back.

The town lay quiet, its streetlights glowing dimly as they passed shuttered storefronts and empty sidewalks. As they neared the interstate, a breathtaking sight greeted them.

Behind a wall of dark clouds, golden streams of light began to seep through, illuminating the sky. The sunrise painted the horizon with shades of amber and white, casting a radiant glow across the road. The light danced on the worn hood of the truck, reflecting skyward like a beacon. The blue hues of dawn stretched overhead, vast and serene.

Sky's breath caught in her throat. The sun was waking the world, reaching out like a comforting hand to the earth below. The clouds fell away, revealing the full brilliance of morning.

She grinned, feeling the warmth of the light wrap around her. Strength surged through her as the first rays of sunlight bathed the truck in a heavenly glow.

Ryan glanced at her and smiled, his hand tightening around hers. Sky returned his gaze, their unspoken understanding as strong as ever.

Sixty-Four

Thirty hours. It would take them thirty hours of driving to reach the sanctuary—thirty long hours on the road, not counting breaks. Over two thousand miles stretched out between them and the haven they hoped would become their new home. Sky and Ryan knew that this journey would be far from easy. They had packed multiple bags filled with snacks, bottled water, and enough food to last the trip. The plan was to make it in three days.

Day one was easy—or at least it started that way. They spent most of the morning singing along to the radio and swapping stories, their laughter filling the cab of the truck. Every new town they passed was another marker that they were truly leaving their old lives behind.

Their first major stop was in St. Louis, Missouri. Sky had practically begged Ryan to pull over so they could take a picture by the famous Gateway Arch. He pulled into a nearby park, and they got out of the truck, stretching their legs as they approached the gleaming monument. The early light of sunrise left the area rather empty, no people to be found.

"Why just take a picture?" Ryan asked, his grin mischievous.

Sky's eyes lit up. She knew exactly what he meant. In minutes, they were airborne, soaring toward the very top of the arch. They perched on the narrow ledge at the peak, the city sprawled out below them like a living painting.

Sky pulled out her phone and snapped several pictures, capturing the breathtaking view and their beaming smiles. She even took a few playful selfies, Ryan making goofy faces behind her. She couldn't help but laugh, the sound of it carried away by the wind.

The elevator inside the arch whirred as it moved past the observation deck below.

Sky stood up, stretching her wings. "Race you back to the car!" she called, her voice daring.

Ryan laughed and stood, his competitive spirit flaring. "You're on!"

Sky leaped off the arch, wings tucked tightly as she dived toward the ground. The rush of air roared in her ears. She flared her wings at the last second, landing in the parking lot with a soft thud.

Ryan landed seconds later, breathing heavily. "You know peregrine falcons are the fastest birds in the world, right?" he said between breaths.

Sky grinned. "I do. And they've got nothing on me."

They hopped back into the truck, Sky's hair still wild from the wind. Their next stop was Topeka, Kansas—a slight detour from their route, but Ryan insisted.

"What's your obsession with Topeka?" Sky asked as they parked by the city sign.

Ryan laughed as he ran over to stand by the sign, striking a ridiculous pose. "There was this one show I watched as a kid—you know, the one with the house of imaginary friends? Anyway, in one episode, they kept saying 'Topeka' like it was the hottest place on earth. I swore that one day, I'd visit."

Sky rolled her eyes but smiled, taking a picture. "You're such a nerd."

Ryan jogged back to the truck, beaming. "And proud of it."

They drove for hours, watching the landscape shift from the bustling cities to the vast, open plains of the Midwest. As the sky deepened to twilight, they decided to stop for the night in Omaha, Nebraska.

The neon sign for "Webbler Inn" flickered unevenly, casting an eerie glow over the parking lot. The motel was small, with chipped paint and narrow balconies. Ryan pulled into a parking spot near the entrance, both of them careful to pull their jackets tight around their wings.

Ryan approached the front desk and asked for the most inexpensive room available. The desk clerk, a tired-looking man with glasses perched on the edge of his nose, handed him the key to room 207.

The room was modest—two twin beds, a small dresser, and a TV that looked older than both of them combined. Sky dropped her bag on one of the beds and immediately started unpacking their takeout from Panda Express.

"I thought we'd never find a place that had decent food," Sky said as she opened her plate of orange chicken and chow mien.

Ryan returned with a duffel bag slung over his shoulder, laughing when he saw how much Sky had already eaten. "You're going to eat us through all our cash before we make it out of Nebraska."

Sky shot him a grin, a forkful of noodles halfway to her mouth. "Better eat yours before I take it too."

Ryan shut the door behind him, set the bag down, and grabbed his own styrofoam plate of food. They sat cross-legged on the beds, balancing their plates as they watched one of the Fast and Furious movies on the tiny TV.

Sky barely paid attention to the plot, too busy texting Nia updates and sending her pictures from the arch and Kansas. Nia's replies came quickly, filled with laughing emojis and excited comments.

Ryan noticed Sky's amused expression and nudged her with his foot. "Movie's almost over. Ready to hit the hay?"

Sky stood and stretched. "Yeah, but I need a shower first. Long day on the road."

She grabbed her pajamas and headed to the bathroom but paused at the door, a playful smile on her face. "I'm surprised you didn't ask for a room with one queen bed."

Ryan's face turned red. Sky laughed and closed the door behind her. The sound of running water soon filled the room.

While she was in the shower, Ryan moved the two twin beds together, creating a makeshift queen bed. When Sky emerged in a puff of steam, her navy-blue star-print pajamas clinging to her, Ryan couldn't resist teasing.

"Do you shower with lava?" he asked, grinning.

Sky shook out her hair, letting the damp curls fall to her shoulders. "The hotter, the better."

She eyed the rearranged beds and plopped onto the nearest one. "I see we have a 'queen' bed now."

Ryan rubbed the back of his neck, his face still red. "I figured I'd fix it since you complained about the setup."

Sky arched an eyebrow. "I wasn't complaining. I was just pointing something out." She grabbed her brush and ran it through her hair, securing it with a claw clip. Ryan watched, amazed at how long her hair was when wet.

"I didn't know your hair was that long," he said, emphasizing the last word.

Sky smirked. "It's always been this long. You just never noticed."

She slid under the covers and reached for the bedside lamp, clicking it off. Ryan did the same, scooting closer until they met in the middle.

Sky's voice was quiet. "Shouldn't we be sleeping?"

Ryan wrapped an arm around her waist, pulling her closer. "It's kind of cold in here," he murmured. "Staying warm sounds like a good plan."

Sky didn't respond, settling into his embrace as she pulled the blanket up to her nose. The soft hum of the TV faded into the background as they drifted off, wrapped in the warmth of a day filled with memories and the promise of the journey ahead.

Sixty-Five

Soon the sun rose on their next day of travels. The dawn's golden light was nowhere to be found; instead, thick clouds stretched across the sky like a woolen blanket. The air carried a chill, and small flurries of snow began to fall, dotting the windshield as Ryan drove steadily along the nearly empty interstate. Shadows from the overcast sky made the world seem muted and somber.

Sky shifted in her seat, boredom seeping into her bones. Their energy from the day before had faded, replaced by a shared grogginess from the restless night in the motel. The only sounds were the hum of the engine and the occasional sigh from Ryan.

Sky glanced at him. His eyes were fixed on the road, but she could see the weariness behind them. Dark circles framed his eyes, his grip on the steering wheel tight. The truck drifted slightly to the left before he corrected it.

"How are you holding up?" Sky asked, concern evident in her voice.

Ryan kept his eyes forward. "Fine for now," he muttered, though his voice sounded strained.

Sky frowned. "Why don't I drive for a while?"

Ryan shook his head. "I'll be fine," he said, though his shoulders sagged. "I just need to focus."

Sky watched him closely, noticing the slight swerve of the truck again. She wasn't convinced. As they passed a green sign that read, "Lakota Reservation — 2 miles," Sky made an executive decision.

"Why don't we take a rest stop?" she suggested. "Looks like there's a spot coming up."

Ryan hesitated but eventually nodded. "Alright."

The truck rolled into a small gas station just outside the reservation. Snowflakes drifted lazily down, settling on the roof of the old building. Ryan stumbled out of the driver's seat, rubbing his eyes. Sky rushed around to his side.

"You need a nap. Right now," she insisted.

Ryan didn't argue as Sky led him to the passenger seat. He slid in and reclined the seat as far back as it would go, practically lying flat. The frosty air nipped at his skin, but the soft hum of the truck's heater lulled him into relaxation.

"I'll be right back," Sky said. "I'm going to grab a few things."

Ryan barely managed a nod before closing his eyes. His thoughts, however, refused to quiet. The night before had been long. While he had loved having Sky close, his mind had been restless, tangled with a hundred worries. What would his parents think when they realized he was gone? Had they noticed yet? Did his father even care? And what awaited them at the sanctuary? Would it be a safe haven, or would they arrive to find nothing but empty promises?

He shifted, pulling a fuzzy gray blanket over himself. The weight of the unknown pressed on his chest, but the scent of Sky's lingering lavender shampoo still clung to the fabric. Slowly, his tense muscles relaxed.

The soft click of the driver's door pulled him halfway out of his thoughts.

"Already asleep?" Sky's voice was warm.

Ryan chuckled without opening his eyes. "I wish."

Sky set two drinks in the cup holders and settled into the driver's seat. "I just met some cool people in there," she said, adjusting the rearview mirror.

Ryan's brow furrowed. "I thought we were keeping a low profile."

Sky rolled her eyes as she started the truck. "It wasn't like that." Her voice softened. "It was… different."

She drove along, replaying the encounter in her mind.

Inside the convenience store, the air had smelled of freshly brewed coffee and pine incense. The cashier area was a small counter lined with local crafts—hand-carved wooden figurines, beaded necklaces, and colorful knit scarves.

The woman behind the counter was short, with a strong but weathered frame. She wore a dress made from soft leather, adorned with embroidered patterns that shimmered in the dim light. A vibrant woven scarf was draped around her shoulders, its colors as bold as a sunrise. Her tanned skin bore fine wrinkles, especially near her kind, dark eyes.

The woman had stepped out from behind the counter and rested a gentle hand on Sky's shoulder.

"Excuse me, dear," she said in a soft, crackling voice. "Are you from around here?"

Sky had smiled politely. "No, ma'am. Just passing through on a road trip with my friend."

The woman's eyes crinkled as she smiled. "My, my," she said. "I bet you have magnificent wings under that jacket."

Sky's cheeks burned. "I—I don't know what you're talking about."

The woman chuckled. "Dear, I know a blessed spirit when I see one. Just look at my granddaughter."

Sky's gaze drifted to the young girl behind the counter. She had long, furry ears nestled in her dark braids, and her bright eyes shimmered with curiosity.

"You're Humanimals?" Sky asked in awe.

The woman nodded. "I'm not, but many in my family are. We believe they are chosen for a higher purpose. Those with the strength and spirit of animals are meant to lead us toward a better future."

Sky had never thought of her wings that way. She had always seen them as a genetic accident, a byproduct of disaster.

The woman reached behind the counter and retrieved a small linen bag. "Here," she said, pressing it into Sky's hands. "Some nuts and berries my granddaughter picked this morning."

Sky tried to protest. "Oh, you don't have to give me anything—"

The woman held up a hand. "Take it. No payment needed. Just stay safe on your travels. The world has yet to understand people like you."

Sky's throat tightened as she nodded. "Thank you."

Now, as Sky drove, the bag of berries sat in the cup holder, its earthy scent filling the cab. She glanced over at Ryan, who had finally fallen asleep, his face peaceful for the first time in hours. Her heart swelled. The kindness of strangers still existed, even in the most unexpected places.

She turned on the radio, hoping to stay alert. Static crackled as she tuned through stations until she landed on a news broadcast.

"Twelve are dead, and another twenty injured in a terrorist attack by the ReFramers group. The Denver airport is on lockdown as authorities search for the suspects responsible for the bombing in the west wing parking deck."

Sky's breath caught in her throat. The reporter's voice was grim.

"This latest attack comes just a day after the rally shooting in Pennsylvania, where thirty-two were injured and four were killed. Presidential candidate Luke Drackett remains in critical condition after sustaining multiple lacerations. He is currently being treated at Grants-Mill Hospital."

Sky's pulse quickened. Her knuckles whitened as she gripped the steering wheel. The chaotic images playing in her mind—flames, shattered glass, panicked faces—made her feel sick. She turned off the radio.

Her eyes flitted to the speedometer, and she realized she had been pressing the gas harder. She eased up but kept driving fast enough to feel like she was escaping the horrors she'd just heard.

The sun dipped toward the horizon as they reached the outskirts of Bozeman, Montana. The beauty of the place took Sky's breath away. Dense forests surrounded the city, their evergreen trees standing tall like sentinels. Snow-capped mountains loomed in the distance, their peaks brushing the clouds. A river, its surface like glass, rushed over smooth stones, flanked by clusters of delicate purple flowers.

She passed signs for Yellowstone National Park and scoffed at the memory of her parents attending some prestigious conference there years ago. They had been surrounded by nature but too absorbed in their careers to notice its wonder.

Sky drove aimlessly for a few minutes, soaking in the serene beauty before pulling into the lot of a stone-built hotel that towered fifteen stories high. Warm yellow lights glowed from the windows, casting a soft halo against the evening sky.

She reached over and gently nudged Ryan. "Hey. We're at our stop for the night."

Ryan groaned and rubbed his face. "Ugh. Okay."

They stepped out into the crisp mountain air, their breaths forming small clouds. Ryan sluggishly grabbed their bags while Sky held the door for him.

The front desk attendant greeted them with a polite smile. She wore an orange uniform and handed over their key card with practiced efficiency.

Their room was on the fourteenth floor. As the elevator ascended, Ryan leaned heavily against the wall, eyes half-closed.

"You really need to get some rest tonight," Sky said gently.

Ryan nodded without protest.

When they reached their room at the end of the hallway, Sky opened the door and set their bags down. She took Ryan's hand and led him to the bed nearest the window, pulling back the comforter. He sank onto the mattress and was asleep within seconds.

Sky stood by the window, watching planes take off and land in the distance. She imagined herself leaping into the sky, soaring alongside them, her wings cutting through the night air.

With a sigh, she turned to the other bed and flicked on the TV. The news channel showed scenes from the earlier attack—flames licking at twisted metal, firefighters trying to control the blaze, people weeping in the chaos. White sheets covered still bodies, scattered like fallen petals. Blood stained the grass and pavement.

The screen flashed with a video from the rally. Luke Drackett stood tall at the podium, a powerful presence with his distinguished, short gray hair and piercing blue eyes. His short, canine-like ears, blending seamlessly into his hair, twitched slightly with each roar of the crowd. He had always exuded confidence, even a touch of defiance. His tailored navy suit hugged his broad shoulders as he gestured passionately to the crowd. His voice—calm but commanding—had once silenced an auditorium of critics.

The camera panned to the chaos that erupted. Screams filled the air as gunshots rang out. Security scrambled to shield Drackett, but not before the impact of bullets sent him crashing to the stage. Blood seeped through his suit as he tried to push himself up, his strength faltering. Black bags now covered bodies dispersed across the bleachers and field, their shapes eerily still. The grass was stained crimson, and the slow drip of blood from the podium sent alarm through the screen.

Sky turned the channel to a live feed of a river, its waters dancing over the rocks. The peaceful sight was a relief to her exhausted mind.

She took a quick shower and climbed into bed; her damp hair fanned out on the pillow. As she reached for the bedside lamp, she whispered a silent prayer—for the victims, for herself, for a world that felt increasingly fragile.

Tomorrow night, they would reach the sanctuary.

With that hopeful thought, she drifted off to sleep.

Sixty-Six

As morning arrived, Ryan woke feeling well-rested, his limbs lighter from the deep sleep he'd finally gotten. Sunlight streamed weakly through the thick clouds, painting the room in soft gray tones. Across the room, Sky stirred beneath the blankets, groaning as she rolled over and fell to the floor with a dull thud.

"Ouch," she muttered, half-asleep.

Ryan chuckled as he walked over, extending a hand. "Someone needs more sleep, huh?"

Sky groaned again but accepted his help, standing up and rubbing her hip. Ryan headed to the bathroom for a shower while Sky began packing their belongings. The room was quiet except for the soft hum of the heater and the sound of water running behind the closed bathroom door. She paused for a moment, taking out her notebook and pen. Sitting on the edge of the bed, she let her thoughts flow freely onto the page, her pen moving swiftly across the paper. Each word felt like a release—fragments of excitement, fear, and hope formed into a long, detailed poem.

The bathroom door opened, releasing a wave of steam into the room. Ryan stepped out, dressed in comfortable loungewear, towel drying his hair.

"Writing, I see," he said, a grin tugging at the corners of his mouth.

Sky smiled but kept her eyes on the notebook. "Yep. Just needed to get some things off my chest."

Ryan stepped closer, trying to peek over her shoulder. "Ooo, what are you saying about me?" he teased.

Sky quickly pulled the notebook to her chest, narrowing her eyes playfully. "Who says I'm writing about you?" She stuffed the notebook into her suitcase, giving him a mischievous smile.

Ryan bumped her shoulder with his. "I'm irresistible—you have to be writing about me."

Sky rolled her eyes and finished packing. Within minutes, their bags were in the back of Ryan's truck. Sky climbed into the passenger side, immediately reclining her seat and grabbing the gray blanket from the back. She curled up, letting her eyes flutter shut.

Ryan adjusted his rearview mirror, glancing at her with a soft smile. Her tired eyes and quiet breathing tugged at his heart. He reached over, running his fingers through her ponytail.

"It's your turn to rest," he whispered before kissing the top of her head. He started the engine and pulled onto the highway.

The miles rolled by beneath the tires as they headed west on Interstate 90—the last stretch of their 2,000-mile journey. The radio played softly, a mix of popular songs and old rock classics filling the cabin. Sky had fallen into a deep sleep, her face serene.

Ryan drove for hours, stopping for lunch in Missoula, Montana. The town was surrounded by rolling hills and snow-dusted trees. He pulled into a McDonald's drive-thru, ordering two burgers, fries, and sodas. As he waited, he noticed the colorful signs nearby. One depicted a family rafting down a roaring river, another showed skiers descending a snowy mountain with wide smiles.

"Man, I'd love to be doing that right now," Ryan muttered to himself.

After getting their food, Ryan drove out of the parking lot. As they left Missoula behind, a billboard caught his eye. It had an illustration of a father and son in a small fishing boat. The son held a fishing pole with a small fish wriggling on the line. The father's hand rested proudly on his son's shoulder, both of them grinning. Above them, bold letters read: "Great Father-Son Bonding! Come Fishing at Missoula Lake!"

Ryan scoffed, his hands tightening on the steering wheel. "My dad would never..."

A memory surfaced, unbidden.

He was six years old, standing next to his father at the edge of a large pond near NisenX headquarters. The sun reflected off the water, making it shimmer like a million diamonds.

"Son," Mr. Daniels had said, his voice calm yet firm, "there are two types of people in this world—those who eat and those who are eaten. Just like the animal kingdom, there's a hierarchy. Predators and prey."

Ryan had looked up, his small hands clutching the fishing net his father had handed him. "So... we're going fishing?" he asked, eyes wide with excitement.

His father shook his head, staring out at the water. "No, son. It's a metaphor." He pointed at the pond. "Humanimals are built differently—like birds of the sky or fish in the sea. You, my son, are a Golden Eagle—one of the fastest predatory birds in the world."

Ryan followed his father's gaze and saw a splash in the center of the pond. A long, blue tail fin broke the surface before vanishing beneath the water.

"I see a fish!" Ryan had shouted.

His father's smile was thin. "Look closer."

The water rippled as the fin emerged again. This time, Ryan noticed the iridescent shimmer of scales and the unmistakable shape of a young woman leaping from the water. Her red hair fanned out like fire, and shimmering blue-green scales trailed down her arms. Instead of legs, she had a long, powerful tail that ended in butterfly-shaped fins.

Ryan's jaw dropped. "She's a fish, Daddy!"

Mr. Daniels' expression darkened. "She's much more than that. She's the start of my company's vision to change the world." He crouched down to Ryan's level, his voice low and sharp. "But remember this, Ryan. She's trapped, forever swimming in this pond. You, on the other hand, are the eagle—a predator. People like her should fear you. Never forget your strength."

Ryan had stared back at the girl in the water. She met his gaze, her eyes wide and fearful.

The memory faded as the truck passed under a bridge, snapping Ryan back to the present. He inhaled deeply, shaking off the lingering sting of his father's words.

Lolo National Forest stretched out before him—a vast expanse of green, white, and gold. Snow-covered pines stood tall on either side of the road like guards. Sunlight filtered through the clouds, dappling the forest floor in patches of warmth. They were now just three hours away from the sanctuary.

Ryan glanced down at Sky, who was still curled beneath the blanket. Her chest rose and fell steadily, her expression peaceful. He smiled softly, his heart swelling with affection. Every mile, every hour brought them closer to the life they'd dreamed of—a life free from fear and pain.

He turned his gaze back to the road ahead, the sky brightening with golden streaks as the clouds began to part. The sight filled him with a quiet sense of hope.

"Almost there," he whispered to himself.

Sixty-Seven

They had made it into Idaho, passing through a quaint town called Eagle. The early afternoon light bathed the small town in a soft glow, making everything look simply peaceful. Sky stirred awake, stretching her arms and legs out as far as they could go.

"Uh, where are we?" she asked, her voice groggy from sleep.

Ryan laughed at her disheveled state. "Good morning to you too. We just passed Eagle, Idaho."

Sky brought her chair to an upright position and blinked at him with a grin. "Dang it! We should have stopped there!"

Ryan raised an eyebrow. "Why? It's just a small town."

Sky leaned toward him, mischief glinting in her eyes. "Because those are your people! Eagles, right?"

Ryan shook his head, chuckling. "Oh gosh, Sky. You're impossible."

Sky pulled out the map from the glove compartment, the edges now worn from her constant handling over the past two days. She traced their path with her finger, stopping at the red star. "Almost to the Panhandle of National Forests! Just gotta keep heading north."

Ryan nodded confidently. "Will do!"

The road narrowed as they left civilization behind. They drove for another hour until a large billboard came into view, advertising "Idaho Panhandle National Forests!" Sky squealed softly with joy, her excitement bubbling over.

Ryan followed the signs leading to a series of camping grounds. The truck rumbled over a dirt path that wound deeper and deeper into the forest until it reached the very last spot—a secluded clearing where the road ended and the trees thickened into a dense wall of green.

Sky jumped out of the truck, stretching her wings wide. They caught the afternoon light, glowing with a soft white hue. The crisp scent of pine and fresh earth filled the air. Ryan stepped out and inhaled deeply, savoring the richness of the forest. It already felt like home.

The sight before them was breathtaking. Towering evergreens stood like ancient guardians; their trunks wrapped in soft moss. Sunlight filtered through the canopy in golden beams, casting intricate patterns on the forest floor. The breeze rustled the leaves high above, creating a soothing symphony. Occasionally, the shadows shifted as birds darted between branches, and the faint rustling of a rabbit in the underbrush added to the quiet life surrounding them.

Ryan broke the silence. "So, how far from here are we hiking?"

Sky tilted her head, scrutinizing the map's faded markings. "I'm not sure... the star is just smack dab in the middle!"

Ryan walked over and peered at the map. His brow furrowed. "Wow. Yeah, I don't know either."

Sky sighed, stuffing the map back into her jacket pocket. "I guess we better get started."

Ryan pulled their large bags out from the truck bed, grunting as he slung two over his shoulders. Sky grabbed the bags from the back seat—one filled with snacks—and wrapped the fuzzy gray blanket around her shoulders. She glanced at the duffle bags and her suitcases, realizing how much she had packed.

"I think I packed too much," she admitted.

Ryan shot her a knowing look as he hefted her two suitcases. "You think?"

Sky chuckled as she slung Ryan's two duffle bags over her own shoulders. "Guess I'll carry yours, then."

Ryan turned and laughed at the sight of Sky, wobbling slightly under the weight of the bags. "What's so funny?" she asked, her voice muffled behind the straps.

He shook his head, still smiling. "Nothing."

The two began their woodland hike. The first hour passed easily enough. The sun warmed their backs as they followed a narrow trail winding through the trees. Ryan kept stealing amused glances at Sky as she adjusted the bags over and over.

By the second hour, the novelty had worn off. Sky's pace slowed, her steps growing heavy. Ryan noticed her stumbling and stopped to take one of the duffle bags from her shoulders.

"Now who looks like the pack mule?" she joked, breathless.

Ryan rolled his eyes, checking his watch. They were still heading north, just as the map indicated.

Three hours passed. The sun dipped lower, its last golden rays slipping away. The forest grew darker, shadows stretching across the path. Sky reached into the snack bag and retrieved two flashlights, passing one to Ryan. The beams of light created circles that illuminated the surrounding trees but cast everything else into deeper gloom.

The air grew colder with each step. The chill seeped through their clothes, and even the usual hum of insects had stilled. The forest felt unnaturally quiet, save for the crunch of leaves and branches beneath their boots.

Ryan glanced at his watch again. "11:11," he muttered, stopping in his tracks.

Sky blinked at him. "No way. We've been walking for six hours?"

Ryan set the luggage down. "I think we need to stop for the night."

Sky's legs trembled as she tried to stay upright. Her face was pale, her breath coming in quick bursts.

"No, we can't stop now... must... keep going," she panted.

Ryan walked over and eased the duffle bag off her shoulders as she knelt down. "You need a break. Right now."

Sky gave a half-hearted shrug. "I could go another hour or two."

Ryan gave her a look. "Sure."

He cleared an area of forest floor, brushing away branches and sharp rocks. From one of the bags, he pulled out a small tent and made quick work of assembling it. Once it was up, he tossed their belongings inside.

"Come inside the tent," he said gently. "It'll block the breeze."

Sky shuffled in, wrapping herself tighter in the blanket. Ryan grabbed a few extra blankets and draped them over her. She reached into the snack bag and pulled out a few bags of chips but struggled to open them, her fingers too cold to feel properly.

She groaned in defeat and tossed the snacks aside. "I give up. These are my crunchy pillows now."

Ryan laughed, using a duffle bag as his pillow. He sat propped up against the tent, listening to the night sounds. The wind whispered through the treetops, scattering leaves across the ground. The forest smelled fresh and alive, a stark contrast to the artificial air of home. The tranquility brought a content smile to his face.

Eventually, he drifted off to sleep.

Sixty-Eight

In his dreams, he soared through a sky painted with hues of gold, pink, and blue, his wings spread wide as they caught the wind. The sun warmed his shaded brown feathers, and the world below was a breathtaking expanse of forests, rivers, and distant mountains. Ryan spiraled through the air, laughing with pure exhilaration as he executed flips and daring rolls.

"Slow down," came a soft, familiar voice.

He turned to see Sky flying beside him, her wings shimmering like starlight. Her eyes sparkled with joy as she caught up to him, their laughter blending into the melody of the wind.

But in an instant, the sky darkened. The vibrant colors drained away, replaced by thick, rolling clouds of black fog. The air became thick and heavy, pressing against his chest. His laughter died as panic set in.

"Sky?" he called, his voice trembling.

Sky's face contorted in pain. She clutched her head, her wings flapping erratically as she let out a heart-wrenching scream. Ryan flew toward her, arms outstretched. "Sky! It's me—Ryan!"

She lifted her head slowly. Her eyes—once full of life—were now pitch black, devoid of any light. Her expression twisted into something unrecognizable, monstrous.

"Sky... please," Ryan whispered, his voice breaking.

Behind her, a towering shadow emerged, its presence suffocating. His father stepped forward; his stature lengthened by jagged wings as black as night stretching from his back. His smile bleak and bitter. "She's fine, Ryan," he said, his tone deceptively calm.

Ryan's heart pounded in his chest. "What did you do to her?!"

Mr. Daniels' eyes glinted with a sinister gleam. "I helped her evolve—made her stronger. Just like I can help you."

Ryan's fists clenched as fury surged through him. "She doesn't need your help. Neither do I. You're killing her!"

Mr. Daniels stepped closer, his wings unfurling like a dark storm. "You don't understand, son. One day, you will."

The black fog coiled around Sky, pulling her deeper into its shadows. Her screams echoed, fading into the void.

A faint voice pierced the darkness. "Ryan... help me."

His heart twisted in his chest. "Mom?" he whispered, his voice cracking.

Far in the distance, he saw his mother in her hospital bed, frail and reaching out to him. Her eyes were filled with sorrow.

"No!" Ryan shouted, tears streaming down his face as the fog engulfed her too.

His father's cold smile widened. "There are things more important than love, Ryan."

Ryan's wings flared with defiance. "You're wrong! You always were!"

The fog crept toward him, icy and sharp. He felt it sting his feathers, wrapping around his arms like barbed wire. Desperation surged through him as he called out for Sky, his voice raw and broken.

The fog thickened until everything went black.

Ryan shot awake, drenched in sweat, his chest heaving. The quiet of the forest surrounded him. Sky was still asleep beside him, her breaths slow and steady. He pressed a hand to his chest, willing his racing heart to calm.

"Just a dream," he whispered, though the fear lingered.

A crack echoed from the woods outside. Ryan froze, straining to listen. Another crack. Closer.

Whispers.

He swallowed hard, reaching out to gently shake Sky awake. She stirred, blinking up at him in confusion. He placed a finger to his lips, signaling for silence.

Her eyes widened as she read the tension on his face. She mouthed, "What's wrong?"

Ryan pointed toward the trees. "Someone's there."

Sixty-Nine

Ryan's heart pounded as he unzipped the tent as quietly as he could. The crisp night air poured in, carrying with it the faintest whispers of leaves rustling in the distance. His pulse quickened. Whoever—or whatever—was out there wasn't making their presence subtle.

He motioned for Sky to follow. Her wings twitched as she prepared to make a silent escape into the starry sky. Ryan stepped outside first, scanning the shadowy tree line. The moonlight scattered across the forest floor, highlighting the gnarled roots and rocks but revealing no clear figure.

Ryan extended his hand back to Sky, who moved slowly, careful not to make a sound. Each step felt like navigating a minefield. As Sky emerged from the tent, her breath caught in her throat. The raw mountain air clung to her skin, sending shivers down her back.

A flash of light reflected off something metallic in the shadows—a brief glint that set every alarm off in her mind. She raised her hand to point at the source of the glimmer. Ryan nodded in understanding.

"On the count of three," he whispered, his voice barely audible. "We fly."

Sky gave a slight nod, her wings unfurling as she braced herself.

Ryan whispered, "One..." Sky's heart hammered in her chest.

"Two..." A rustling sound grew louder behind them.

"Three!"

Sky leapt into the air; wings extended. For a brief moment, she was weightless, free—and then, with a sharp snap, something coiled around her midsection. She crashed to the ground with a muffled cry.

Ryan turned mid-leap, horror spreading across his face as he saw the bola wrapped tightly around Sky's waist and wings. The weighted cords had pinned her arms to her sides, and she writhed, struggling to free herself.

"Sky!"

Before Ryan could react further, he felt a heavy net slam over him, knocking him off balance. The cords tangled around his wings and limbs, dragging him down into the dirt. He kicked and fought, his wings thrashing beneath the weight of the net.

"Who's there?" Ryan shouted; his voice defiant despite the panic rising in his chest.

A shadow moved into the moon's beams—a tall figure with pointed ears that twitched as he stepped forward. His silhouette was broad, his movements slow but calculated. The figure's tail swayed behind him, thick and bushy. The glowing sky highlighted his sharp cheekbones and faint scars etched across his jawline.

The figure spoke, his voice low and gravelly. "What business do you have out here?"

Sky wriggled in the dirt, panting as she tried to loosen the bolas' grip. "We're looking for the Humanimal sanctuary—the safe place we heard about!"

The figure stepped closer, and the moon illuminated his face fully. His skin was a pale contrast to the shadows, his eyes glowing with a fierce, animalistic green. His pupils were wide, like a predator in the wild. His pointed ears flicked toward every sound, hyper-aware, and a faint silver ring glinted near the tip of his right ear.

Ryan narrowed his eyes. "Who are you?"

The figure's eyes flickered to Ryan, measuring him. "I could ask you the same thing," he growled. His voice held the unmistakable cadence of someone accustomed to command. "How do I know you're not spies from NisenX?"

Sky's eyes widened. The fact that he knew about NisenX only deepened her unease. She struggled to sit up. "We're not spies! Daren gave us a map and told us to come here. He said there was a safe place for Humanimals deep in the forests of Idaho."

The guy's wolf-like ears stood tall at the mention of Daren's name. He stepped back, suspicion warring with cautious curiosity.

A new voice pierced the tension, light and melodic but firm. "You know my brother?"

Both Ryan and Sky turned toward the source. A girl stepped into the clearing; her silhouette graceful against the backdrop of trees. Her black hair was intricately braided down her back, with streaks of fiery orange woven throughout. Her eyes gleamed like molten gold, glaring in the moonlight. Wisps of white fur framed her face along her cheekbones, almost like whiskers.

Her dark, smooth skin had a warm, earthy glow, and she moved with a confidence that felt almost regal. The tips of her fingers were sharp and claw-like, though her posture radiated calm.

Sky felt her breath catch. "Are you... Delilah?"

The girl smiled, revealing a row of sharp but friendly teeth. "That's me."

Delilah turned to the wolf-like man, who still stood tensely with his arms crossed. "If Daren sent them, then they're not a threat. You know how cautious my brother is."

The man's jaw tightened, his tail flicking once behind him before he stepped back. "Fine," he muttered. "But if they make one wrong move—"

Delilah rolled her eyes and walked toward Sky. "Don't mind Grey. He's... protective." She crouched down and began unwinding the bolas from Sky's wings with nimble fingers. "Sorry about this. He takes security way too seriously."

Sky stretched her wings as soon as she was free, shaking off the ache. "Thanks."

Grey stepped toward Ryan and began to untangle the net. Ryan brushed the net off before Grey could finish, rising to his feet with a tense stance. The two stood face-to-face, their postures mirroring each other in stubbornness.

Ryan's jaw clenched. "You didn't have to trap us. We're not here to hurt anyone."

Grey stared at Ryan for a long moment, his glowing green eyes unblinking. Finally, he muttered, "You can't be too careful."

"Cut it out, Grey," Delilah scolded, though her tone remained warm. "Let's get moving before these two freeze."

Grey huffed but turned away. "Follow me."

Delilah beamed and threw her arms wide. "Welcome to the woods around our campus!"

She led the way as Ryan and Sky gathered their bags. Ryan kept his distance from Grey, who picked up two of the heavier duffle bags without a word. Sky noticed the tension in Ryan's shoulders—the anger he was holding back.

Delilah fell into step beside Sky. "Grey's bark is worse than his bite," she whispered. "He acts all tough, but he's really just a big softie."

Sky whispered back, "He seems territorial."

Delilah giggled; her golden eyes gleaming. "That's one way to put it."

The path wound deeper into the woods, the towering trees casting long shadows in the early dawn light. The air grew warmer as the sun began to rise, painting the sky in soft hues of lavender and cerulean. After an hour of steady hiking, the forest opened up into a vast clearing.

Sky's eyes widened as she took in the sight before her. A sprawling campus emerged from the trees, nestled within the valley. Red brick buildings with ivy-covered walls stood in neat clusters, their windows glinting in the sunlight. Pathways wound between them, lined with blooming wildflowers. A sparkling lake sat at the center, its surface reflecting the pastel sky.

Ryan stood beside her, his hand finding hers instinctively. They both squeezed tightly, sharing a moment of awe and disbelief.

Delilah bounded ahead, her laughter ringing through the clearing. "Welcome to Nick State University—home of the Humanimal sanctuary!"

Sky felt a rush of emotion flood her chest. She wasn't sure if she wanted to cry or cheer. After everything—the fear, the uncertainty, the miles of endless road—they had finally arrived.

Ryan squeezed her hand once more and whispered, "We made it."

Sky smiled, eyes glistening. "Yeah. We're safe."

ABOUT THE AUTHOR

Mc Randall developed a boundless imagination from an early age. Inspired by epic tales of heroism and exploration, she began crafting her own stories, weaving together adventure and heart. Writing became not just a passion but a way to bring her creative visions to life.

Now residing in Moody, Alabama, Mc Randall enjoys family life with her husband and three children. When she's not writing, she's busy managing the beautiful chaos of motherhood or finding time to soak in more sci-fi inspiration. As a published poet and the author of two children's books, Mc Randall has built a versatile writing repertoire.

Mc Randall continues to write with the hope of inspiring young readers to dream big, embrace their unique paths, and believe in their own inner heroes.

Made in the USA
Columbia, SC
20 April 2025